A History of the Island

A NOVEL

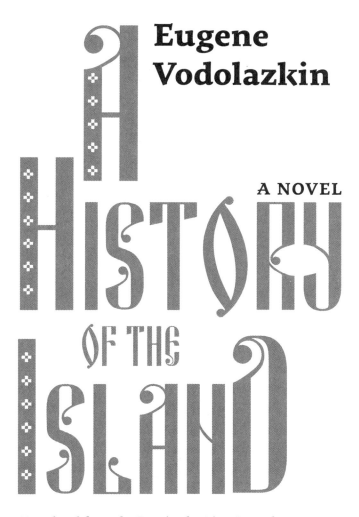

Eugene Vodolazkin

A NOVEL

A HISTORY OF THE ISLAND

Translated from the Russian by Lisa C. Hayden

Plough

Published by Plough Publishing House
Walden, New York
Robertsbridge, England
Elsmore, Australia
www.plough.com

Originally published in Russian as Оправдание Острова.
Copyright © 2021 by Eugene Vodolazkin.
This translation published by arrangement with the author and Banke,
Goumen, Smirnova Literary Agency AG.

English translation copyright © 2023 by Lisa C. Hayden.

ISBN: 978-1-63608-068-0
27 26 25 24 23   1 2 3 4 5

Library of Congress Cataloging-in-Publication Data
Names: Vodolazkin, E. G., author. | Hayden, Lisa C., translator.
Title: A history of the island : a novel / Eugene Vodolazkin ; translated
  from the Russian by Lisa C. Hayden.
Other titles: Opravdanie ostrova. English
Description: Walden, New York : Plough Publishing House, 2023. |
Summary: "Eugene Vodolazkin, internationally acclaimed novelist and
  scholar of medieval literature, returns with a satirical parable about
  European and Russian history, the myth of progress, and the futility
  of war." -- Provided by publisher.
Identifiers: LCCN 2022050891 | ISBN 9781636080680 (hardcover) |
ISBN 9781636080697 (ebook)
Subjects: LCSH: Islands--Fiction. | Prophecy--Fiction. | Middle
  Ages--Fiction. | LCGFT: Satirical literature. | Novels.
Classification: LCC PG3493.76.D65 O6713 2023 | DDC
  891.73/5--dc23/eng/20221021
LC record available at https://lccn.loc.gov/2022050891

Printed in the United States of America

To Tatyana and Natalia

TABLE OF CONTENTS

And the ground will shake,
and black water will ignite in the North,
and a fiery water will begin to flow in the South.
And ash will float from the heavens,
and your hearts will turn to ash.

Agafon's Prophecy

News of the continuation of *A History of the Island*, our country's renowned first historical chronicle, has recently piqued the interest of the Island community. Discovery of the continuation made publication of a new and complete edition of the chronicle a necessity.

A History of the Island has been published more than once in its previous form. It is part of the curriculum at schools and universities and has long been widely quoted. "We shall see how this all ends." "He understood that war is capable of resuming, for he was one of those who wished to resume it." "Happy are the times that do not enter the annals." "It, time, has nowhere to hurry." These phrases have entered our everyday life so firmly that not everyone remembers that they date back to the chronicle.

We requested that Their Royal Highnesses Parfeny and Ksenia have a look at the full text of *A History of the Island*. Their opinions of the published work felt extraordinarily important to us and they agreed to share them. Their notes unexpectedly took on a journal-like character, which pleased us inexpressibly, for any word from the royal couple is the word of history itself. With the authors' permission, we have divided the notes into chunks and published them as a running commentary on the text of the chronicle.

Events of the last year changed our initial publication plans: we have now lived long enough for ancient prophecies to begin coming true. One cannot call this time joyful but it has taught us a great deal. We have become wiser and, as Ecclesiastes tells us, in much wisdom is much grief.

The whole world has looked at what has taken place on the Island and reflected on the essence of history. Not only about our history but about history in general. The recent release of the film *Justification of the Island*, directed by the great Jean-Marie Leclerc, furthered those reflections. It was initially a surprise for many that the film's main characters agreed to be consultants for the French director, but the movie's grand success confirmed that they made the right decision.

The release of this book into the limelight has a special purpose now, as our people stand at a crossroads. And so: into the limelight, from the darkness of our time.

FEODOR

Long ago, we had no history. Memory preserved isolated events, but only those events with a propensity for repeating. Our existence thus seemed to take a circular path.

We knew that night follows day and spring follows winter. The luminaries floating in the firmament create those circles and their wayfaring is limited to one year. The year was also the natural boundary of our memory.

We vaguely recalled dreadful hurricanes and earthquakes, fierce winters when the sea froze, and internecine wars and invasions of other tribes, but we could not specify when they were happening.

We said only: That happened one summer. Or: That happened in spring, many springs ago. And thus all hurricanes blended into one large hurricane and internecine wars became for us one unending war.

With Christianization, we heard the word of the Holy Scripture, though previously we heard only one another's shabby old words. Those words crumbled to dust, for only that which is written is preserved and we had no written language before Christianization.

Books arrived on the Island later and we then learned of events that occurred before us. This helped us to understand the events of today.

We know now that human history has a beginning and is hastening toward its end. With these thoughts in mind, we shall set about to describe the years and events that flow past.

Bless us, O Lord.

PARFENY

Monks wrote *A History of the Island.* Nothing surprising
there: only someone focused on eternity is capable of
depicting time, and one who thinks of the celestial is the best
person of all to understand the earthly. Time was different
then, too: boggy, viscous. Not as it is these days. Time is slow
during childhood, it lingers, but later it takes a running start
and then, toward the end of life, it flies. That is pretty much
common knowledge. Isn't the life of a people rather similar
to the life of an individual person?

People suppose that the chronicle's first chapters are the
work of Father Nifont the Historian. In the entire history
of its existence, the manuscript never once left the walls
of Island Monastery of the Savior. That was most strictly
forbidden.

In the chroniclers' opinion, when a history was located
within a sacred space, it was protected from forgery. People
handle a history more freely now: anyone at all, in any place,
writes history. Might the reason for numerous falsifications
lie there?

The prohibition on bringing the chronicle out of the
monastery did not preclude the possibility of familiarizing oneself with it inside the monastery's walls. For the
ruling princes, at any rate. It was thought (as now, too) that
knowledge of the past is essential for those holding power.
That notion seems fair to me. True, it is also fair to say that
knowledge of history has yet to prevent anyone from making mistakes.

The Island was Christianized in the days of devout Prince Feodor. The prince was named Alexander until that time and not Feodor. And he was not devout. And he ruled only the northern part of the Island but seized the southern part during internecine war and became prince of the entire Island.

In the eighth year of his rule, he said:

Everyone gather on the Sandbank and you will be baptized there.

He said:

Whoever does not accept baptism is not my friend.

Everyone – or nearly everyone – was baptized, understanding that it is a difficult matter to not be a friend of the prince.

KSENIA

According to Byzantine Emperor Justinian's *Novel 47*, historical events are dated based on the current length of the reign of the emperor in power. Following the Byzantine tradition, Nifont the Historian (as well as all subsequent chroniclers) dates events with the ordinal number denoting how many years the prince has reigned. As is commonly known, we did not have emperors.

The Gospel was brought to the Island and read to people, and everyone learned of the life of our Lord Jesus Christ. It was ascertained about old gods that they were wooden idols, that they did not need to be defended since if they were gods they would defend themselves. And nobody particularly clung to them beyond the few sorcerers who served them.

When the pagan gods were burned, sorcerers said the day would come when words in books would also burn. No one believed them since everyone thought they spoke from powerless malice. And also, perhaps, because they had never known written words. The words they uttered hung in the air until the next wind, when they were carried off.

In the twentieth year of Feodor's reign, historical books were sent to the Island. We store them most carefully: There is nothing worse than remaining without history at a time when you are only beginning to understand what history is. From those books we discovered that history is singular and universal and, even when it is mislaid on an unknown island, it is one branch of our common tree.

We also learned that history was predicted in prophecies that encompass both its entire whole and its minor parts. A prophecy surmounts time and thus opposes the ordering of time. The great prophet Elijah, who rose to the heavens in a fiery chariot, was freed by the Lord from death and time, which, when all is said and done, are one and the same.

The people of the Island have a prophet of their own, by the name of Agafon the Forward-Looking. He speaks according to inspiration, not according to books, for there are not yet books about the Island. He gives predictions covering a long period, thus there has yet to be an opportunity to verify them. Nonetheless, Agafon's way of thinking and overall degree of concentration speak to his forecasts coming true, so we place our trust in them. Particularly the prediction that the hostility wracking this piece of dry land will be broken for a long time when two princely lines come together as one.

I think enough has been said about prophecies. We will not delve deeply into the future and, remembering that history recounts the past, we shall return to what has already been stated.

PARFENY

Agafon the Forward-Looking taught that a prophecy does not imply limitations to the freedom of future generations. It stands to reason that they, our descendants, are unrestricted in their actions insofar as circumstances allow. The reason for circumstances, says Agafon, is people, not God.

It is hard not to agree with him: long life has convinced me that people themselves create their own circumstances. Obviously, they are most often unfavorable. God sees them and reveals them to people through prophets. Sometimes.

And so, through Agafon, it was revealed to us when hostilities would break out on the Island. Nifont the Historian refers to that prophecy as not yet coming true. It is now known to all that it did come true. It was, so to say, a medium-term prophecy.

There was, however, one more of Agafon's prophecies that touched on distant times. It did not reach us. Unlike the others, which carried a more or less private character, this one was devoted to the fate of the Island in its entirety. Unfortunately, we haven't the slightest sense of its insights. Or perhaps that is fortuitous, though that can only be decided after reading it.

Saint Agafon dictated his principal prophecy in the literal sense, into the ear of chronicler Prokopy the Nasal. Agafon, who by then had reached the age of one hundred and twenty, had very strictly forbidden the one writing to loosen his tongue. For Agafon's part, that of a person who was (if it may be expressed this way) of a mature age, this was a joke to some degree (after all, nobody prohibited saints from joking) since Prokopy's tongue was cut off for using foul language back in the years of his youth. One did not need to worry about asking him to hold his tongue.

Prokopy, however, acted unexpectedly, in a way that required no tongue. After taking apart the manuscript of the chronicle, he removed the prophecy and, according to rumor, secretly forwarded it to the mainland, to a likely (as people now say) adversary.

Prokopy's deed – if reports are true – suggests that the secret information did not look especially optimistic for Island residents. It's possible it could have somehow strengthened the aggressive designs of those on the continent – nothing raises an adversary's spirit like a prophecy received in a timely fashion.

The only possible way to pass judgment on Prokopy the Nasal's goals would be to familiarize oneself with the prophecy's text but, as has been stated, it was lost without a trace. Why did he not rewrite it instead of pulling it out of the manuscript? After all, his action deprived his compatriots of the opportunity to read it.

It cannot be ruled out that the chronicler's actions aimed to exact revenge on his strict motherland for the loss of his tongue. That was an appreciable loss for Prokopy: the deceased loved to talk. He somehow contrived to do so using the bit that remained in his mouth. (A tongue, they say, grows back slightly.) Come what may, the story of the theft of the prophecy from the manuscript was discovered only after his death. This is striking evidence that people were not especially interested in the chronicle during Prokopy's time.

If I am to be brief, books brought to the Island have informed us of the following about the past.

On the first day, God created the heavens and the earth, the earth was unseen and unembellished, and the Spirit of God was moving over the waters, enlivening the watery essence. And God said, "Let there be light," and so there was light.

In the next days, He made the sea, rivers, and heavenly bodies. When filling the world with water, He left islands and lands in order to delineate dry ground before the creation of the sun, that people not deem the sun a god because it had dried the land.

God created fish and birds at the same time for they are akin, with but the difference that fish swim in water and birds in the sky.

And God created man and woman in order that he leave his mother and his father, and cleave to his wife. And God gave all earth's dry land to them to possess.

Seven days of creation, however, were still not time. Time was revealed at the Fall and the banishment from paradise, and history began together with time because history exists only within time.

At the age of 230, Adam sired his son Seth; all the years of Adam's life were 930. And children began to be born and from Adam to Noah there were counted ten generations and 1468 years. When Noah turned 600 years old, there was a flood on the earth.

And upon God's command, Noah struck a semantron and birds and beasts began to gather at the ark he had built, every creature in pairs, except the fish, for water did not frighten them. When all had entered, Noah closed the door to the ark and the windows of the heavens opened. And rain poured down for forty days and forty nights so there was no dry land left and even our island went under water. In the place where clouds now hang there were in those days rolling waves.

In one of the nonbiblical writings, it is said that the devil, wishing to sink the human race, transformed into a mouse and began to gnaw the bottom of the ark. Noah then prayed to God and a lion sneezed, releasing from his nostrils a tomcat and a she-cat, and they strangled the mouse. That is how cats, who are still a rarity in our land, came about.

PARFENY

In Nifont's text we find apocryphal pieces of information that the modern reader will regard as steeped in legend: I have in mind the story of cats. The details, which show the difference between storytelling and Darwin's ponderous prose, are wonderful and all that is wonderful is true in some way.

And there it is: the origin of a species, without being dragged out over hundreds of pages. What can be seen clearly here are cats, and there you have them: flying out of a lion's nostrils, meowing as they flip in the air and land on four paws. Without forgetting their super-objective, they end up next to the mouse in one leap and then scritch-scratch! I say *scritch-scratch* because I have in mind that the duel was unusual to the highest degree. Did the cats know who they were up against? That's a good question.

It is true that these pieces of information do not fully correspond with Darwinism but that's more likely a problem with Darwinism. Its founder simply would not have understood the story about cats. It seems to me that he didn't know how to smile.

On a serious note. Given my considerable age, I am often asked about my attitude toward Darwin. What can I say? His ear that caught the rhythms of evolution turned out not to hear the pulse of metaphor and (more broadly speaking) poetry. Only Charles's inability to hear metaphor can explain his pouncing on the Holy Scripture. Only his insensitivity to poetry prevented him from understanding that he was not contradicting a biblical text. I think the deceased now understands that.

The Lord gave water to us Island residents both to assist and to punish. Since time immemorial water has carried our cargo ships to distant corners of the inhabited world, to the line establishing the limit of sea and earth. But at the time of our spiritual devastation, water rose to a threatening height, drowning people and flooding fields. So said our forefathers. Given that the entire world was flooded with water, one can only be astounded by the degree that humans fell during Noah's time.

And on the fortieth day, Noah opened a window of the ark and sent forth a raven to learn where the water had receded. But the raven alit on dead bodies floating upon the water's surface, began pecking them, and did not return. And then Noah sent a dove. The dove returned, holding an olive branch in its beak, and Noah understood that the water had begun to subside.

Noah died 350 years after the flood; all the years of his life were 950.

KSENIA

The unthinkable longevity of our forefathers might seem to some to be the result of a misunderstanding, perhaps an incorrect transposition from one chronological system to another, a scribe's error, etc. Strictly speaking, there is

11

no need for these sorts of conjectures. Everything has an explanation.

People were still filled with a paradisiacal timelessness. Standing with one foot in eternity, they were still becoming accustomed to time. Their lifetime shortened as they became more distant from paradise. That said, one should not think that longevity ended with our forefathers. Parfeny and I are now three hundred forty-seven years old and that surprises no one.

Yesterday I answered a survey. In response to the question *What is your age?* I said: "Three hundred forty-seven."

They didn't even smile.

I used to feel shy about my age but that stopped after one hundred fifty. Some people simply live longer, for various reasons.

And so, the earth was divided among Noah's sons Shem, Ham, and Japheth. It should be supposed that we are related to Japheth's progeny and our island belongs to Japheth's portion.

It is 3324 years from Noah to Abraham. When the Lord turned His gaze to Sodom and Gomorrah, Abraham asked:

If they find fifty of the righteous in this place, wilt thou really destroy them?

The Lord said:

If I find fifty righteous there, then I will spare all the place.

And Abraham said in reply:

Behold, I have taken upon me to speak to the Lord, I who am but dust and ashes. And wilt thou destroy all the city if there shall lack five of the fifty righteous?

The Lord said:

No, if I find there forty and five, I will not destroy it.

And Abraham spoke further and asked about forty and about thirty and about twenty and about ten. And the Lord promised him He would preserve this place even for the sake of ten righteous but He found not ten there and so He rained brimstone and fire out of heaven on Sodom and Gomorrah and the entire surrounding area.

Historical books describe many other events too, but I have referenced only the primary ones.

In the thirty-ninth year of his reign, Prince Feodor presented himself to the Lord. Upon Feodor's death, his son Konstantin reigned.

Chapter the Second

KONSTANTIN

During the third year of the reign of His Highness Prince Konstantin, on the seventh day of the month of March, after night had deepened over the City, rumbling and moans began to sound on the streets. Those who exited their homes in order to understand the nature of those sounds were struck by flaming arrows. And the arrows continued to rain down during the day too, sent by heavenly horsemen who remained unseen. Only their horses' white-hot hooves were visible.

And because it became clear to all that the horsemen were sowing death, the residents of the City did not leave their homes and everything ceased during the evening of that same day. At the time, no one could explain either the reason for the occurrence or its purpose, other than blacksmith Agapit, who said:

By the looks of the horseshoes that miraculously appear, I conclude that this vision bespeaks nothing but war, for horseshoes such as this arise only before a war.

In Konstantin's fifteenth year, Prince Yevfimy, whose forbears once ruled the southern part of the Island, divulged his true genealogy. Its truth consisted of the fact that Yevfimy's bloodline apparently descended from Emperor Augustus, something the previous genealogy, which had been passed down orally, suppressed.

The true genealogy described how Augustus' flotilla washed up on the Island during a sea crossing, due to a storm. And that storm was so severe and prolonged that Augustus was unable to go out into the open sea for three days and three nights. The emperor was taken in by a local princely family and Princess Melania herself

attended to him. And, in the words of that true narration, *Augustus'*
heart had been stricken by her beauteousness and on their first night,
Prince Yevfimy's ancestor, Prince Irakly, who became the forefather
of the Island's dynasty, was conceived.

Yevfimy found the new genealogy in the hollow of an old oak
tree while hunting a spotted deer. In saving itself from Yevfimy's
pursuit, the deer ran off through a field where there stood a lone
tree with a secret hiding place. The deer's flight was so swift that
Yevfimy's arrows did not reach it but the animal stopped suddenly
by the oak as if rooted there, and said to the prince in our language:

Here you will find your true genealogy.

Yevfimy showed the oak tree and the deer to others but the scroll
with the genealogy is what was important, for it is difficult to doubt
the written word.

Ruling Prince Konstantin, however, doubted. In the twentieth
year of his princely reign, he asked Yevfimy why the spotted deer
spoke no more in our language or in any other language at all, and
why the skin on which the charter was written looked unusually
fresh. He also saw a certain similarity between what was written in
the charter and descriptions in Greek chronicles that had recently
become available on the Island. Konstantin thought Yevfimy's
explanations were imprecise and so Yevfimy was confined to the
Monastery.

In Konstantin's twenty-sixth year, a charter containing Konstantin's new genealogy was found in the hollow of the same oak
tree. The difference in the second acquisition consisted of the deer's
absence. A certain person who had learned of Yevfimy's find went
off to the oak in order to see if any other sort of scroll remained in
the hollow. To his great surprise, he found such a scroll and hied off
to hand it over to Konstantin.

Konstantin's new genealogy also mentioned the arrival of Augustus on the Island but it spoke, too, of the emperor's second night in a royal home. He spent that night with Princess Ilaria and the fruit of their all-consuming love, Prince Roman, became Prince Konstantin's forefather.

The Monastery's brethren subsequently told of how Yevfimy met the news of Konstantin's lineage with *displeased eyes* and apparently even announced that he had ransacked the hollow in all his zeal, though it contained nothing more within. No one outside the Monastery's walls, however, heard his objections, for Prince Yevfimy suddenly breathed his last after two days had elapsed.

PARFENY

Yevfimy justified the deer's further silence by saying the animal had already made the most important utterance in its life. What, really, could have been added to what it had already articulated? With regard to the freshness of the charter, the prince reasonably raised the objection that there was nothing to compare to the document he found because there were no other ancient scrolls on the Island.

When the lucky find resulted in determining that Konstantin's line also descended from Augustus, some seemed to think the two documents contradicted each other. In fact, Konstantin's genealogy offered a compromise. Speaking of Konstantin's ancestor's conception by Augustus on the second night did not exclude that the speedy emperor had a chance to conceive Yevfimy's ancestor on the first night.

Prokl, Yevfimy's son and heir, however, did not agree to the compromise and did not consider sharing his kinship.

In Konstantin's twenty-eighth year, stones and ash the color of blood fell from the heavens. This sight frightened all, for it boded nothing good. The stones were hot to the touch and some were so fiery that houses in the City burned from them.

A year hence, small silver ingots began falling from the heavens. And although they were cold, people feared gathering them because no one knew what force had tossed them down. Several daring people began gathering them and everyone looked at them in terror. Nothing, however, happened to them; they only grew rich. And many people then envied them. Hieromonk Avksenty said in the ninety-sixth year of his life:

We shall see how this all ends.

And everyone calmed.

In Konstantin's thirty-ninth year, Prince Prokl, the eldest son of Yevfimy, came to Konstantin's Palace. There he announced that their bloodline had an advantage over Konstantin's, for his ancestor Irakly had been conceived by Augustus one day before Roman, who was Prince Konstantin's ancestor. And according to those around him, Konstantin's eyes also became *displeased* and they reflected a wish to send Prokl to the Monastery.

Prokl silently pointed at the windows and everyone became aware of rumbling that carried from the City's Main Square, as if from rolling ocean waves. This was not, however, waves but a human crowd that had come to the Palace with Prince Prokl. The crowd dinned and seethed and everyone inside approached the windows to look silently at those on the square.

And then Prince Konstantin smiled and took Prokl by the arm, sitting him down on a tall chair. He himself continued to stand behind Prokl, who was sitting.

Konstantin said:

Brother of mine, it is not the night of conception that is

significant but the day of birth. Ilaria gave birth two weeks before Melania and you know that.

Although Prokl did not know that, he had nothing to say in response. At first he wanted to stand but Prince Konstantin placed his palms on Prokl's shoulders and forbade him to do so.

He said:

I call you a brother for we both trace back to the same ancestor, a most august Roman emperor. I see that you lack for the esteem which you deserve by right of your birth. I appoint you to be my confidant and henceforth you will share a meal with me each day.

Such was the power in the palms of his hands and his speech that Prince Prokl could neither stand nor refuse. And from that time on he shared a meal with Konstantin on all days, although those days were few, three to be exact. On the third day, Prince Prokl felt ill after lunch and toward evening he departed this life.

The next day, armed people began to gather at dawn in the southern part of the Island. Judging by their speech, they did not believe Prokl had died naturally, and they did not hide their intentions to avenge his death. They informed Frol, Prince Prokl's younger brother, but he assured them that even without human participation vengeance would be exacted on those who were guilty.

The situation changed toward noon. Prince Frol himself went out to the crowd, his face wet with tears. After saying the time had come to dry tears (and so he dried his), Frol summoned those who had gathered to take decisive actions, although he did not explain exactly what actions he had in mind. Without waiting for explanations, Prince Konstantin ordered his troops to prepare to march south.

A short while later, a funeral service was held for Prince Prokl. The Island's bishop, Feofan, forbade armed people from making an appearance there, explaining that the deceased's good deeds were now weaponry for capturing the Kingdom of Heaven.

Prince Frol demanded that last rites be read for the Lord's servant Prokl as for one who was murdered, but the bishop refused him since there was no direct confirmation of murder.

After showing the blue face of the deceased, however, Prince Frol shouted:

If this is not a confirmation, who will tell me I am wrong?

Feofan answered:

Accept and mourn now but leave the investigation to Him who never errs.

Frol mourned but did not accept, and the final words of the graveside psalms had not yet quietened when he threw a harsh accusation in Konstantin's face.

Prince Konstantin kept silent, as if coping with his rage, but then he uttered:

Grief has clouded your reasoning, brother. Your reasoning should be especially sharp now, when we are but a step from internecine battle. Let us leave and discuss how to salvage peace on the Island.

Well, you are not inviting me to lunch, smiled Prince Frol, though there was no merriment in his smile. And you are no brother to me. My kin descend from Emperor Augustus and your ancestors – please do not take this amiss – are evil swamp spirits and we have nothing in common, just as light and dark have nothing in common.

And so the conversation between Konstantin and Frol did not take place, for how could it take place after such words?

And the Island divided into northern and southern parts, as in times long gone, and confrontation that all seemed to have forgotten was renewed. There had been no animosity between the people of the South and North, and many were related, so why did they go to war against one another? Would it not have been better for the princes to resolve everything in peaceful conversation?

19

KSENIA

Thus began the war that was subsequently called the War of the Genealogies, though I suspect its reason did not lie in genealogies at all. After long wavering, Frol decided that a convenient moment had arrived to seize power, though Konstantin (who also wavered) thought the threat should be nipped in the bud, without waiting for its intensification. He was essentially the one who began the war, assuming he would be dealing with a handful of people devoted to Frol and certainly not foreseeing that all the residents of the South would go over to Frol's side. Astonishingly, even the residents themselves did not foresee that, since they were busy with nonmilitary matters.

Were there war preparations? Not in the usual sense of the word. It's clear that Prince Yevfimy did not find his genealogy in a tree hollow, though for some reason he needed that. But was he planning to wage war? Certainly not: he had no troops. Perhaps he wanted to raise his status. Prince Prokl was also not thinking about waging war, nor, even, was Prince Frol. The thought entered Frol's mind only when armed people began gathering around him, people who had been farmers, craftsmen, or sailors only the day before.

What made these people throw away their prosperity, exchange a calm life for the gravest of ordeals and, finally, arrive at the complete destruction of that life? The idea of justice? But why had that thought not beaten in their hearts so powerfully before? They came to support someone whose slights had basically left them disinterested, someone who had asked nothing of them. War had not entered Prince Konstantin's plans either. It had not entered into anyone's plans but it began anyway.

Sudden dissonance – not too loud, like the sound of an instrument's snapped string – united everyone to act together. Did this happen because of the sound? Yes and no. Sometimes every string snaps and nobody hears. Why did they hear it now?

His Highness Prince Konstantin opened military operations. In the forty-first year of his royal reign, he advanced his troops to the southern part of the Island but did not call this a war because he considered the entire Island his ancestral land. Bishop Feofan went out toward the troops, holding his hand on a pectoral cross.

He said:

In the name of our Lord Jesus Christ, crucified on a wooden cross, I forbid you to move farther, for I hope for the peace to be preserved.

Similar to you, Bishop, objected Prince Konstantin, I hope for that as well, and have thus set my troops in motion. There is treachery in my royal domain, and so why do you prohibit me from tearing out its root in the person of Prince Frol, who betrayed us? I assure you I need no one but Frol, although coups and wars will shake the Island until his capture.

The bishop stood firm and responded:

Tearing out one root, you damage many other roots. Do you, Your Highness the Prince, not see how they have intertwined? And here is my final word to you: kill me first and only then act of your own free will.

The horseman looked down upon Feofan, who stood on the earth, and His Highness's gaze clouded with rage. He shook the reins but Feofan seized a stirrup and was pulled behind the horse.

21

His legs slid along the earth, he did not let go of the stirrup, and there were tears in the eyes of those who saw this. And when Konstantin set the horse to a gallop, Feofan fell under the hooves but remained unharmed due to the intervention of an angel.

Prince Konstantin stopped after beginning to ride off. He did not order that Bishop Feofan be killed but rather commanded riding past him. And the warriors rode around Feofan, and he stood as if he were a dead tree stump on a sandbank, with a rapid stream flowing around him. He resembled a dead tree stump, too, motionless, disheveled, mute, his aged arms stretched out.

The troops had long been behind his back and even the dust they raised while walking had time to settle as Feofan remained immobile. He prayed for his people, concentrating all the strength within him on the prayer. And so great was the exertion of his spirit that sometimes it seemed he was taking flight. When the bishop realized that did not simply seem to be happening, he ceased praying because he did not wish to lose the ground beneath his feet. It is also said that when Feofan broke away from the earth, there appeared the angel who had saved him from the horse's hooves.

The angel said:

Your prayer, O holy leader, is powerless against the sins of your people. A wish for war is not outside them, it is born within the heart of each of them.

How can one wish pain and death, Feofan wanted to ask, but the angel's sorrowful face became the answer to his question.

Konstantin's troops moved, meeting no opposition and generally meeting no one. Only empty villages were to be found: residents fled, knowing the prince's harsh disposition. Konstantin was not met by his subjects. He fell into a rage and ordered their homes be burned, supposing those who fled had joined Prince Frol. That was not, in fact, the case, as they only joined Frol after losing their homes, since they had nowhere to return. And after hardening their hearts, they became Frol's most embittered warriors since one evil draws upon another.

Konstantin's troops continued to advance south, moving deeper into the Forest during the forty-third year of his royal reign. It is known, after all, that the Forest's thickets in that locality are dense and difficult to penetrate, and there are no large roads, only narrow paths. The troops moved forward for a long time, stretching over a distance of several miles before stopping in front of a multitude of felled tree trunks on the path. When those riding up front dismounted to drag away the tree trunks, clouds of arrows suddenly began to fly at them from the right and from the left, and Konstantin realized he had fallen into a trap.

His troops could not even retreat because those in the back were unaware of the ambush and pressed at those in the front. What had happened, however, quickly became obvious to them, too, because the arrows also flew at them and those riding abreast and at all of Konstantin's dispersed troops. They shot from trees and from behind bushes and fallen tree trunks. The arrows' points were soaked in the juice of poisonous plants so that even a light wound inevitably provoked death. Those shooting were invincible.

And so Konstantin's troops began to retreat to where the trees seemed sparser, whence no arrows flew. Some of the troops covered that retreat as the main troops rushed, unhindered, to the less dense part of the Forest. A meadow soon appeared behind the trees and Konstantin ordered that all advance there, in order to deploy into battle formation.

When the horsemen entered the tall grass, water squelched beneath the horses' hooves and the meadow proved to be a swamp. Pressured by Frol's people, they could no longer return to the path and so continued moving forward because the water seemed shallow to them. It is said that there were shallow places and routes for escape if one carefully chose one's way, but fear drove Konstantin's troops. Horses began slipping into the bog, bringing riders down with them. Feet constrained by the mire could not free themselves of stirrups.

And there was a horrible moaning, for the mire engulfed them, as if it were a living creature, and this reminded many of infernal torture. Mud slowly closed in over those screaming and their screams turned to bubbles. Frol's people stood on the dry spots and shot those escaping, prompting Bishop Feofan to deprive them of communion for twenty-nine years.

Those of Konstantin's troops who managed to survive by wandering the Forest for several weeks returned home with no strength and, I shall add, with no desire whatsoever to wage war. And so the Island found itself definitively divided into two parts and Prince Frol now ruled the South.

Upon assuming power, Frol began fortifying the earthen wall around the Fortress, for in the absence of wars, the earth crumbled from it and trees began to grow at its top. From the Mainland, the so-called Continent, the prince also summoned people well-versed in the art of war and entrusted his troops to them. He understood that war is capable of resuming, for he was one of those who wished to resume it.

KSENIA

Family lore mentions that even during the first war Frol initially wanted to continue the attack on Konstantin but then dismissed the idea. He recognized that what succeeded in the forest would not be easy to repeat in an open space. Beyond that, a significant portion of Konstantin's army did not take part in the unfortunate march and thus had not been demoralized. Finally, Frol did not have his own trained army. And so he made a priority of getting down to creating one.

In the fiftieth year of the reign of His Highness Konstantin, a woman by the name of Angelina, who prepared food for Bishop Feofan, was found to be with child and gave birth nine months later. Coming out to the Main Square, she announced for all to hear that Feofan was the father of the child.

And Konstantin's people came to Feofan and said:

Grieve not, O Bishop, for this is an everyday matter. Life without women is difficult and anything can happen during an hour of food preparation. Our prince is wise, he will not hold this against you but rather summon you to the Palace for a private conversation. As for Angelina, whose life story has never been angelic, he will, believe us, force her to disavow her accusations.

But Bishop Feofan refused to go to see the prince, saying:

The woman is telling an untruth and here I place my trust not in the prince but in our Lord Jesus Christ, to whom all people's matters and designs are known.

His words were drowned out by shouts from the street, demanding another bishop for the Island's residents.

Upon receiving Feofan's answer, Prince Konstantin shrugged his shoulders and left the Palace to go out to the crowd, walking with the gait of a just person. He looked silently at the crowd for some time. People shouted to him that they could not kiss a bishop's hand if it had caressed women. As Konstantin began to speak, he seemed to choke with righteous anger and he expressed his understanding of the matter to those who had gathered. Before too long, he made an effort to gain control of himself and said that nothing could be undertaken without an investigation. The crowd blessed his soft-heartedness but demanded he bring in for investigation all participants of the events and so all of them, including the two-week-old baby, were brought in.

In order to prove her rightness, Angelina stated that the bishop had a large mole on his left hip. The bishop's bathhouse attendant was quickly called in; he confirmed the presence of a mole. A hush fell, for many had been hoping for Feofan's acquittal until they heard the bathhouse attendant's testimony.

Feofan remained silent and prayed.

Harsh accusations and substantial evidence have been brought forth against you, O Bishop, said Konstantin. How shall you answer them?

I will not answer them but the baby will, answered Feofan, and laughter rang out in the crowd.

I fear that the child's evidence will not be comprehensible to all, surmised Prince Konstantin, who was not laughing. It will be comprehensible only to those who are but two weeks from birth.

But the bishop walked over to the baby and called out to him in a loud voice:

In the name of the Son of God Jesus Christ, tell me if you are my son.

And the baby answered him in distinct speech:

No, O Bishop, I am not your son.

And thus Bishop Feofan's innocence was declared. When requested to ask the baby who his father was, Feofan said that one need not turn to the baby to learn that, as it was sufficient to ask Angelina.

PARFENY

People said that Konstantin cut off the inquest too quickly.
That circumstance gave rise to rumors that the prince was
involved in the child's conception or at least the accusation
against the bishop. The motive for that action might have
been Feofan's disagreement with Konstantin's march south,
in which case revenge was at issue.

I do not rule out, however, that revenge was beside the
point here and the reasons were purely pragmatic: the prince
simply did not want another, future, clash between worldly
power and spiritual power. There's good reason the chronicle
writer notes the private conversation that Feofan valiantly
turned down. In this case, it must be supposed that a new
march did not seem impossible to Konstantin at the time.

I n Konstantin's fifty-fifth year, there was a great drought. The
seeded fields did not give rise to new crops and the sun's
scorching rays singed what did sprout. Summer forest fires also
began, particularly on the southern tip of the Island, where strong
winds from the sea are common. The smoke carried to the Island's
interior, where it stood some days like a continuous shroud, con-
cealing the sun.

Nobody remembered such fires as far back as the memories of
the living could reach, and indeed lore mentioned nothing similar.
The movement of the fires along the coastline from the North to the
South was also worthy of surprise because it appeared as if someone
had lit the Forest afire, although no one permitted thoughts of ar-
son, for at a time of widespread burning one might ask, Who would
think of lighting a fire? In the fire's unusual motion, people saw

the conscious power of the one who had been fighting the human species since time began and so they turned to Bishop Feofan.

The bishop said:

There is no necessity, my children, to search in otherworldly realms, for vile desires are also born in the hearts of people. It is the fire that troubles me, rather than who is to blame, be he the prince of this world or, let us say, simply a prince. I shall share my apprehensions with Holy Archangel Michael.

And why Archangel Michael, those present wondered in surprise, for after all you prayed to him in the post-war time about preserving the peace; how could he now halt a fire?

I am attempting to halt a worse fire, answered the elder, and I propose considering the present time a pre-war time.

When alone, Feofan began to pray.

Ten months later, the angel he had seen before appeared before him again and the angel said:

I was sent to announce to you that the path to war is already blazed in the Forest and, well, of course, in the hearts of people. Favor will be shown to you and it will be expressed to you only in the fact that you will not see war. And so then, Feofan, take care that there will be a coffin for your body – you have been taking care of your eternal soul all your life.

Feofan began to weep upon hearing that. Not because he feared dying but from the pain he felt for his people. Beginning that day, he saw to preparing a coffin. Since he was making it from oak, a hard wood, the work did not progress quickly, but the bishop was in no hurry.

Two years later, when the bed of the coffin was finished, Feofan began using it for nighttime sleep. During the months that he worked on the cover, he successfully smoothed those places in the bed that caused discomfort. The bishop liked sleeping in the coffin and his dreams there were always unclouded.

He dreamt primarily of his childhood, spent by the sea, for he was born into the family of a fisherman. The colors and smells were so fresh that they sometimes awakened him, and then he would hurry to fall asleep again because what appeared in his dreams was enticing. He told of seeing the azure sea at dawn and then he happened to sense the smell of the resin his father used to varnish the boat. As in childhood, he pushed away from shore and, laying down the oars, lay in the salty nets and watched the sky as the boat rocked so that the sky seemed to him the sea and the sea the sky. And then he began to call his coffin a boat, asserting that he sailed off in a boat each night.

One morning Feofan did not leave his cell. People dared not enter to see him but stood silently until Elder Avksenty was brought in – he was nearly one hundred and four years old and had neither aged nor died. He entered the bishop's cell and, after spending some time with him, he appeared with a smile on his lips.

He said:

Last night God's seafarer Feofan sailed beyond the skyline whence there is ordinarily no return for sailors and travelers.

He also said:

Carried by an amicable current, Bishop Feofan wishes you long life.

PARFENY

The description of the fifty-fifth year of Konstantin's royal reign is noteworthy first of all because *A History of the Island* shifts into the hands of another chronicler. This can be ascertained not by a change in style, something that is roughly

29

identical for all chroniclers, with the possible exception of Prokopy the Nasal, but simply because a series of sources announces the death of Nifont the Historian that year.

We know next to nothing about Nifont. All that remains of him is a name, though this could have been worse, because not even names remain for a number of other historians. Medieval authors were usually anonymous, since they presented not their personal view but a general one, inspired by faith. More specifically, a general view that was simultaneously personal.

Unlike us, who are people of, as they say, the old school, it is difficult for a person in the modern era to understand how that is possible. The thing is that God was at the center of the world during the Middle Ages but the individual is now at the center of the world. There is one God for all and thus the view during the Middle Ages is a view from above, since only a view from above can encompass everyone. That view reflects the sole God, hence it is also the only view. But now, with the individual at the center of the world, there are many views, just as there are many people.

In the sixtieth year of the reign of His Highness Prince Konstantin, the great drought continued, due to our sins.

That same year, Afanasy was installed as the Island's bishop.

In the sixty-first year of Konstantin, there was again no harvest due to the great drought. Since foodstuffs were routinely stored in the northern part of the Island, residents of the southern part were the first to experience the shortage. And then Bishop Afanasy called on the prince to send a small part of the stored grain to the South, in order that people living there not die.

Prince Konstantin replied:

The South split not only from the North but also from food-stuffs. How can I feed others when there is nothing for my own people to eat tomorrow?

In the sixty-third year of Konstantin, rains began in the spring. Toward the end of May, after the rains abated, the prince moved his troops to the South. This time, he set off along the burned part of the Forest and met no hindrances other than small trees that had sprouted on the fire site.

They went farther along a field planted with long-awaited cereal plants and came across no one there, save one aged peasant, Elevfery, who said:

Why are you trampling a sown field? I would probably compare you to a locust but I fear a cruel death.

Some warriors wanted to kill Elevfery but Bishop Afanasy, who had set off with the troops to soften hearts, protected him with his own body.

KSENIA

The prince's troops went along the sown field not by chance, just as the march itself was not by chance, having begun in May, when the first sprouts appeared in the fields. Konstantin understood that the chances of his victory over Prince Frol would decrease sharply if that harvest was gathered. He knew how painstakingly Frol had prepared his defenses, thus hunger was Konstantin's primary ally.

As Konstantin's troops neared Frol's Fortress, they came across ever more villages and farmsteads and all of them were empty, for the residents had escaped to the protection of the Fortress's walls. There they hoped to find at least some sort of sustenance for themselves, though after the long drought there was also nearly nothing at the Fortress. Prince Frol had shared the small bit of food he had with soldiers from his own troops. And so the men among the refugees joined the troops since only thus could they feed their families.

Upon approaching the Fortress, Prince Konstantin was surprised at how it had changed. He knew from scouts that Frol had been working to rebuild it, but he had not expected such changes. The moat with water surrounding the Fortress was broader and the walls had become so high that it seemed to Konstantin that the clouds floating past were grazing their battlements. And he asked those standing with him if they would graze them. They answered as if in one voice:

No, they will not.

Arrows flew out when the forward detachment neared the Fortress's northern wall for the first time. Smoke from unseen fires rose from behind the wall and soon cauldrons on wooden hoists came into view. Mobile hoists moved the cauldrons so they appeared over the wall's outer side. The cauldrons swung on chains and from time to time they poured out their contents: tar and boiling water.

The River flowed through the Fortress, so there was plenty of water inside. There was also no shortage of tar since many people in those parts were fishermen and tarred their boats. And so Prince Konstantin's forward detachment retreated beyond the distance of an arrow's flight and the main troops also did not advance farther.

And then Bishop Afanasy said to Konstantin:

You see, Prince, that the Fortress is well defended and can be taken only with great sacrifices. Subdue the proud spirit within yourself and return to the City; may that be your sacrifice to the Almighty.

The prince answered:

Of what sacrifice do you speak? How do I return after the God-hating Frol sacrificed the unity of the Island?

The bishop objected that no unity is worth human life. If unity pleases God, He will return it even without you, but if it does not please Him, then why should it be returned?

Prince Konstantin, however, did not listen to the bishop. He moved his troops on the Fortress at the hour of dawn, cutting short their pointless stand. Konstantin devoted the passing time to preparing rafts on which they could surmount the watery moats. He brought some from the City and ordered that others be made on the spot. Before the start of battle, he turned to the bishop for a blessing but Afanasy refused him.

I will, he answered, ask only that the heavenly angels screen all those fighting, using invisible shields.

The prince looked at him, his gaze lingering.

He said:

It is important, O Bishop, that there be enough angels for all. And shields, too, since I have heard that some angels fly empty-handed.

Arrows showered down from the wall as soon as Konstantin's troops began to put rafts in the water. And although those attacking attempted to cover themselves with shields, arrows found a way to their bodies. And again, as before, in the Forest, poison had been applied to the arrows' tips and the slightest scratch turned to death.

After some of the troops managed to conquer the moat and those out front began to place ladders against the wall, boiling water and tar were poured upon them from above. And it was frightful to see the scalded people fall from the ladders and hear screams that no longer sounded human. Flesh peeled from their bones and it was black from tar, as if they had been born in those countries where

33

people were said to have a black color. The scalded writhed spasmodically on the ground and some rolled down into the moat and drowned because the water's cold depths alone could deliver them from the unbearable pain.

And then, raising a cross, Bishop Afanasy went to the moat and shouted with all his might:

In God's name, I order everyone to stop!

But his voice drowned amidst the shouts of those battling and the groans of those dying. And so he stood as arrows flew past him and not one of them grazed him, for an angel with a shield had been at his right shoulder and those pure of heart saw that angel. When it became clear that those fighting were deaf to the bishop's appeal, his words were repeated in an angel's voice. And that voice was as thunder from the sky that makes everyone tremble, and no one could find the strength within to disobey.

Prince Frol came out on the wall, screened by nonangelic shields. Over the course of three days, he had silently observed the bishop with his angel as well as death, which reigned below. The bishop stood on one of the rafts. He made the sign of the cross over himself and then slowly rowed toward the Fortress wall.

He said to Frol:

Allow me to take away the wounded and bury the dead.

Frol kept silent but did not impede, instead signaling to the Fortress's defenders that they not shoot. Seeing that, the bishop and Konstantin's people began placing the dead and those still living on the rafts. From a knoll, Konstantin watched the mournful arrival of the rafts and tears washed over his face, though he thought that no one could see that.

His tears so glistened in the sun that they did not escape the notice of Frol, who said:

Is this what you wanted, Konstantin?

Frol uttered that quietly but somehow Konstantin heard him. Perhaps with his inner ear, which, as they write in books, is present in any person.

He answered just as quietly:

No, not that, Frol.

He also answered:

I wanted unity and I will achieve it.

And the wind inserted his words into Prince Frol's ear but Frol only shook his head. He also wanted unity but only if he were in power.

Prince Konstantin continued standing on the knoll and watching as the rafts moored for the hundredth time, delivering maimed bodies.

He whispered:

I have read books about great empires and about peoples who accepted a life-saving yoke. Why has that not occurred on the Island, where there live not various peoples but one? Unity will improve their life and so why do they not understand that? Nothing good awaits them now.

The siege of the Fortress began that day.

The weather that year was favorable for arable farmers and the harvest promised to be abundant on both parts of the Island. Wheat had come up well where Prince Konstantin's troops did not trample the fields. The Fortress's defenders saw that from the walls but were cut off from their fields.

Prince Frol knew that nearly no foodstuffs remained and he initially wanted to buy up a stock of grain from the Mainland. Foreseeing this, Konstantin ordered his navy into the sea, stopped the vessels carrying grain, and threatened to burn them if there was a next time. And so the vessels turned around and sailed off to the Mainland, never to return.

Then Frol promised a considerable sum of money to two ship-
owners, convincing them to deliver grain at night. Konstantin's
people intercepted them and burned the vessels. They burned at
night as if they were two torches and those who saw that from the
Fortress walls wept.

And so starvation set in at the Fortress. A horse's head cost
ten dinars but even that was soon impossible to buy and so dogs,
pigeons, and rats became their food. People boiled leather belts, sad-
dles, and boots. When all that had been eaten, there was no smoke
over the houses, even over those where something was still left
because smoke betrayed the fact that food was present in the house,
and then bandits arrived. Those who still had supplies of flour ate
raw dough in order not to reveal themselves.

In the eighth month of the siege of the Fortress, people began to
eat other people, lying in wait for them on the street at night, killing
them, and eating them, especially children. It was said that a mother
of five children killed her baby in order to feed her older children
and then she lost her mind. Others said she had lost her mind
before that and was already mad when she boiled the child. Bandits
who came because of the smoke confirmed it: they were horrified at
what they saw and left without touching anything. And dead bodies
lay everywhere on the streets and no one cleared them away. To the
contrary, people cut pieces of flesh from them under cover of night,
in order to eat it.

Deserters told Prince Konstantin about the situation of those under siege and one day he sent his envoy Anisim to the Fortress wall.

After people gathered on the wall, Anisim addressed those standing there:

Our prince, His Highness Konstantin, holds no grudge against
you and will not touch any of you but Frol. Hand Frol over to him

and you will be saved, for you will not survive without food, which has already run out for you.

Voivode Orest answered him, saying the people in the Fortress would hold out as long as necessary for victory over their foe Konstantin, meaning they would not hand over Frol.

Glancing at the voivode, Konstantin's envoy Anisim said:

Your appearance, Orest, is too well fed for those words. I am appealing to the martyrs and sufferers of the Fortress.

Even before those words left the speaker's lips, his chest was pierced by an arrow released from upon the wall. Anisim stood for an instant then collapsed to the ground. Some confusion and struggle broke out on the wall, evidence that not everyone agreed with what Orest said.

A week later, Bishop Afanasy set off for the Fortress. He met with Prince Frol and requested that those eager to leave the Fortress be released. Frol, however, did not agree because he knew too many wanted to leave.

You are making these people into hostages, Afanasy told the prince.

You are mistaken, O Bishop, answered Frol. Konstantin is making them into hostages by condemning people to starvation and so each ruined life becomes a deadly sin for him.

After a silence, the bishop said:

The two of you share the deadly sin but that does not make your part easier.

A month later, revolts began in the Fortress because Prince Frol released no one. A great rage then gripped people and it was a rage of desperation. The revolts were brutally quelled by troops whom Frol fed what little food still remained. When even that was gone, rage spread to the troops like a pestilence. And it became clear to Prince Frol that his primary danger lay not outside the Fortress but within it.

After sending for Bishop Afanasy, Frol announced to him that he was prepared to surrender if Prince Konstantin would safeguard his life and freedom. Konstantin had to swear on a cross to release Frol once he recognized Konstantin's supreme power, also by kissing the cross.

Upon his return, the bishop conveyed Frol's words to Prince Konstantin. After considering what he heard, Konstantin kissed a cross in the presence of the people, saying he would release the prisoner; Frol was informed of that without delay.

And then the gates were opened and the troops entered the Fortress, headed by Prince Konstantin, on horseback. They were greeted with rejoicing, as liberators, and a laurel wreath was placed on Konstantin. Inside the Fortress, the troops tossed out bread, which quickly disappeared into the hungry mouths of the besieged after they tore it apart. People also gathered up fallen crumbs and fought over them, rolling on the ground.

When Frol was led from the prince's chambers, he bowed to Konstantin, lowering his head to the ground.

He said:

Remember, Prince, about the oath on the cross, that after I recognize your seniority, you will release me.

And Konstantin answered him:

I remember, Prince Frol, about the oath, but I will not even wait for your recognition, I will release you this minute.

Having said that, he signaled to a guard, who stepped away from the prisoner. Then a crowd immediately closed in around Frol, just as it had around the tossed bread. And those who had languished in the Fortress so hated the prince that he was destroyed in an instant. The guards had no chance to interfere, but witnesses said they were in no hurry since they had received no direct order to interfere.

When a spear suddenly flew out of the crowd at the mounted Konstantin, he was wearing a laurel wreath. The prince lacked chainmail, for he had not, after all, come to battle, so his chest was unprotected from the spear. And he died an instant death, hanging in the stirrups. In the turmoil, no one noticed who had dispatched the spear, though some said it was dispatched by the hand of an angel, as punishment to Konstantin for his treachery.

And thus ended the great confrontation of Konstantin and Frol, of North and South.

PARFENY

A universal aspiration for unification took shape during the creation of great empires – historians have found reasons for that again and again. But they subsequently explained the collapse of empire using those same reasons, announcing each time that *the reasons are on the surface.* Likely on the surface in the sense that they are all very superficial.

Nobody knows the deeper reasons. We just grope at them, vaguely sensing the rhythm of convergences and re-pulsions. And for now, alas, we study waves, forgetting about the ebb and flow of tides.

A time to cast away stones, and a time to gather stones together. If desired, one can announce (*the reasons on the surface*) that a person is gathering together good stones and casting away the bad; however, that explains nothing about his unusual activity, which he performs out of love for the rhythm rather than for the stones.

Some things cease their existence not because they are bad; their time has simply expired. And they begin their existence not because they are good; their time, to the contrary, has arrived. A time to cast away stones, and a time to gather stones together. Perhaps the answer is time? Time and rhythm.

Paradise was a place of absolute harmony but people disrupted that harmony, dooming themselves to sweat, blood, and death. Were there rational reasons for that? It seems not: I see only a surfeit of serenity and a readiness for escape. But the pendulum swings again and the escapees' descendants dream of lost paradise.

Chess pieces are at their highest level of harmony when in their initial positions: the first move disrupts the harmony. Each subsequent move only aggravates the matter, but it is impossible not to make a move. Such is the inexorable law of chess, something chess players did not think up.

The South of the Island did not experience oppression from the North and Prince Frol was not beloved by residents. They accepted his side, submitting to history's strange rhythm and their own instinctive attraction to motion. Serenity began beckoning to them again when they started to hear a whistling in their ears brought on by the speed of motion.

Konstantin and Frol were made for each other and shared a common cause. In some sense, they were an inseparable couple who died on the same day.

Ksenia and I, too, dream of dying on the same day.

Chapter the Third

MIKHAIL

After the death of Prince Konstantin, his son, Prince Mikhail, ruled the Island. The beginning of his royal reign was not unclouded, for Prince Andronik, son of the dead Frol, took his time acknowledging Mikhail's primacy. He announced that his father's acknowledgement of Konstantin's primacy did not extend to him and so he demanded a meeting with Mikhail.

In their meeting, the princes spoke of the genealogies since that was where the sorrowful confrontation had begun. After arguing for a week, they reached an agreement that consisted of the following: Both princes admitted that Emperor Augustus spent the first night with Princess Melania, the loveliest in the royal family. Augustus, however, sought profundity in relationships and thus spent his second night with Princess Ilaria; his search was not in vain.

In spite of discovering what he had sought, the emperor left the Island the morning after, never to return.

Ilaria was first to give birth, which, according to the princes' agreement, gave her bloodline a preemptive right to power over Melania's bloodline. And Prince Andronik confirmed the declaration of that right, though his facial expression was pensive at the time.

PARFENY

After the War of the Genealogies, the princes came to an agreement. It turns out Augustus spent two rather than three days on the Island. According to Mikhail's and

Andronik's thinking, a possible third dynasty was lopped off along with the third day.

That attempt to protect themselves from a third power might, as it were, be seen as some sort of naiveté. In actuality, though, the argument did not stand up to criticism. It seems that the person who became the forefather of two dynasties in the course of two days was completely capable of starting three or even more dynasties within those same two days. That is from the physiological point of view. If looking at the story metaphysically, then the founding of a dynasty cannot be reduced to conception and it thus indisputably demands a separate day because that day is, in and of itself, an epoch.

It is noteworthy that in the course of achieving the compromise, the loveliness of one of the foremothers was pitted against the other's profundity. One could, of course, be surprised that new details about the women were clarified by the time of the princes' agreement: over the course of centuries, Clio, history's muse, never uttered a sound about Augustus' Island affections.

The treatment of the world as a work of art manifests itself here. Only what is beautiful is veritable or, expressing it in the spirit of the chronicle, deep. And the opposite: only what is deep is genuinely beautiful. In order that a text be believed, it should be beautiful. It is that circumstance that withdraws the question of why Augustus left quickly, after finding depth. It does not matter that he leaves, what is important is that he found what he sought.

Prince Mikhail thought Prince Andronik's pensiveness seemed to be a bad omen. He understood that their agreement was precarious and would collapse under the first gust of wind, as if it were a house built upon sand. He then appealed to Bishop Afanasy and told of his alarm regarding the future.

Be alarmed, Prince, about the present, the bishop counseled Mikhail, for the future arrives in the guise of the present. Only Agafon the Forward-Looking, who disregards time, is not alarmed about the future and can help here.

Upon hearing that, Prince Mikhail summoned Agafon and shared his alarm with him.

And Agafon said:

You, Prince, will have a son by the name of Parfeny, which means *virgin*. Prince Andronik will have a daughter Ksenia, that is to say *foreign*, which can be understood as *unknown to the world*. And they will unite in marriage and upon their union, the internecine strife will quieten.

Will that happen within a foreseeable time? asked Prince Mikhail.

Only eternity is unforeseeable, responded Agafon the Forward-Looking.

After learning what Agafon had said, Prince Andronik began to treat the concluded agreement with greater fervor. Agafon's predictions aroused in him greater trust than Mikhail's promises.

In the fifth year of Mikhail's royal reign, a certain blacksmith sailed to the Island with his blind and speaking dog. The blacksmith took gold rings and necklaces from people, buried them in the ground, and then commanded that the dog find them. And the dog dug up valuable after valuable, taking them in his teeth and returning them to their owners and speaking about each, telling who was merciful and good, and who, on the other hand, was a fornicator and adulterer.

Others, convinced of the dog's clairvoyance, preferred to part with their jewelry and escape unnoticed, anything so as not to hear the bitter remarks the dog uttered. And since the dog never once erred, everyone said he had an inquisitive, albeit sorcerous, spirit. The dog foretold the arrival of pestilence on the Island before sailing off to points unknown with the blacksmith.

Seeing that the dog had not erred previously, all were greatly worried and questioned Agafon the Forward-Looking as to whether the prediction of pestilence was false.

Answering a question with a question, Agafon said to them:

What good is there in knowledge if you stand powerless before it?

And why, Forward-Looking, do you not want to warn us about the fatal pestilence? retorted the people. We would take measures to save ourselves, even if there are not actually such measures.

Agafon answered them with sorrow:

Am I not the one who warns you daily that drunkenness is fatal and who points out effective measures for salvation? So then, do answer me, have you taken many of those measures?

KSENIA

Agafon the Forward-Looking spoke reluctantly to the princes about the impending pestilence and he said nothing about their deaths. He did not like looking ahead. Strictly speaking, the very nickname "Forward-Looking" was not given to him entirely fairly: Agafon looked in all directions simultaneously.

He saw coming events with the same clarity as he saw events that had already arrived. Possibly even more clearly because the imperfection of the human memory had not distorted them. History, Agafon taught, tells much more about the present than the past.

In one of his sermons, he examines the question of the predestination of events. He confirms that there is no predestination. There is a person's free choice, which leads to one event or another.

So said Agafon.

In discussing this chapter of the chronicle, Parfeny and I touched on freedom of choice. I did not understand how unlimited freedom of choice could help but infringe on God's omnipotence.

Parfeny said:

"Why, my joy? It can. It is simply that any – even the freest – choice a person makes is known to God in advance."

I thought: My husband calls me *my joy*. We have been creating joy for one another for an entire eternity. We chose one another freely, although they betrothed us without asking our permission. One might say the choice came about after the fact, in the course of our life together, but that sort of explanation would be frivolous. It would certainly not have pleased Agafon, who disregarded time. The choice came about not after the wedding ceremony but during it.

Much of what Agafon says resonates with me. Every now and then, I anticipate something from the future but do not speak of it. Not because I am hiding it, but because I simply cannot express it. Under no circumstances am I comparing myself to Agafon: he fore*saw* and I fore*feel*. That does not lend itself to words.

In the seventh year of the reign of His Highness Prince Mikhail, his wife, Princess Zoya, sensed she was with child during the days of May. At that same time, in the month of May, Princess Yevpraksia became pregnant by Prince Andronik.

In the month of August during the seventh year of Mikhail's royal reign, pestilence gripped the Island. It began on the Mainland and was carried to the Island by ship rats.

And then Prince Mikhail and Prince Andronik asked Agafon:

Why, one might ask, were our children conceived if they are doomed to perish from the pestilence?

In all things related to conception, which comes about between two people, questions to a third party are not completely warranted, responded Agafon. I can say but one thing: the children will be saved.

In the course of a week, plague had gripped the entire Island, and there was no escape anywhere. Some went into the Forest, in the hope the terrible illness would not overtake them there, while others built shelters on the deserted shoreline. But life's necessities forced them to visit their homes, if only occasionally, and then they returned, already carrying within themselves deadly plague particles, which became obvious upon their return.

A person struck by plague first and foremost felt what seemed to be the blow of a spear under the shoulder blade or in the chest, opposite the heart, and became ill and began to hack up blood. Then it was as if the person was being burned by fire and still later began shivering. And the glands swelled up in various places, on the neck for some, on the thigh for others, though some had it under the arm or under the cheekbone or perhaps under a shoulder blade or in the groin.

In the plague's first month, Priest Ioann died after courageously taking deathbed confessions and then reading the funeral services.

He began slowly sinking while performing a funeral service and was caught under the arms and led to a bench, but even when they carried him away to his home, he did not interrupt the funeral service and soon he met his Maker with a prayer on his lips.

Goldsmith Yevlogy, whose jewelry was worn by the Island's nobility, died. His hands forged the candleholders in the Church of the Transfiguration and gilded cupolas that seemed to burn with fire in clear weather, to the joy of the devout and the fright of the faithless.

The head tax collector, Yevmeny – an incorruptible person who toiled with great zeal, for which he was regarded with deference, though, truth be told, not loved – died.

After them, there departed Vissarion, the head of the City's guard, whose heavy fist was familiar to many City citizens. And such was the power of his habit that even during the funeral service, Vissarion's threatening right hand suddenly took on the form of a fist. I imagine many might have sighed in relief at his demise, had they not been looking into the face of that which is more fearsome than any guard.

A great, great multitude of others died; their names are known to God.

And the living had no time to bury the dead and there were not enough healthy to look after the ill, so one healthy person tended ten of the ill. Many homes already stood empty or there was only one person left inside, sometimes a child.

In those days there was a head of the City, an eparch, a person by the name of Amvrosy. He walked the City each day, block by block, in order to understand where there was the most trouble, so he might dispatch help there. He did not keep for himself even a dinar of the money entrusted to him – this was not the usual practice on the Island – but rather gave everything to fight the plague, adding his own funds as well.

This Amvrosy himself checked empty buildings to be certain no one had been forgotten inside, and he had no fear of touching ill bodies, for he wished to determine if life was still within them. Residents revered Amvrosy as a righteous man: such people are rarely found among eparchs. The fact that the dead were buried, even if not immediately, and help was offered to the living was in great part due to his efforts. His firm fulfillment of his duty saved many people then, though of course many were not saved.

And the plague raged for three months and no one then counted the dead although it was clear to all that the number was in the tens of thousands.

In late September, after taking the schema, Prince Mikhail departed this world.

In early October, having also taken vows, Prince Andronik met his Maker.

And the Island was left ravaged and deprived of a leader.

One other death, however, was added to these. In the middle of October, after the pestilence had already begun to quieten, Agafon the Forward-Looking met his Maker. Judging from the fact that in the last months of his life Agafon took pains to pray and fast more than ever before, he knew of his own quick death. And he said nothing to anyone. And his most honest body was buried in the Monastery's Church of the Transfiguration.

His death brought great sorrow to the Island, for Agafon was a just person. Island residents grieved since the only person who had known the future was now gone. And although he had been powerless to avert anything, everyone had felt slightly more at ease from the very thought that the future was known to someone.

Recalling the agreement between the princes who reposed in the Lord – and even more so recalling Agafon the Forward-Looking's prediction to the bloodlines of Roman and Irakly, whose dynasties descend from Augustus' sons – it was decided to set aside the question of power until the birth of the royal children and their first birthdays. It would be necessary to appoint a regent when the newborns had clearly established themselves on this earth.

In order that the Island not be struck by the plague of another lack of governance, the people of the Island, along with both dynasties, appealed to Bishop Feofan with an entreaty to take governing upon himself until that time. After hearing the words addressed to him, Feofan locked himself in his cell and prayed all night on bended knees. He emerged with the first rays of sun and told the people awaiting him:

If it please God, then so it shall be.

Chapter the Fourth

YUSTIN

It is unlikely that a pen will be found that is worthy of describing the royal reign of devout Yustin, the prince-regent, who after long requests agreed to accept the position of guardian for Parfeny, a minor, the son of Yustin's brother Mikhail, who departed before his time. If such a pen is ever even found, it will be difficult – oh, so difficult – for it to form the letters of the official words *guardian* or, for all we know, *regent*, although devout Prince Yustin became *a second father* to the lad Parfeny from the very first day.

That pen will begin scraping as if it were an unlubricated axle, begin writhing across the paper, stumbling like a horse sensing a wolf, and preferring the warm word *father* to the bureaucratic term. The first father, the second father – who will attend to that counting and who will even count that as attentiveness? The primary thing is *father*. For that word was the first to fly from the orphan's lips, when the child began speaking at the proper time.

His second word was *mother*, addressed to the right-believing Princess Glikeria, Prince Yustin's wife. With a youth full of disquiet behind her – poor but honest, complex but wonderful – the princess became for the child a model of what never fades. With a glimmer of the unprecedented, and with moderation and bounds.

KSENIA

Regarding choice. This chapter was written by a person who simultaneously made two mutually exclusive choices. I am speaking of Prokopy the Nasal, who described the reign of

Prince-Regent Yustin. The description is distinctive because of the particular style of the narration, which someone aptly called "animated." It is unlike the other chroniclers' style.

Many years ago, an astonishing – one might say sensational – manuscript was found. It is entitled *The True History of Prince Yustin, Written by Prokopy the Nasal*. It was noticed in a crack in the chimney in Prokopy's cell.

The stove in the cell had not been used since the monastery began heating with one large stove in the basement (this happened even before Prokopy's time), and by all appearances, the chronicler decided to use the chimney as a hiding place. I will note that Island Monastery of the Savior is restored from time to time; only God knows what other finds we can expect . . .

Storing the manuscript in the hiding place was not an empty whim on the author's part: it contains pieces of information that, put mildly, contradict what he himself says in the chronicle. Based on the document that was discovered, Prokopy had been intending to divulge it. It likely remained in the hiding spot due to the author's sudden death.

There is a mysterious codicil inserted on the manuscript's last page. In its published form it looks like this:

By Agafon's coffin will not find a prophecy are so vessel is the source of information about the future of the Island.

That line has an unusual construction and its meaning is obscure. All that is clear is that it is somehow linked to Agafon the Forward-Looking's prophecy. But how?

And so after stealing the Island's predictions about the future, Prokopy simultaneously enriched it with knowledge about the past. Even from the title of the discovered text, it follows that the history in the chronicle is *untrue*. Since two

51

stories were written in parallel, it worked out that Prokopy's choice came true simultaneously in favor of truth and falsity.

Prokopy did not seem to stop after separating truth from falsity in his writings. It is possible he even assumed that truth and falsity would change places with the passage of time (something that happened during his lifetime) and he left independent assessments to posterity.

T
he children, for whom it lay ahead to enter into marriage, were betrothed at the age of three. They truly became the pride of the Island, our land's two loveliest flowers. Everyone thought radiance emanated from their very heads and they were like two small suns. Their appearance outside in dreary weather drove away the clouds, so one might say that three suns shone at once, warming everyone. Their love for Yustin and Glikeria warmed the children themselves, the blessed Parfeny and Ksenia.

Parfeny's behavior may have resembled that of other children his age, but matters worked out differently with Ksenia. She did not like children's games and avoided them, which might have seemed unsociable or even rather outlandish to those who lacked any subtlety of feelings. In fact, that apparent unsociability reflected her attention to the lofty rather than the earthly. Glikeria, a beacon of chastity and purity, served as a model for her from the very cradle.

Glikeria was Yustin's second wife. His first wife, Agafya, had turned out to be infertile and so the prince needed to part ways with her. Yustin and Glikeria had previously attempted to cure Agafya's infertility, but since their efforts turned out to be as fruitless as Agafya herself, with heavy heart, Yustin had to take Glikeria as his wife.

Ksenia's Auntie Klavdia, who whiled away her time at the Coast, took on the girl's care. It was, however, decided not to separate the children and so they usually spent time together, either at the Palace or by the sea.

I am left feeling distressed that I lack the ability to describe the kindness and wisdom of people who take the guardianship of small children upon themselves. How can one not weep for oneself, for having never visited Athens or studied at academies, and for possessing crude intelligence and low feelings? For having not initially understood the deepest educational essences when observing games, when playing, shall we say, odds and evens with a pious couple and seeing their wonderful progeny who in their earlier years had learned to tell the odds from the evens, something not even titled people can distinguish?

In the eighth year of virtuous Yustin's regency, the tutee Parfeny came into the habit of playing a knife game. That game developed the precision and dexterity a future leader so needs. The art of flinging a knife in order that it arc, something the right-thinking Glikeria taught Parfeny, was a means for fighting clumsiness – something that was, to a certain degree, characteristic of the aforementioned orphan – and that sort of art is always, as they say, of some general use anyway in public life. Teaching the child to throw knives began when any sort of learning comes easily.

We adults are another matter, incapable as we are not only of learning to throw a knife so it will arc but also of memorizing a small number of outlanders' words. This is why we stand mute and tongueless before visitors from the Mainland, powerless to even greet them, and I shall keep silent regarding complex topics such as philosophical discourse or, loosely speaking, constructing syllogisms. Without language, you cannot enter into either simple friendship or closer relationships, which is why there are still so few international marriages here. But we shall set discourse aside and return to the previous topic.

Glikeria was a true second mother during the knife game, tire-lessly following, ensuring not one of the knives flew toward the heir to the princely throne. When a knife by some devilish instigation flew in his direction anyway, tender-aged Parfeny was saved by the shout of she who was designated to be his wife, the tender-aged Ksenia. She was strolling at that time with her kin, by the sea. While walking past a cliff that reminded her of a tower, she briefly shouted:

Knife!

And that was enough. Forestalling his unwieldiness, the boy managed to take a half-turn and the knife flying toward his heart pierced his forearm.

This turned out to be sizeable knife, and it had been tossed skillfully, so if not for the shout, all might have ended lamentably for Parfeny. Beside herself with rage, the commonsensical Glikeria immediately ordered that the head of the lad who had incautiously thrown the knife be chopped off. Several liars or simply uninformed people recall that the chopped-off head allegedly spoke. If one takes into account *what* exactly it said (and I do not wish to repeat it), then the story of the talking head appears to be completely unreliable.

KSENIA

I did not see the actual knife game (we were too far from those playing) but I felt what they were doing there at the time, on the northern part of the Island.

We were walking along the seashore near our castle. Leading us was Auntie Klavdia, my dead father's sister, who handled my upbringing. She was walking along the edge of the surf line, lifting the hem of her dress. She held it with both hands, high and above her knees, but part of the hem slid along the sea sand even so and kept submerging into the trembling sea foam. I noticed Klavdia's legs that day. They were, to put it in contemporary language, knock-kneed. I suddenly felt a jab of uneasiness and, without understanding what I was doing, I shouted:

"Knife!"

"Why did you shout 'knife!'?" asked my aunt, without slowing her pace.

"And why are you knock-kneed?" I said, answering her question with a question.

Klavdia did not understand either my shriek or the question, and I myself did not understand either of them – they simply blurted out. Essentially, I was not there. I saw Parfeny in the distant city and heard words in the impenetrable future. The same thing, however, also happened to Klavdia, who once called me a *problem child*. I think that runs in our family.

My shout saved Parfeny. He heard it in some strange way (my intended heard my words from any distance) and turned toward me. That was enough for the knife to hit his shoulder rather than his heart. Of the two versions of the event that Prokopy the Nasal offered, the one in *The True History* is closer to the truth.

In the twelfth year of Yustin's regency, his devoted wife Glikeria, a veritable vessel of chastity, founded the House of Piety as lodging for women who formerly sold their bodies but had set off on the path to redemption. In order that the women not give in to temptation and return to their sinful ways, she removed men from the House, all save one doorman, Yevlampy, who was ninety-two years old. The repentant women (they called one another sisters) sewed everyday clothing. Once a week, on Sunday, one of the sisters went to a bazaar where sewn items were sold and the money earned went to the women for foodstuffs.

In the fourteenth year of the regency under Prince Yustin's rule, Glikeria, a beacon of benevolence, founded yet another home, and then more and more. Morals on the Island improved so much that some began to fear that childbearing would cease here when all was said and done. Or that it would be fulfilled in a less sinful manner, such as budding. Meanwhile, the ruling pair's primary destiny – rearing the royal couple – was being fulfilled in an extraordinarily responsible manner, albeit slowly.

In the eighteenth year of righteous Yustin's rule, events developed, as always, rather slowly. During the eight years that had passed since the day of the memorable knife game, young Parfeny and Ksenia had only become one and a half years older. This testifies to the child-rearing challenges of pious Yustin and Glikeria.

They rightfully decided that in cases such as these, there was no reason to hurry, as the natural slowing of time for Parfeny and Ksenia should not be overcome artificially in any way. Yustin and Glikeria had observed that time is leisurely during childhood. That discovery allowed them to count the years for Parfeny and Ksenia in a special manner, dividing them by three, sometimes even by four. That, of course, forced them to remain in power longer than intended, but these people had been created such that they could not leave their wards undereducated.

As Yustin sometimes said, if it will take one hundred years for proper upbringing, that means we will labor over it that long.

I am convinced that there is no need to compare time for various people or to say "this one lived long but that one did not." Each lived as long as necessary for attaining his or her life goals. It is known to all what muddle arises as soon as we begin speaking about time, age, and suchlike matters. And right then, there it is: the explanation is that each person has his or her own time, and so it is very difficult for people to find common ground.

This is why not everyone's age is known. Families where everyone's age is unknown are not a rarity, although they do realize, let us say, who in the family is oldest. If they are in the dark in that regard, then they come to an agreement about age. Time is good in that it can always be agreed upon.

In the twentieth year of the reign of the most wise Yustin, he hunted hares. And he had not yet had the chance to set his snares when a huge snake fell from the sky and everyone was terrified. And there was thunder, the earth groaned, and people scattered. And the prince realized this was a sign from above, in order to thwart his hunting of hares, an impious pursuit. He never went hunting again.

In the twenty-fifth year of the reign of the most noble Yustin, the Hellenic philosopher Eusebius visited the Island. Seeing the prince's righteous life, Eusebius changed his way of thinking and was christened. Being a person of some means, he gave the prince three hundred dinars for improving the Island. Moved by love for his people, Yustin, who had no interest in personal gain, wasted no time in spending it all, to the last dinar, on good deeds and gave Eusebius a charter with the promise that the donated money would be returned one hundredfold in the Great Beyond.

A year later, Eusebius suddenly passed away and the aforementioned charter was placed in his hands when he was buried. Several weeks later, he appeared in one of Yustin's dreams and said: Take your charter. And so they dug up the grave and found Eusebius sitting with a scroll in his hand. When they attempted to take that scroll, the deceased would not give it to anyone but the prince. After Yustin took the charter, Eusebius lay down again. And everyone read what was written in it: *I, Eusebius the Philosopher, confirm to blessed Yustin, with a signature from my own hand, that the debt was paid back one hundredfold.* Learning of this astonishing event, many well-to-do people fearlessly and, one might say, joyfully, gave money to Prince Yustin.

In the twenty-sixth year of Yustin's reign, a snake crawled into a pitcher of wine and drank all the wine. This made the snake swell so much it could not crawl out. When the pitcher was brought to the sage Yustin, the prince smiled meekly and told the snake:

First give us back the wine you drank and only then will you be able to crawl out.

The snake spewed forth the wine and freed itself shortly thereafter. Those in attendance fell to the ground when that happened and glorified the prince's wisdom.

In the thirtieth year of Yustin's rule, there occurred a great misfortune: the Royal Palace went up in flames one September night. Much time was required to extinguish the fire and when that was finally accomplished, two charred bodies were found in the royal bedroom. These were the bodies of Yustin and Glikeria. That is how the two beacons of piety burned and the bedroom became their burial vault.

PARFENY

Not everything Prokopy says in his chronicle should be considered a lie. Prokopy rightfully points out that each person has their own time and that time can even change during the various periods of a life. He is also correct that longevity and rhythms of time are given to each person according to need. On occasion, more time might be needed in order to understand something or, to the contrary, explain it to others.

Yes, all people have a common time but that time is nothing more than a dotted line connected to the personal time of each one of us. This is why some live twenty years, some two hundred. Or nine hundred. Their personal time is a reality but that common time is a pure invention. A wish to pretend that everything is connected. In some sense, it is even unexpected that Prokopy understood that.

As for Yustin and Glikeria's unlawful ambition to rule as long as possible, that did not revoke the correctness of their calculations. It was as if Ksenia and I felt (she certainly felt) that our life would be longer than expected, so we were in no hurry to mature.

Unlike other chroniclers, Prokopy tried to remain close to the royal court, explaining that by saying that as a historian, he needed to receive first-hand information. From time to time, he even showed the prince what he had written, which, frankly, is difficult to explain as some sort of necessity.

Prokopy justified himself by saying he did so because his heart told him to, that he was powerless to conceal his love for the ruling personages. As Prokopy's secret manuscript shows, however, what his heart told him could change beyond all recognition in the course of a day.

Yes, there was a certain duplicity in Prokopy: even contemporaries unfamiliar with *The True History* called him *a person with two tongues*. Like the majority of artistic statements, that image did not square with reality, for we know the historian did not have any tongue at all. In the non-tongue sense, the reality was also not as simple as it appears at first glance. Liberalism was not a strong suit in the

Middle Ages and Prokopy's experience speaks to the fact that sometimes even one tongue is a lot.

Needless to say, the radical difference between Prokopy's two versions of history creates an unfavorable impression. It seems as if the two histories ought to complement one another, but when one combines them the volume of truth does not increase because neither one nor the other sets out to seek the truth. This differs slightly from what we (meaning Ksenia and I) were accustomed to in the Middle Ages.

History in that distant epoch was, to a greater extent, history because it looked at things with less bias. Contemporary historical thought, though, is formulated by circumstances that are distant from the events described. It depends on political expediency, which turns historical writings into a tool for a fight. This is why, to some extent, the modern-day historian participates in events with a sideways view. A medieval historian, though, looked from above.

Prokopy the Nasal did not observe from above and he was thus ahead of his time. Perhaps this is the reason why the publishers of *A History of the Island* made the decision to publish *The True History* as an addendum to the chapter on Prince Yustin. It is the right decision.

It is curious that what Prokopy himself considers truth in the official history is only the story about Ksenia and me. He writes about us sympathetically and I won't hide that this is nice. I send him my sincere greetings, to that part of the other world where he is now (various options are possible here).

The True History of Prince Yustin, Written by Prokopy the Nasal

Well, well, whoever plans to describe the deeds of Yustin and Glikeria needs a strong pen indeed. Deeds, misdeeds. Any pen is liable to break from descriptions of these sorts. I write about that ungodly couple at night, when no one sees. After writing all those daytime panegyrics, I now write about how they were actually snakes in human form.

What I wrote about the children, Parfeny and Ksenia, is the small bit in the chronicle that is truth. I am unworthy and do not disavow what I wrote there. Children cannot help but call forth love, particularly Ksenia, an unusual and strange child for whom the unknown was known and the unseen was seen. She always shuns childish diversions, as only holy children shun them. If ascending the royal throne will be granted to Parfeny and Ksenia at some time, they will become merciful and wise rulers. Unlike Yustin and Glikeria.

Yustin. A brainless adulterer, bribe-taker, and usurper. It had been decided in advance that after the babies were born, Bishop Feofan would become the Island's ruler for a year. But that Yustin could not tolerate even one year; he began mercilessly crowding out Feofan.

He conversed with him, admonished, noted that he would be regent a year later anyway, and so why hem and haw, would it not be better to transfer power immediately to him, Yustin? The bishop silently listened to him, simply looked at him and waggled his eyebrows, then a month later, he left the Royal Palace just as silently and returned to the Monastery.

Glikeria. An exceptional whore and that is the best that can be said about her because in some sense Glikeria is even worse than her husband.

If anyone found out that I am now writing all this, I would not live another hour. But that is exactly what draws me to write with particular force – I cannot resist it. And I pity the descendants too: I fear they will believe the conjectures I was forced to place in the chronicle.

About, for example, the first words Parfeny spoke. No babies I am familiar with began speaking with the words *father* and *mother*. The words *mama* and *papa* exist for that, in that particular order.

Glikeria means "sweet." . . . Her sweetness was tasted from the age of fourteen and by many, I shall note, for there has not been in the history of the Island such a b– . . . One might think my terms are intolerably strong but that is not the case. No matter what terms I use, I am certain they will be too mild.

She sold her body on streets and public squares, in noble homes and in barracks. Especially in barracks, where the quantity of participants drew her in and she was the last to tire from those orgies. When the soldiers had no money to pay for her obliging body, she offered it at no charge. And whoever explains that as unselfish would be mistaken, for her irrepressible lust was the only explanation.

The Island's worldliest libertines were astounded by her knowledge in the field of romantic delights and they felt themselves pathetic ignoramuses in her presence. From time to time, when Glikeria realized she was pregnant, she attempted to rid herself of the fetus using every means she knew. Those failed her twice and she gave birth.

It is unknown exactly what happened to those children. It is said, however, that years later, when she was already a princess, some sort of person came to the Palace gate, asserting that he was her son. The constables wanted to turn him away but Glikeria hindered them. Instead, she ordered them to bring the person to one of the basements, where she allegedly intended to speak with him. No one ever saw him again.

In speaking of how disinterestedness was not a force for change in Glikeria's life, I will mention only that it was she who established brothels on the Island and she herself who received the profits. By bitter irony, she called those establishments houses of piety, where priestesses of love were allegedly reeducated.

Glikeria personally led the investigation when three of the reeducated women from one of the houses became pregnant all at once and the entire Island learned of that fact. Suspicion fell on Yevlampy, a ninety-two-year-old porter. In a public inquest, the aforementioned Yevlampy could not remember either the women with whom he had purportedly sinned or even how that was done.

The pregnant women, however, recalled him and announced that at the moment of their seduction he was utterly perky, persistent, and inventive. Many doubted Yevlampy's persistence when they looked at him, for he resembled a dry branch in the wind. The seducer's runny eyes focused on the nearest cloud. His entire appearance testified to his weak understanding of what happened. Yevlampy was found guilty and put to death.

However, what point is there in speaking of Yevlampy when Glikeria carried out multiple attempts to kill her ward Parfeny? Fortunately, a guardian angel drew her hand away from the lad each time. The best-known such incident was the knife game when the princess incited one of the boys to fling a knife at Parfeny. Glikeria explained that by saying Parfeny was wearing chainmail under his shirt (although who wears chainmail below a shirt?) and nothing would happen to him, and that the prince needed to grow accustomed to anything unexpected and that flinging knives is the best medicine for treating notorious juvenile clumsiness. She was a great master of muddling another's head, was that Glikeria.

When murder did not occur thanks to Ksenia's shriek from the other end of the Island, the princess wasted no time chopping off the little boy's head, moreover she shut his mouth in an obvious way while waiting for the executioner. Glikeria had not, however, expected that the head would begin speaking even after being chopped off. Lying on steps red with blood (in the absence of a scaffold, the execution took place on stairs) alongside the puny body of a child, the head spoke of Glikeria's request and of chainmail and of so very much else.

It is astonishing, shouted Glikeria, astonishing the stupid things that head says! There is no doubt the lad was insane.

Yes, he's simply lost his head, said the flatterers and toadies, watching as blood spurted on the steps from the aorta.

And no one dared shut the head's mouth and then Glikeria rushed to the stairs, unafraid not only of talking heads but also of the prince of this world himself. When she bent toward the head, her foot slid on a step slippery from blood. As she fell, the princess's forehead touched the chopped head and her forehead turned scarlet. They say that blood did not wash off her forehead for forty days. How else can it be explained that she never left the Palace and no one saw her during that time?

Did Glikeria hate Parfeny? I suppose not, despite desiring to kill him. After lust, her primary passion was a hunger for power, and all her other passions were somehow a continuation of those principle ones. Parfeny was a meek child and would not in his own right have caused Glikeria to wish to kill him, but he stood in her path to power and therein lay his great fault.

I am certain that in the end she would have killed Parfeny without wavering, but her thoughts changed when she noticed the lad was living according to a different time, one far longer and more spacious than her own. Glikeria realized that Parfeny was not an obstacle for her but rather protection.

Parfeny's time made his rise to power a distant event, while his death would have returned all the princes to a struggle over the royal reign, a struggle the simple people would have entered into, and the people (here Glikeria could not console herself with hopes) would not have found themselves on the side of Glikeria and Yustin.

After rereading what I wrote, I will correct myself in terms of her hunger for power, which was, after all, stronger than lust. All the same, those two passions united and led to her unparalleled elevation.

She wormed her way into the trust of Yustin's then-wife Princess Agafya, who suffered from infertility. Glikeria assured the unfortunate woman that it would be easy to cure her of infertility and that would avert the danger of her husband rejecting her. After saying she needed to light special incense in the royal bedroom, Glikeria sent Agafya to lie in the bath with an herbal infusion, moreover warning the princess that she would come for her at the necessary time.

The quack healer, meanwhile, hid in the bedroom, as she had planned, to wait for Yustin. Unlike herbal matters, which she was unfamiliar with, there were no secrets about matters of love. The Royal Gentleman of the Bedchamber told of Glikeria's indecent motions but her gaze was even more indecent. It was that which inflamed Yustin and something happened between him and Glikeria that the artless Agafya, lying in water long-cooled, simply did not expect. Glikeria shared Yustin's bed that night and Agafya did not return to that bed. It was said that Glikeria cast a spell on Yustin although it is more plausible that the prince was spellbound primarily because of her bedroom skills.

Agafya wandered the Palace for another week, like an apparition. She would find herself by the bedroom doors in the evenings and stand there, pouring out tears until one day Glikeria struck her in the face with a silver candlestick. That blow broke Agafya's nose and gashed her brow, which made the tears on her face mix with blood.

That is how Prince Yustin found her near the bedroom chambers. In his presence, Glikeria struck Agafya yet again, splitting her lip and shattering her front teeth. She would have beaten the unfortunate woman more since she was aiming for her eye, in order to remove it, but the prince stopped that infernal spawn.

Glikeria then began shouting that he should execute his former wife immediately since Agafya would not let him live in peace. Everyone feared that Yustin, who had fallen fully under Glikeria's influence, would do just that, but since he wished not for his wife's death (even if she was his former wife) he ordered her confined to a convent.

Tearful Agafya thanked him for his magnanimity and repeated that, toothless, she was no wife for his highness the prince and so she wished him joy and prosperity with Glikeria since her master's happiness was paramount for her.

Several days later, Yustin demanded that Bishop Feofan marry him to Glikeria. Feofan answered that this union was illicit and would not have the bishop's blessing. Yustin looked at the bishop with a copper gaze but said nothing, and everyone saw an ill omen in that silence.

The worst assumptions were borne out a week later, for Feofan suddenly passed away and Filaret was installed as bishop. And he, who was more silent than a fish, performed the marriage ceremony. Glikeria was punished for her evil deed since, like Agafya, she could not become pregnant. She had cut short too many pregnancies in her youth to be capable of giving birth.

After Feofan, the next to suffer was Eparch Amvrosy, whose selflessness saved many lives during the time of the plague. Unlike other officials, he brought no gold to Yustin in order to retain his position. The memory of his selfless devotion during the plague days had not faded in his countrymen's hearts: it remained fresh, and he even continued to irreproachably fulfill his eparchial duties.

Yustin became more and more annoyed about not receiving tributes from Amvrosy. I shall remain silent about the great jealousy that the prince experienced due to the people's love for the eparch. Propelled by those ignoble feelings, Yustin had long sought grounds for removing Amvrosy. Yustin found no such grounds in reality and so contrived something.

At that time, it was reported that the Royal Bible decorated with gemstones had vanished from the Monastery – this was the Bible on which the princes took their oaths upon ascending the throne. Amvrosy was accused of the theft. The basis for the accusation was in the testimony of two monks who had allegedly seen the eparch carry the valuable book from the Monastery under cover of darkness.

One of the witnesses was the Monastery's cellarer, who was capable of witnessing anything possible for anyone possible: he was a money-hungry person devoid of piety, someone whose soul held nothing holy.

I was the second testifying monk . . .

It is grievous for me to acknowledge this lie but what could I do? When Yustin asked me if I had seen Amvrosy carry the Royal Bible from the Monastery, I answered that I had not seen him. I also asked how the eparch could appear at the Monastery archive at night. The prince was silent for a moment and then said:

Who could have ended up there at night? Only you. Only you yourself could have removed the Bible from the library. And the father cellarer will confirm that he saw what happened.

Could I have avoided false testimony?

After gathering Island residents at the Main Square, Yustin
asserted for all to hear that the eparch's activity had always aimed
to destroy the Island via complete submersion but this particularly
appalling incident was one of the links in the chain of Amvrosy's
crimes. Yustin indicated that this link was crucial since what else
would the princes swear upon when ascending to the throne? It
worked out that now they could not rise to the throne, and so Yustin would need to remain there, against his, Yustin's, wish. Hearing
that, I realized the full scope of what Yustin had thought up.

Amvrosy was initially sentenced to death but the response to
the sentence was a storm of indignation that quickly swelled on the
square. Seeing his people this way for the first time, Yustin made
haste in reversing the sentence, which calmed people somewhat.

Glikeria recommended he execute the eparch in secret but the
prince was afraid of irrevocable actions for he understood that the
day could come when the crowd would demand he bring forth
the live eparch. As a precaution, Amvrosy was not executed. That
evening, he was blinded and taken away, to the South of the Island.
This person's future fate is unknown to me.

Afterward, when confessing on his deathbed before the brother-
hood of the Monastery, the father cellarer admitted that, per
Yustin's secret request, he himself had taken the Royal Bible out
of the Monastery and delivered it to the Palace and then falsely
testified against the eparch.

Yustin and Glikeria, whom one can call nothing other than
viper's spawn, were, however, loathsome in their own various ways.
Glikeria, as stated, was the incarnation of lust; Yustin was captured
by the passion and greed for money. After appointing himself the
Island's supreme judge, he approved any court decision made on the
territory entrusted to him. And he made those approvals only upon

receiving recompense, giving preference to the side that brought the most money. And this was both surprising and incomprehensible to all, since never before had a prince of the Island been venal.

But Yustin also contrived to demand money from wealthy people, allegedly for good deeds, promising them that they would receive their gift back a hundredfold in the Great Beyond. Something similar truly had happened with the philosopher Evagrius in Alexandria – the prince learned of this from a manuscript I brought to him. He enjoyed the story so much that he ordered me to write it out on a separate sheet, and when choosing his next victim to target for an offering, he would read that story aloud and then demand money. I do not know if they all believed what was written, but no one refused to donate.

I write these lines several days after the great fire in which Yustin and Glikeria, who were hateful to all, burned. It is said that the Palace was set afire in five spots. That is easy to believe. It is significant that they burned in their bedroom, where their sinful union began.

Three years before the horrible death of Yustin and Glikeria, a notable incident occurred that many jokingly called *Saint Yustin and the Dragon*. It is described by me in the chronicle, after Yustin himself ordered it. Being short on intelligence, he seemed to think this incident clearly displayed his wisdom. In fact the incident embodied the rule of Yustin and Glikeria.

They were a two-headed dragon that drank up all of the Island's juices: many small trunks with gold coins were found in a hiding spot behind the bedroom. On top of one of the trunks there lay the Royal Bible, miraculously untouched by flame. Perhaps it is sinful to speak of this but I shall say it: all that remains is to rejoice that, unlike the snake in the pitcher, Yustin and Glikeria will never crawl out of their grave.

Chapter the Fifth

YEVSTAFY

Upon the death of Yustin and Glikeria, the regent for the juvenile Parfeny became the right-believing Prince Yevstafy, younger brother of Mikhail and Yustin.

In the first year of Yevstafy's reign, certain seafarers brought the prince a gift of wondrous fish. Wishing to have a look at them, Yevstafy approached the marble water reservoir near the Palace, fell into the water, and drowned. The overall time of his rule was three days.

PARFENY

The entry is brief and does not even seem to correspond to Prokopy the Nasal's wordy style. On the other hand, could you really write much about this sort of occurrence? Some might say it would have been simpler to not write anything at all, that three days of rule don't count, but that would be incorrect. This isn't a matter of Yevstafy and his three days, which truly have no historical significance.

The point of a separate mention for Yevstafy's rule lies elsewhere. The Middle Ages did not tolerate the absence of links in a chronological chain. In any chain, be it composed of the Olympiads used to date events in some chronicles, or of emperors, or simply of years. Lost links broke the integrity of time, which organized God's world and anticipated eternity. Russians and the Irish even indicated *empty* years, those which passed without events. Year such-and-such: Nothing happened. *And there was great calm.*

For Prokopy the Nasal, who was neither Russian nor even Irish, the entry about the three days of Prince Yevstafy, who is now forgotten by all, was for an *empty* year. Yes, I will repeat that the text is lapidary; it is not in Prokopy's style. It is possible that the chronicler wanted to underscore the unusualness of what happened to the prince using an unusual style: he went out, as it were, to have a look at the fish. . . . This is Prokopy's hand and this is his entry.

That same hand recorded Saint Agafon's prophecy way back when. Had Agafon predicted the fate of the text he himself dictated? If so, then why did he dictate it to Prokopy? Were there no other scribes at the monastery? Sometimes I think that in trusting the prophecy to Prokopy, Agafon wanted to make its content unknown until the time was right. Until such time as it would become necessary and then found again. Time will tell.

Ksenia once told me, for no apparent reason at all, that the prophecy would be found.

"How do you know?" I asked.

"I feel it."

That is a weighty argument for me. What Ksenia (fore)feels usually comes true. I got used to that back when we were children.

It's amusing that I'm called *juvenile* in the announcement of the new regent. In general terms, Ksenia and I were about thirty years old at the time. But we truly did have our own time so over all, there is no mistake there.

This is Prokopy the Nasal's final entry. It was made on the day Yevstafy died, which also became the day of Prokopy the Nasal's death. Prokopy's joy over the death of Yustin and Glikeria was probably too great for his heart to bear.

All the days after the fire he flew rather than walked. At the evening prayer for the newly departed Yevstafy, he suddenly grabbed his heart and slid heavily down the wall to the floor. Brother Melety, who was standing next to him, grabbed him under the arms and dragged him to the door, out into the air.

We were at that service and also hurried outside, along with several monks. Prokopy lay on the grass. Brother Melety held his head but Prokopy's unblinking gaze left no hope. Snippets of psalms resounded through the open doors. We stood, shaken, because this was the first time we had seen a person's death.

Bishop Filaret came outside a minute later. After taking a careful look at Prokopy, who lay there, the bishop closed Prokopy's eyes. He closed them with his thumb and ring finger, with a confident and precise motion, as if he had been doing this his entire life. After reciting a prayer, he told Melety that from now on he, Melety, would take the deceased's place as chronicler. Melety continued to hold Prokopy's head as he bowed his own, accepting the bishop's blessing.

A month later, the bishop was forced to leave because he had not been pardoned for marrying Yustin and Glikeria, even years after the fact. The bishop left but the blessing remained and no one removed it from Melety.

It was Melety, by the way, who established that Agafon's prophecy about the Island had been removed from the chronicle. At first he simply noticed a pagination error in the sheets and then from conversations with the brothers (he conducted those discussions purposefully) he determined that the removed text was the prophecy.

Prokopy oftentimes tossed out enigmatic phrases, saying texts disappeared now and then, that not all the prophecies reached their addressees, or, for example, that prophecies can be useful when conveyed to an opponent in a timely manner. Prokopy said various things to various people, hence no suspicions arose in his regard. Yustin and Glikeria's celebrator turned out to be a natural-born big mouth, to the degree, of course, that was achievable, given his situation. Generally speaking, it was believed that his mind worked about as well as his tongue and since Prokopy's tongue was not his strong point, that somehow carried to his mind too.

Meanwhile, Prokopy was not especially artless. After collecting incoherent statements from the tongueless man, Melety reconstructed the course of events, not unlike how a mosaic is restored by gathering up strewn stones. He realized that the deceased had not only removed a sheet from the manuscript but had also sent it somewhere on the mainland.

There was one thing Melety said he did not understand: why Prokopy had made those dangerous hints that could unmask him if there were to be a certain confluence of events. One can only assume that this was a game for him, and it became particularly gripping as he came closer to unmasking himself. That tickled Prokopy's nerves, just as *The True History* most likely did when he wrote it simultaneously with the untrue history. The longer Ksenia and I live, the more surprised we are at how what's true in the world is interwoven with what is not true.

Such was Prokopy the Nasal, who had a reputation for being a person with two tongues though he did not have a single one, someone who hated political power yet sought to be in its proximity, who wrote in secret but spoke of the secret – he was once alive but now is dead. A part of our life departed forever – he will never again be.

KSENIA

What is most surprising of all is that we are still living. We are now doing that at our country home, where we've gone for the summer. In the evenings we walk along deserted beaches.

Today Phillip, who's publishing *A History of the Island,* came to visit. Phillip comes about once a month to cheer us up. He's proposed we not limit ourselves to our existing comments about the chronicle, that we write about other things. About whatever we want.

We promised to think about it. We actually are writing but it's more like personal notes. Do those need to be published?

When we were saying goodbyes, I showed Phillip the cliff that resembles a tower: it looks as if there are battlements at the top. It was near that cliff that I once shouted:

"Knife!"

Whenever Parfeny and I walk past it, I whisper:

"Knife!"

And Parfeny sharply turns each time, though not as sharply as before. What surprises him most of all about that story is my observation about the knock-kneed legs.

During our conversation with Phillip, a woman came out from behind the cliff. And, yes, she had that same sort of legs. She waved when she saw we were looking at her. Parfeny squinted as he scrutinized her: "The spitting image of Auntie Klavdia. Something draws them to this spot."

We all waved to her in response. Sometimes it seems to me that the very same people – or very similar people – are born with each new century.

Phillip called on his mobile and his car pulled up a minute later. He sat in the backseat and waved again, this time to us. Surprisingly, everyone waved a lot that evening. When his car had driven out of sight, Parfeny and I stood by the highway for some time. Cars of unfamiliar makes rushed past us. The woman who'd been standing by the cliff walked up to us.

"We've learned to differentiate cargo vehicles from light vehicles," Parfeny told her, "but for some reason, that's our limit. We can't learn the makes."

"It's age," the woman answered. "You're at the age when it wouldn't even be right to state your age."

Parfeny hung his head, as if he were offended. When he raised it again, it became obvious that he was smiling.

He said: "We don't feel a day over a hundred and twenty."

Chapter the Sixth

GAVRIIL

I t is not without trepidation that I set to work on my entries.
Not long before his death, Saint Agafon the Forward-
Looking said to me, the sinner Melety:
Be joyful, for you will be a describer of bygone years.
I bowed to the ground before him. I answered:
Glory to the Creator.
And he said:
Concentrate, since the pen is not granted to a person for idleness.
I again bowed.
He summoned me once more when he was on his deathbed:
Keep watch, O Melety, over the unity of time flowing past.
I promised to and though I did not fully understand what he was
saying, the request seemed justified to me.

On the day of Prokopy the Nasal's death, a work of penance
was imposed on me: to describe the changing of years and events. I
interpreted my assignment in the most painstaking manner. I asked
myself if it would have occurred had I not held Prokopy's head and
had I not then caught Bishop Filaret's eye. And I also answered myself: it would have; otherwise, why had Agafon instructed me?

Upon Yevstafy's death, Prince Gavriil, uncle of Princes Mikhail
and Yevstafy, was regent to Parfeny, who was a minor. And although
Parfeny's age had long not fit with being a minor in the usual sense
of the word, everyone understood that being a minor is simply
the state of having lived only a minor number of years. But major
and minor are fluctuating concepts. One hundred years is a minor
number for one person, but one year could be a major number for

another. The answer to those who questioned when the betrothed would come to the throne was: at the appropriate time.

In the first year of Gavriil's rule, Feopempt was installed as bishop. The Church had experienced a rather difficult time under Filaret and so Feopempt had set his sights on restoring its original beauty.

In the fifth year under Gavriil, darkness dwelled for six weeks due to our sins and so the sun was not visible and fish died in the water and birds fell to the ground, for they saw not where to fly.

In the seventh year of Gavriil's rule, someone at the bazaar presented to the prince an apple of unusual size that had been brought from the Phrygian Land. Surprised by the apple's size and also its beauty, Gavriil gave it to his wife, Princess Arkadia.

When Arkadia received the apple, she recalled the dignitary Pavlin, who was a mutual and unselfish friend to her and Gavriil. Pavlin had been ill and Arkadia sent him the prince's gift since she supposed that large apples are of great use during illness.

As a loyal subject, however, Pavlin decided to give the remarkable fruit to his prince and sovereign.

When Gavriil recognized his gift, he summoned the princess and asked about the apple she had received. Arkadia answered that she ate it. Threatening earthly and heavenly retribution, the prince repeated his question and appealed to his wife to repent. But she had lost her senses from fear, continued to stand fast, and even swore on the cross that she was not lying. When Gavriil showed her the apple, Arkadia fell to her knees and told what actually happened. Since she could no longer be trusted, Pavlin was executed that day.

A short while later, Arkadia asked her husband to allow her go on a pilgrimage to the Holy Land and he did not impede her. And so she died in Jerusalem, leaving behind memories of devout deeds. Before her death, the princess confessed and received communion, and it became clear that she had remained faithful to her husband.

In the fifteenth year of his reign, Gavriil reminisced about Pavlin and bitterly regretted his death, for Pavlin was a childhood friend. The prince complained to those around him that fate had acted harshly with him, taking away his close friends. No one disagreed with him about that.

For the edification of future generations, Gavriil ordered that all apple trees on the Island be chopped down since (as he said) that tree was the source of all woes. The prince also found ardent support for this among those near him, other than one Bishop Feopempt, who said:

The apple trees are not to blame.

There were many on the Island who repeated after Feopempt, whispering:

The apple trees are not to blame.

But others repeated this without whispering and it ended up becoming a saying. For now, we have no apple trees.

In the seventeenth year of Gavriil's reign, the sea overflowed its banks during a horrible earthquake. After picking up ships by the shore, a wave carried them to dry land, where they lie to this day since there is no possibility of delivering them anew to the water. Just before the wave hit, the sea, on the other hand, ebbed several poprishches, revealing the seabed. Thinking that the sea would no longer return, many people blithely walked along the seabed and collected outlandish bottom-dwelling creatures that only an experienced diver could see.

A short time later, a wave whose height was reminiscent of a mountain range appeared on the horizon. It approached with horrifying speed and swallowed not only those walking on the seabed but also many residents of the Coast since few had time to run to a safe place.

In the eighteenth year of Gavriil's rule, he happened to ride along a street on the outskirts and see a person sitting by the ruins of a building. The person was wretched and blind. He was grubby, in clothes so shabby that the body he had wearied shone through holes. Hearing the horsemen ride along the street, the wretch began shouting:

Give alms to the defender of the great City!

Surprised by the oddity of the utterance, Gavriil stopped and asked:

Who is this man and what do his words mean? I perceive a certain mystery behind them.

The prince's entourage scrutinized the blind man and someone suddenly recognized in him Eparch Amvrosy. Right then the prince recalled Amvrosy's doleful life, including pestilence and the harsh blinding. The prince and his suite did not know of his current stay in the City since they did not usually ride along streets on the outskirts. According to inhabitants of the street, the stay was long-term and one could not say it had gone unnoticed. The wretched man shouted his unusual words many times a day but nobody had suspected the eparch was behind them.

And then Gavriil dismounted and said to the wretched man:

O Eparch, because you have taken on many and guiltless sufferings, I will bring you to the Palace, dress you in the finest clothing, and sit with you at table, as it should be for you, according to rank. You will be a wise advisor for me in matters and you will enjoy a deep rest after your anguished life.

Our life, O Prince, is a funeral service, answered the eparch, and who will enjoy themselves at a funeral service? Further, I am a defender of the great City, and so how am I to relinquish my duty?

There are many other defenders of the City and you, honestly, should rest.

The eparch blindly smiled and said:

But I speak of Heavenly Jerusalem and it can never have too many defenders.

The prince was surprised by the man's firmness and left him to his chosen duty. After Gavriil shook the reins, Amvrosy asked him if the lost prophecy had been found.

No. After saying that, Gavriil threw up his hands. And you know, it is unlikely to be found.

In the nineteenth year of Gavriil's reign, a dragon flew through the sky one night. And it was as bright as day and even brighter because the dragon's sheen was so vivid that everyone squinted. The dragon came from the direction of the sea and thus was visible for an extended time. And all prayed that its appearance would leave the Island without casualties and havoc. After flying over the City, the dragon tumbled down into the Forest and the trees were charred for several poprishches around. And although everything ended without casualties, all understood the dragon's appearance boded ill.

Looking at the flying dragon, Prince Gavriil said:

It means nothing beyond my death.

He said:

The time has come for Parfeny and Ksenia to marry in order to ascend to the princely throne after uniting the two ruling branches.

KSENIA

It's interesting that this chapter – for the first time in the chronicle – is accompanied by a miniature. Melety illustrated the story about the comet, obviously in the form of a winged dragon. The chronicler drew it with a pen and colored it with ochre, placing it in an onion-shaped frame with clouds.

While visiting us today, Phillip (who has become our regular guest) admired the miniature for a long time. It occurred to him that he can put the miniature on the cover of the future edition of the chronicle, the one with our comments. Checking the miniature's size against a book taken at random from the table, he expressed his amazement at the naiveté of the Middle Ages. He did not hide his progressive smile.

Later, while drinking tea, Phillip asked us how we perceive such a radical change in notions about the universe. Parfeny (geniality itself) answered that he had not noticed radical changes. Phillip (polite patience) poured himself more hot water. He did not understand how one could not see differences between the Middle Ages and modern times. They give opposite answers to all basic questions.

"There is only one basic question," said Parfeny, bringing a cup to his lips, "and it concerns the circumstances of the world's creation. The Middle Ages answer that the world was created by God. What do modern times answer?"

"Well, first of all . . ." Phillip's hand moved in an arc.

"Modern times say: I don't know," Parfeny cued him. "And for some reason, it seems to me that science will never have another explanation."

The din of an airplane resounded outside; the airport is not far away. Phillip involuntarily spoke louder and the conversation suddenly became a debate:

"Why, I wonder won't there be?"

"Pure logic. Science studies only the physical world but in order to explain that world as a whole, one must leave its confines. And there's nowhere for science to go."

The plane seemed to have frozen in the air. It will hang there until progress becomes obvious to all. Phillip leaned back in the chair. His gaze slid over the miniature.

"I have a very simple question. Were comets thought to be dragons in the Middle Ages? They did take it that way, right? You won't deny that?"

"I cannot deny the obvious."

"And now?"

"And now a dragon is taken for a comet."

G avriil's words were followed by a wedding ceremony and a festive celebration of the wedding. The Island had never known such festivities and everyone understood the wedding would be entered into history with gold letters.

The young people rode up to the church in a carriage harnessed to three pairs of white horses. Upon their arrival, three white doves landed on the roof of the bell tower and everyone rejoiced, as this was considered a good omen.

Overcoming the difficulties of years lived, Bishop Feopempt married the royal couple. And here something occurred that left everyone speechless.

When the bishop asked if God's servant Ksenia wished to be the wife of God's servant Parfeny, she said, after hesitating:

Yes.

In answering the question of whether she was connected to another groom, the bride did not answer, as if her lips were sealed.

As a common gasp scudded through the church, there sounded the word *no*. Prince Averky, the bride's paternal uncle, uttered it in a loud whisper. Sidling over to Ksenia, he angrily rolled his eyes and continued repeating his *no* as if he himself were the bride.

Or *yes*, hissed the uncle after thinking. The main thing is to answer.

At that very instant, several bats darted down from inside the cupola. They flew over those standing below then vanished in the narthex. All seemed to regard that as an ill omen and a second gasp scudded through the church. And the brows of many rose in bewilderment and alarm, as only the bishop remained calm. He again questioned about promises to another groom, be he from the Island or a resident of the Mainland. And then the bride quietly said:

No.

And a third sigh, a sigh of relief, resounded in the church.

Upon leaving the church, Ksenia's uncle inquired of the bishop the reason the doves and bats had flown and also, more important, what this signified. Feopempt looked at the uncle and smiled.

He said:

They mean nothing. They simply flew.

Surprised at the flippant answer, Prince Averky retorted:

They flew within the church and outside it, so this cannot help but be a sign.

The aforementioned Godly creatures, answered the bishop, are given to flight, as you are to walking. If you, let us say, walked around inside the church, what does that mean in and of itself?

Other incidents involving animals took place on that day. In honor of the national festivities, a talking cat was brought in. It opened and closed its mouth as it meowed, so that distinct phrases could even be heard. And that surprised many, although others alleged that the animal meowed more than it spoke. Various people, after all, understood what the cat said in various ways. When the cat uttered *harmony and love* at the mention of Parfeny and Ksenia, the most mistrustful were satisfied on the strength of the cat's words.

Encouraged by the people, the cat began uttering proverbs that befit the situation. *Where harmony is treasured there is pleasure. Even light is not lovely when there is no lovey.* The cat wavered before adding: *He fell in love like a mouse dropped from above.* After that, however, as soon as members of the audience brought the feline performer some catnip tea, his lips began to loose certain non-celebratory utterances.

After growing solemn, the cat purred out: *They married me off without me, I went off to the mill* and also *Love is rarely smart, one may fall for a hardened heart* as well as other unseemly expressions. After all that had been proclaimed, people finally began hurriedly ushering the cat out, for animals are like people when inebriated and do not realize what they are saying, and are thus capable of inflicting harsh insults on those around them.

The whole world escorted Parfeny and Ksenia to the marital bed-room, which was decorated in flowers and herbs whose fragrance spread over the entire Island. Drowning in that divine scent, the Island's population sang the praises of the unity in marriage of two God-loving hearts.

That evening a great feast was held for all. Evening flowed into night and all were happy since the marriage of Parfeny and Ksenia strengthened the union of two dynasties, giving hope for a long and solid peace.

And five hundred sheep were slaughtered, though some speak of a thousand, plus four hundred pigs and endless numbers of various fowl. Twenty carts of fish, our sea's riches, were brought from the Coast. And all was roasted outside and set on tables that were knocked together on the spot. Pitchers of wine made from the sweetest Island grapes were also set out. And there was no one who did not feast or did not feel the overall joy as they blessed Parfeny and Ksenia.

The next morning, relatives and the Island aristocracy waited for the newlyweds at the doors of the princely bedchambers. The spouses came out late and everyone understood the night had been sleepless and so they were delighted. When the sheet, crimson with blood, was brought out after the couple, everyone was assured of Ksenia's virginity, something that had never previously been doubted. Knowing her great piety and angelic purity, others even doubted the very possibility of the union, in accordance with human nature, of a maiden and a man.

Prince Gavriil died six years later, in the twenty-fifth year of his rule. And it is difficult now to understand if the dragon's appearance was an omen of his death since he needed to die at some time, independent of the dragon. All one can firmly say is that His Highness the Prince died. And with him the many years of the regency epoch ended and that was announced on the very day of his death.

PARFENY

Left in the bedroom, just the two of us, we sat next to one another on the huge marital bed. The celebrants' shouts carried from outside, making the quiet in the bedroom all the more piercing. Neither Ksenia nor I disturbed it.

Somewhere there, below, people walked around with torches whose crimson reflections flashed on the ceiling. They served only to emphasize the duskiness in the bedroom. Only one dim lamp had been left for us, so we might thus see only the contours of objects and not be embarrassed by the sight of our nakedness. The word *nakedness* knocked in my ears like a metronome and that rhythm responded in my body in sweet waves. Nakedness. Na-ked-ness.

We sat, clothed. I placed my hand on Ksenia's shoulder. Her shoulder trembled. Her warmth was palpable even through the thick fabric of her dress. Her fragility too. And nakedness.

KSENIA

Parfeny placed his hand on my shoulder. His hand trembled. I experienced a fervid tenderness for him. And compassion. I carefully took his hand from my shoulder. I touched his fingers to my lips. I said:

"Please don't."

Then we sat silently for a long time. He asked:

"Do you find me unpleasant?"

And I revealed to him that I had chosen another Groom. That servant-maid Fotinya would bring me a cloak that hid my face and take me out of the palace. A covered cart would be waiting for us outside.

I was prepared for his rage, interdiction, even a beating. That did not happen. He simply began to weep.

And later he asked what would now happen to the Island, whose peace, according to Agafon's prediction, depended on our marriage. I wanted to answer that – remembering the prophecy – I had decided to marry first and leave later. But after his question, I no longer knew if that was the correct answer.

PARFENY

She took my hand from her shoulder and stood.

I thought that my touch was unbearable for her; everything within me broke. I began to feel more pained because of the exultation outside. It even smelled of roasting meat in the bedroom.

Ksenia took a travel bag from the corner. She said she needed to leave me.

"How can you leave me?" I asked. "After all, you are my wife."

She looked me in the eyes for the first time:

"I am Christ's bride and he awaits me at the convent. Do forgive me."

I wanted to say something to her but the words caught in my throat because she was my great love. I kept silent and felt tears flowing down my cheeks. And Ksenia wiped them away. I do not know how long we stood that way because I lost my sense of time from the sorrow. It was as if I was watching, in my sleep, as her maid, Fotinya, entered the room and dressed her in the black cloak.

When Ksenia approached the door, I reminded her of Agafon's prediction. I no longer hoped to hold her back, I simply asked what I should do.

After noticing the doubt in her eyes, I knelt before her. I said I would never touch her, may she simply stay. I promised she and I would live a perfect love: remain brother and sister, as before our marriage. Fotinya knelt with me, too, and also prayed for Ksenia. And we all wept.

Then Ksenia took Fotinya aside and spoke quietly with her about something. After that she turned to me and said:

"Promise before my heavenly Groom that you will preserve me as a virgin and not desire me and never touch me."

I promised. I could not help but desire her because that is beyond human nature, but I have never once touched her.

KSENIA

I now thank the Lord that I did not leave then. The many years spent living with Parfeny have been a time of happiness. The highest happiness.

I will say something unexpected, perhaps even an unlikely thing. I sometimes think the path I chose was not the only one possible. Insisting on a life of perfect love, I deprived Parfeny and myself of something important.

I regret nothing, neither my faith that burned within me then nor how our life has passed. My faith is ardent now, too, but it is now an internal burning that demands no harsh actions. Years (centuries) later, I understand that there is also wisdom in following a common path. It is, in its own way, no simpler than the path for those who are chosen. At times, it is more complex.

Fotinya helped us very much that night, not only by supporting Parfeny. When she left the palace before dawn, my loyal servant-maid found a street where a sheep had been slaughtered and collected a pitcher of its fresh blood. It was that blood which we poured on our sheet.

We recall Fotinya with tenderness but with, of course, a smile because that woman's devotion could only compete with her wit. To our amazement, it turned out that it was Fotinya who trained and released the three white doves that opportunely soared to the roof of the bell tower. Compared with the doves, which she said long had no wish to soar up, the work with the sheep required no great efforts.

Where do her bones now decay? Most likely nowhere. I think they have already turned to dust.

Back then, the bloodstained sheet confirmed both our marital relations and the virginity I had preserved for my husband. And so it remains, preserved.

PARFENY

Upon the death of Prince Gavriil, Parfeny ascended to the royal throne.

In the first year of Parfeny's royal reign, the Island's people experienced great fear. All, though especially those residents living near the sea, had noticed a dark cloud approaching from the Mainland. It stretched as far as the eye could gaze and concealed the rising sun. And judging from its attributes, it was clear that this was not a thundercloud and not even a cloud at all but a swarm of locusts. Seeing it move slowly over the sea, many stood in tears, for the appearance of locusts portended nothing but hunger, suffering, and death.

After hearing that the locusts were nearing, Parfeny and Ksenia walked up the belltower of the Church of the Transfiguration with Bishop Feopempt and prayed to the Lord and the Most Holy Mother of God for deliverance from this misfortune. And in the morning hour, all was shrouded by an impenetrable gloom in which only moaning and prayers could be heard.

After flying over the belltower and the entire Island, the swarm descended to the sea and was swallowed by waves ten poprishches from the shore. And for several weeks, bloated locusts washed up on the Island and the sea resembled kasha. A layer of locusts a cubit high blanketed the shore and a stench spread over the entire Island as they rotted.

Once the danger had passed, services of thanksgiving were held, for everyone understood that a miracle had been delivered. People saw the prince's chosenness and the blessing that lay on his reign in the fact that the miraculous salvation occurred in Parfeny's first year of royal reign.

As a swarm creature, it is said that locusts have no individual will, only a common will for the swarm, which is led by a guide. After landing on the ground, these creatures devour everything that grows upon it. Occasionally, however, the guide happens to err and then the entire swarm dies in the sea, clotted, and none are saved because they cannot escape the swarm. Are locusts similar to people who dissolve their will into the will of the crowd and disappear in the waves of the worldly sea without a trace?

In the seventh year of Parfeny's royal reign, Prince Averky, Ksenia's uncle, was troubled by the couple's lack of children. He made it a habit to express his concerns in public, maintaining that the absence of heirs threatened the agreement between the dynasty of Roman's bloodline, which represented the northern part of the Island, and the southern dynasty of Irakly's bloodline. He said that after the death of Parfeny and Ksenia, there would be no common heir for the two dynasties and power would thus be turned over to Roman's dynasty.

A short while later, Averky's words reached the ruling couple, saying that as an infertile wife Ksenia should yield her place to another woman, one capable of reproduction. That thought seemed sensible to many and so Averky began to have devotees. It seemed that Parfeny and Ksenia noticed nothing and the silence of their response was replete with dignity.

Prince Averky decided to speak openly on the sacred day of Christmas. At the conclusion of the Christmas service, he unexpectedly walked up to the pulpit and asked for everyone's attention.

The ruling couple's infertility looks especially dispiriting on Christmas, said Averky. In speaking of the couple, however, I mean Ksenia, for the sheet clearly proved Prince Parfeny's reproductive capabilities. As her close relative, my heart is pained to say that Ksenia should go to the convent and spend the remainder of her days there, praying for forgiveness of her secret sins. For infertility is a punishment and the sins are the reason for the punishment.

Ksenia calmly looked at her Uncle Averky. Parfeny exchanged remarks in a low voice with someone who was in front of him, as if he had not heard Averky.

Feopempt was sitting in the bishop's throne, hands folded on his crosier, chin resting on his hands. And it seemed to many that he understood little. Feopempt was old.

And a significant part of the church began to shout that another woman, a woman from Irakly's dynasty, ought to represent that bloodline; it was later revealed that Prince Averky had coached them. Here shouts were heard that it was Parfeny's duty to take Aglaya, Averky's daughter, for his wife.

So be it, she is ready, replied Averky. It is the bishop's turn to speak. If he is a pastor to his people, he will support us.

And so all and everything in the church rejoiced because Prince Averky's speech was beautiful and it spoke in everyone's name, so all felt their own significance.

Feopempt stood. A quiet set in and he slowly moved toward the pulpit.

Without looking at Averky, he asked:

Are you saying that your daughter Aglaya is prepared to become Prince Parfeny's wife?

She is, O Bishop, said Averky, bowing to Feopempt.

Feopempt pointed his crosier at Averky:

This person himself explained his intention and course of action to us. I consider both shabby.

Averky began speaking altogether quietly but his every word was audible.

You, Bishop, are sowing future quarrels. My niece Ksenia is an utter disgrace to our bloodline, where all the women have given birth very shortly after matrimony.

And words emerged from the thick of the crowd, saying they had given birth even without marrying, as had Averky's daughter Aglaya.

Who here dares to lie, shouted Averky.

The crowd parted and everyone caught sight of Fotinya, Ksenia's servant-maid.

I have served this house for many years and thus know its secrets, although my lips have always been sealed. Seeing how you destroy my mistress, I feel now is just the time to unseal them. Answer me, O Prince, what child are they hiding there, where our deep River, which divides into numerous branches, falls into the sea? I am prepared to kiss the cross on that which is truth, but are you prepared for that?

But Prince Averky was not prepared.

After thinking, the bishop said:

At least it is good that you did not kiss the cross.

Those attending the service that day were themselves surprised later that they had supported this Averky, for in their souls, they loved Ksenia for her kindness and pureness of soul.

They said:

Incited, he must have been, by the devil.

They spoke, too, after the bishop:

At least it is good that he did not kiss the cross. For he could have.

KSENIA

I secretly hoped on that day that my crafty uncle would carry out a little palace coup. At that time, I still had not parted with the thought of taking the vows – the occasion seemed fitting to me. The main thing is that Parfeny was spared from humiliation: far-sighted Averky did not forget to compliment him. He only underestimated Feopempt. Well, and Fotinya, too, of course.

Nothing, however, would have worked out for him. During my uncle's speech, Parfeny, who is usually meek, whispered an order to seize the plotter at the church's exit. Yes, he later waved it off since it was no longer needed.

That's who he is, my Parfeny.

In the twentieth year of Parfeny's rule, news came from the Mainland that a significant portion of territory had been captured by the Apagonian emperor, Nikifor, and that no one had the might to resist him, though some powers surrendered without opposition. And Island residents rejoiced that the sea separated them from the Mainland.

In our land, nothing worthy of notice happened during all those years. Is that not a sign of the authorities' wisdom? Happy are the times that do not enter the annals. Blessed is he whose rule is unmarked by historical events, for nearly all of them are born of blood and suffering.

In the twenty-second year of Parfeny's reign, Bishop Feopempt went to eternal rest, leaving behind a blessed memory of himself. His kind deeds came to his burial because many of those whom he secretly helped had gathered. The farewells to Feopempt before his final journey were filled with sorrow and tears although it was clear to all that they were seeing the bishop off to his heavenly native land and that those weeping for him were still residing in a foreign land.

After Feopempt, Yevsevy became the Island's bishop.

In Parfeny's twenty-fifth year, strange and frightening sounds began emerging from the abandoned castle standing by the River on the southern part of the Island. As befits a castle, it stood on a high hill and because of its elevated position, those sounds carried without the slightest impediment. People heard them primarily at night and they were so loud that soon the residents of that area began giving the castle wide berth.

In reality, they did not often need to give it wide berth, for the castle lay far from the roads so it was enough not to approach. But those boating on the River past the castle told of being horrified by the moans and underground thuds emanating from inside. And it was obvious to all that some evil spirit was straining to come out of the ground and moaning because it could not break its way to the surface.

One night, the earth shook harder than usual and the moans were so desperate that nobody in the neighboring villages could fall asleep. In those villages where there were churches, people gathered for prayer and asked the heavenly powers not to allow the underground forces to be released to the surface or wander that location, lest they wreak havoc on the residents. At exactly midnight there sounded a thud of such strength that the earth shook under the feet of those standing in prayer. At that exact same hour, the castle and the hill collapsed into the River and blocked its flow. The water overflowed and flooded many villages and adjacent fields but the moaning and underground thuds ceased that day. Deposits of copper and iron were discovered on the spot where the hill had slid into the River.

Bishop Yevsevy arrived shortly thereafter and examined what remained of the base of the hill. The nature of the base of the hill convinced the bishop that the spot was now safe and the forces hostile to man were locked under the earth thanks to the copper and iron.

The Mountain, which was located in the South and had been quiet for more than one century, aroused the bishop's unease.

Legends stated that there was a time when it had shaken and fiery rivers had flowed down its slopes and the whole Island had swayed.

Yevsevy said:

I fear the Mountain may awaken in the future, for all lofty places are connected underground and if this small hill made so much noise, what can one say about a great Mountain?

He said:

As for the River, although it temporarily overflowed, it will soon break a new course for itself, since the earth here offers every opportunity for that. I wish only to caution everyone requiring metals not to begin mining them here. The content of the minerals speaks to the fact that they should not be dug out because that pursuit is ruinous.

Certain people experiencing a need for iron and copper did not listen to the bishop. They arrived with spades and shovels, and set to their work. And then the earth parted with a horrifying scraping sound and devoured the diggers alive.

In Parfeny's twenty-seventh year of rule, envoys of the Apagonian Emperor Nikifor arrived on the Island. The emperor wished Grand Prince Parfeny good health and alerted Parfeny that he, the emperor, had united the entire enlightened world under his scepter. His crown, however, lacked one pearl, which was the Island entrusted to his brother Parfeny by God and people. His Imperial Highness was inclined to relax the burden of responsibilities imposed on Parfeny and to assume power over the Island. Parfeny would be elevated by comparison with his present position and would be appointed His Imperial Highness's Governor General on the Island.

Prince Parfeny heard out Nikifor's ambassadors and asked them to convey to the emperor that he had expressed his fraternal gratitude for the concern shown. However, not wishing to increase the excessive weight of imperial duties, Parfeny advised Nikifor that he was prepared to continue bearing the burdens involved with governing the Island. As far as the possible advancement, Parfeny replied that he considered himself unworthy of such a gift and preferred to remain in his current humble position. After the meeting with the prince concluded, Nikifor's ambassadors were immediately sent to the Mainland, with all honors.

In Parfeny's twenty-eighth year of rule, Nikifor's envoys were dispatched once again. Their appearance was less friendly and now there was not a word about fraternal feelings in their speech. The emperor informed the prince that the empire he had constructed was deliberate and that he saw an indubitable sign of that deliberateness in the fact that states near and far had submitted to him. According to Nikifor's notion, large empires are created for large ideas, hence small states unite into one large state and only their full inclusion in the empire draws those boundaries.

Foreseeing Parfeny's objections, a most august philosopher pointed out that there is no such thing as too many states uniting since, in the words of Ecclesiastes, *All the rivers run into the sea; yet the sea is not full.* As long as even one river has not fallen into a sea, a sea will still lack water, hence the emperor was not retreating from his goal.

Driven by benevolence, Nikifor proposed that Parfeny not spill blood and not fight the inevitable. He warned the Island prince that this message was his last, that war and numerous casualties could follow.

Prince Parfeny voiced his agreement to the envoys on the point that an empire has its own advantages, also agreeing that large empires are founded for large ideas. All the arguments Nikifor produced certainly applied to the Mainland. Parfeny, however, presented his objections. He pointed out the Island's main distinguishing characteristic, which, in his opinion, was that the Island was surrounded by water on all sides. His country's natural isolation was a sign of the special path foreseen for it and he thought it seemed rash to neglect that sign. As far as the large idea went, it could be incorrect, despite its largeness. All that taken together did not allow him, Prince Parfeny, to accept the emperor's proposal of entering into the empire's fold.

No answer followed from Emperor Nikifor. To be more exact: the navy vessels that appeared near the Island in the twenty-ninth year of Parfeny's royal reign were the emperor's answer. There were so many ships that it seemed they did not have enough sea. The sea seemed to have shrunk in size, making it resemble a pond strewn with autumn leaves. These were not leaves, however, but menacing military ships. At Parfeny's command, the Island fleet was sent out to them, in very small numbers, but prepared to battle to the last.

Nikifor's vessels dropped anchor two poprishches from the Island. They swayed on the waves and the helmets of the emperor's warriors glistened in the sun. The glistening blinded Parfeny, who stood on the foremost ship. Squinting, he counted the emperor's vessels but kept losing track. He then turned to those standing on deck and asked:

Are you prepared to die for our blessed Island?
And those standing there said:
Yes, we are prepared to die.
And he did not utter another word.

When Parfeny disembarked at the shore, a crowd of women greeted him, shouting and tearing out their own hair. They implored that their husbands, sons, and brothers be saved, saying the emperor was powerful and any resistance was futile. They stretched their arms toward the sea and called upon Parfeny to compare the two navies and said the Island's navy was indiscernible alongside the emperor's. And then Parfeny asked them:

Are you prepared to live under the power of outlanders?

We are prepared to simply live, said the women.

And Parfeny looked at them in silence and no one knew what he was thinking.

The two navies stood opposite one another for two days and then Nikifor's envoys arrived on the third day. The emperor notified Parfeny that his troops would not stand idle forever and that they were prepared to take the Island. He offered to meet the prince, warning that the meeting would be their first and last.

And soon one ship separated itself from each navy; they neared one another and stood side-by-side. And Prince Parfeny and Emperor Nikifor conversed without leaving their ships and nobody heard their discussions because, maintaining security, they had agreed the decks would be cleared. It could be seen from the other ships that each stood at the rail of his own ship but the emperor's ship was significantly higher, thus Nikifor looked down upon Parfeny and there was something greater in that than the difference in the ships' heights. The emperor said something and pointed at the Island but Parfeny stood motionless except for the wind tousling his hair. They conversed thus for a long time and then the prince bowed his head and his ship began its slow movement toward shore.

Parfeny was greeted at the shore by a crowd awaiting his word. But no word escaped his lips. And for some reason everyone thought a war was starting and one of the women shouted:

Do not let us die, after all you are acting as our father!

And then Parfeny said:

You will not die. But your father henceforth is Emperor Nikifor.

He pointed at the sea as he walked away. And everyone saw that the Island's ships had turned toward shore, as the emperor's ships were also set in motion. Before long, it was obvious that Nikifor's navy had set a course for the Island.

The next morning, the emperor's troops moved from the harbor into the City. They were met with silence and there was no joy in that silence, however there was also no hatred, only surprise. The city gates turned out to be open and the troops entered, together with the dust they had raised along the way, and their helmets no longer gleamed as before, though their faces gleamed, bathed in sweat.

Inside the gates, only Amvrosy, who introduced himself to the troops as the City's eparch, greeted them. The emperor's warriors felt sad at the sight of Amvrosy, saying to one another that if this was how the City's eparch looked, they wondered how the local paupers looked.

Amvrosy said:

Something tells me that these helmet-wearers will be here for a long time. But where, for the love of all that is holy, will we house such quantities of metal and dust? I fear that many in the City will be forced to squeeze in tightly.

What he said found confirmation in the shortest possible time.

PARFENY

I remember those days as perhaps the most difficult of my life. All the misfortunes and humiliations that Ksenia and I had to relive many years later were personal misfortunes and affected only us. At that time, I was responsible for the whole Island.

I was forced to make my choice where, strictly speaking, it would have been better not to choose. I guessed one hand of someone whose hands were both empty. Unfortunately, I also had no right to refuse to make a choice. The choice consisted, as is wont to happen, of *whether 'tis nobler in the mind to*

*suffer the slings and arrows of outrageous fortune, or to take arms
against a sea of troubles.* I will note that this quotation came
into being during my lifetime.

In the former case, it would have been necessary to
simply allow enemy ships into the Island's harbor and open
the city's gates. *Simply*, what a word . . . *Simply* agree with
being forever commanded from afar, agree with systematic
robbery and, worst of all, agree with constant humiliation
for one's people.

In the latter case, war and death – many deaths – awaited
us. And then, most likely, everything that the first case
threatened, since we could not have fought Nikifor for long.
If this had affected only me, I would have put up a resistance,
if only to avoid feeling shame later.

I thought a lot before making my decision and continued thinking about it after the fact. My decision was to cede
the Island to the emperor.

The emperor was a strong-willed person. He craved
obtaining the Island and he obtained it. Now he is dead and
no longer experiences that craving. The women who asked
me to cede the Island were afraid for their men. They are also
now dead and have nothing to fear.

KSENIA

I am willing to confirm that there had never been a more
difficult time in Parfeny's life. The development of the
situation was absolutely predictable even before Nikifor sent
his first diplomatic envoys. When Parfeny says he thought a
lot about his decision, he means the years that passed from
the rise of Nikifor's empire until they invaded us. And he

continued to weigh his decision for many years after. I think he is still doing so now.

He certainly made up his mind that way when he saw the crowd of women imploring him not to take away their men.

Those women later accused him of betrayal and making a deal with the emperor. About what, I wonder, could Parfeny have made an agreement with him? About being stripped of his power?

Those women laid blame on Parfeny for all woes, bar none. They said they never lived so badly on the Island as under Nikifor and they blamed that on my husband. They just forgot that they had lived. Simply lived. And that was exactly what they asked of Parfeny. And if a war had happened, many of them might not have lived.

Chapter the Eighth

EMPEROR NIKIFOR

U pon his entry into the City, His Imperial Highness Nikifor was declared the Supreme Ruler of the Island and Parfeny was appointed his governor general. Some say that Parfeny initially refused to be governor general, and wanted to leave the Island. Bishop Yevsevy apparently reminded the prince of the words of Agafon the Forward-Looking, about the peacemaking destiny for him and his blessed wife, Princess Ksenia. Only the prince and the bishop know if that is what happened, but the prince remained.

As before, he ruled the Island, but now he obtained permission from the emperor each time he faced decisions that were more or less important. Of the visible changes, I will note only that the prince's troops were merged into the emperor's army and were issued new uniforms. More specifically, the troops received a uniform, for until that time, they had no uniform whatsoever and there was no uniformity either, since each dressed as he wished. The Island's fighters were warned that in the event of war, as part of the emperor's army they could be deployed to any spot in the world. But there were no wars and there was no one to fight, since the entire world now belonged to the emperor's crown.

Enhancement of shipping routes to the Continent should be considered among the visible changes. One could see, ever more frequently, ships sailing out of the port in the direction of the Mainland laden with lumber, ven . . .

PARFENY

Ven is *venison.* The chronicle breaks off for 150 years on that
nourishing word. The 150 subsequent years were simply
cut out. I nearly said *by an intrepid hand,* but the hand had
nothing to do with it; I think it did feel daunted. This was,
however, not the hand of Brother Melety but rather of
Brother Galaktion. The stubs of the sheets stick out of the
binding like a footless person's stumps.

It was Atanas, a minister in the Island's government
many years later, who ordered cutting out the sheets that
described the time of *imperial occupation.* It turned out that
those sheets were not pages from a heroic past. It was inexplicable for Atanas that the chronicle contained ninety-five
sheets of an unheroic past.

As it happened, the minister visited the monastery,
where they showed him the chronicle. He stuck his nose
in it and hit on a snippet dedicated to the Island as part of
the empire. Brother Galaktion, the chronicler at the time,
described afterward how the minister straightened up and
began twitching his mustache. That history did not sit well
with him.

"Scissors," he said, mouthing his command.

They brought scissors and Atanas nodded to Galaktion.
"Cut!"

Galaktion looked at the minister, stunned.

"This is, as they say, history ... It is what it is, and that is
what makes it interesting ..."

"Well?!" shouted the minister.

Galaktion got to work. He opened the manuscript
with a forceful crack, so the spine stuck out unnaturally.

He thought that something unnatural was happening. This was how the arms of an arrested person were twisted. He pressed the manuscript to the table and placed two logs on it so it wouldn't close. He took the scissors in hand, as someone castrating a horse takes up a knife. . . . At that moment, Galaktion felt he was castrating history.

He cut out ninety-four sheets and the first remained in the manuscript because the end of the previous chapter was on the other side.

Minister Atanas pointed at the burning stove:

"Burn it!"

Brother Galaktion tossed sheet after sheet into the stove. They first curled, losing strength from the flame and resisting it. They grew unbearably bright, as if they were emitting all the light amassed in them, so the letters could be read clearly even at a distance, but then the flame devoured them, leaving nothing.

The minister did not hurry Galaktion: he liked monitoring the agonizing death of a text.

"If history is not heroic," he pensively said, "then it is not history."

He turned to his entourage and shouted, joyful about his find:

"You hear that, shitheads: if history is not heroic, then it is not history. Write that down!"

The destruction of the manuscript sheets burned Galaktion from within. He is now in the grave and the flame has gone out. Minister Atanas is also in the grave. His death can be considered exotic since a crocodile was involved. The crocodile is dead too.

KSENIA

If one ponders it, our people carried *the heavy Apagonian yoke* relatively calmly, even in a dignified manner. If not for the significant difference between the Apagonian and Island languages, that yoke would have hardly been noticeable.

Yes, we learned Apagonian: knowledge of a foreign language has yet to harm anyone. I can say it is really not a bad language at all. In some sense, it's even softer than the Island language and thanks to its softness, it sounds as if it is apologizing for the occupant's role: it was not conceived for that.

I would not think of painting a picture of the Apagonian presence in only black paint. It's true that we were on the empire's *periphery*. But the accent could be placed differently, affecting the meaning: the *empire's* periphery. At the time, we received everything that was new in the world, along with the empire. It must be said that the invaders displayed a well-known latitude.

We understood all of that. And we disliked them with our entire beings.

When Nikifor's troops occupied the Island, Parfeny told me he would step down. He thought he had no right to continue participating in ruling the Island. He even considered leaving the Island completely. And he told the emperor that.

Knowing Parfeny's impeccable honesty, Nikifor asked him to stay. There's no doubt the emperor, who was not impeccably honest, valued that quality in other people. Experience told him that those people were predictable and one need not expect dirty tricks from them. And yes,

Nikifor figured, it would be better for Island residents to deal with someone they were used to on routine matters.

Parfeny had not intended to heed the emperor's opinions. It was the bishop who forced Parfeny to change his initial plans. Yevsevy reminded him that Agafon's prophecy linked the Island's well-being with our marriage and nothing there had changed due to the emperor's arrival. And so Parfeny became the emperor's governor general.

In those years, someone was constantly listening in on us. In the absence of today's marvelous electronics, an ordinary cup placed against a wall gave decent results. The listeners' yield, however, was not great since we held our discussions primarily during walks. We developed a passion for walks at that time because it was possible to speak freely by just going outside the palace. Our palace swarmed with spies whose ears were puffy and red from excessive listening. That's how it seems to me now, in any case.

Back then, Island residents didn't even suspect there were secret police who regularly informed the mainland about everything the empire (which wished to exist as long as possible) had gone to the trouble of looking into. This had helped the empire for one hundred and fifty years, though by historical standards that's not such a long stretch.

In the final years of external dominion it was already clear that the empire was falling apart at the seams. As in the empire's other lands, there was an uprising on the Island. This was one of the last and most peaceful uprisings against the empire. An uprising, so to say, for the sake of appearances. To rise up before the empire had fallen.

Parfeny forbade the emperor's troops from suppressing the uprising with force and they obeyed. When the empire ceased to exist, he summoned his fellow citizens to deal with the Apagonian soldiers humanely and then provided them with food and vessels for their return to the mainland.

My gaze falls on what Parfeny just wrote. He refers to Minister Atanas. What was he minister of? It's impossible to immediately recall that now. A remarkable individual, although not in the best sense of the word.

I once asked Parfeny: "Did Atanas actually think he'd conceal history by cutting out the text? There are many other sources. Could he really have thought nobody would find out about the hundred and fifty years of Apagonian dominion?"

"Of course not," said Parfeny. "It was a signal that that sort of history should not exist."

As he left, the minister wondered if the prophecy that Prokopy removed had been found. Galaktion threw up his hands.

"It's too bad," said Atanas. "It's too bad that Prokopy turned out to be a traitor."

I skim over Parfeny's fine but even handwriting ... And here's something I wrote. I notice our hands have become similar. That happens to those who live together for a long time. To everything about people: their handwriting, appearance, sensations, and thoughts become alike. One of the two departs, leaving the second everything that was acquired together. The second departs and all that remains of the two is handwriting, sheets covered with words. Which can easily burn.

Chapter the Fourteenth

PARFENY & KSENIA

I Nektary, a monk of many sins, am continuing my long story and announce with heartfelt joy that the Apagonian empire has fallen. When independence was returned to the Island, our land's citizens wished for Prince Parfeny to rule, for they loved him.

During the years of his single-handed royal reign and as governor general, he showed himself to be a wise ruler and a kindhearted person. Many on the Island remained alive only thanks to his intercession, though my predecessors have already written of that, telling of the emperors' reigns.

At Parfeny's request, his joint rule with Princess Ksenia was announced after the Island was liberated. And although power had previously not belonged to him alone, in his opinion, the announcement of the coregency would have been in keeping with the prophecy of Agafon the Forward-Looking. Moreover, since two princely lines had united in their marriage, coregency was the visible incarnation of that union.

The Apagonian troops left and their departure was just as calm and bloodless as their arrival had been, so long ago. Those who witnessed their arrival and then, long after, their shipping out for home, sorrowfully realized they were a hundred and fifty years older. But such people were very few, for the majority of those who had greeted the ships had long been lying in their graves, as is directed by the natural order of things. And those on board the ships were also not at all the same people as those who had come ashore in their time. Accordingly, the ships had changed too by then, becoming steamships. Even the emperors had changed, and there is a separate chapter of the chronicle devoted to each who served as the Island's ruler.

KSENIA

Alas, alas. After the eighth chapter, we now have the fourteenth and nothing can be made right. Poor Melety (as well as those who followed), who wrote the chapters that were removed, could not have even imagined that someone would burn the pages of the chronicle after all those years.

Is the horrible death that struck Atanas not his punishment for burning history? For his contempt of time lived that, yes, is not an eternity but is still granted for some purpose? Not to mention that in Atanas's case, it is the death of one whose name means "immortal." With a name like that, he had the chance to at least live for a long time, if not eternally.

Carriages, hairstyles, dresses, and other phenomena of little importance were also spoken about in previous chapters. The items mentioned have no independent meaning and take on purpose only as distinctive signs of the time. And so a milepost, no matter how colorfully painted, has but one task: to mark a journey.

What entered into our life under the brief label *fashion* serves to show us all how quickly time moves. I am among those for whom fashion is immaterial, meaning that it is nonexistent in some literal sense. My clothing is always of the same color if, of course, it is not stained, and it is of one cut, if it has not happened to fall apart at the seams.

What do I, unworthy monk Nektary, think, when watching the passage of time? Time is most noticeable when you see the end of those events that began neither yesterday nor today, but, let us say, a century and a half ago. Just yesterday it seemed that history had gone still forever, that it would henceforth consist of small events since everything significant had now settled in forever. But not even two centuries have passed and the empire that devoured the entire world fell apart and from there, as if from the womb of a fairy-tale animal, small powers emerged unharmed. There were no harsh wars and no treacherous plots, yet the empire fell.

Time destroyed it. Just as mountain rocks become weather-worn and sharp cliffs are eroded by waves, empires are destroyed by the passage of time. Time's movement is wavelike. How many iterations need to wash over a fragment of a cliff for it to become a round stone?

The question is superfluous, for it will wash over the cliff as many times as necessary, since it, time, is patient. It, time, has nowhere to hurry. Hurrying is characteristic for us, although if one takes life in its historical dimension, we have not been hurrying.

Did we aspire to rid ourselves of the Apagonian occupation quickly? No, because we did not feel our own captivity: Prince Parfeny took that upon himself, alone, for our entire land. And it turned out that each of us who was behind him was already free. The time has now come for the Island as a whole. And so how is it that we do not know what to do with our freedom? The answer is no longer mine to give, for merciless old age is engulfing me.

In the second year of the joint reign of devout Parfeny and Ksenia, all-wise Elder Nektary, who had grown decrepit, appointed me, unworthy Ilary, to observe time and years.

He said:

History is becoming ever more willful and I can no longer cope with it. But you, O brother, are a philosopher: perhaps you will understand something about it.

What kind of philosopher am I and what will I understand about it? I asked the elder that and told him many other things but he remained deaf to my arguments. He had long heard but a little.

In that same year, something occurred that had never been seen on the Island, namely this: infernal forces made an attempt on the royal couple. This occurred on the Coast, where the pair went during the summertime. After reconnoitering everything about their habits, a scoundrel by the name of Leonid lay in wait for them during their evening stroll by the sea. More properly speaking, there was no need at all for him to reconnoiter, for everyone knew Their Royal Highnesses took evening walks to breathe sea air. It was also known that they did not take a guard with them when leaving the house.

After awaiting his victims behind the trunk of an old oak tree, Leonid stepped out to greet them with a homemade bomb in his hands. Since (unlike the husband and wife couple) he himself was flustered, the bomb fell out of his hands and exploded.

Before understanding the essence of what had happened, Parfeny and Ksenia rushed to the injured man, whose feet had both been torn off. Ksenia took the scarf from her head, tore it in two, and wanted to bandage his legs, meaning what was left of them, but Leonid would not allow her to come near him. He pounded his legs on the ground with all his might and shouted something incomprehensible as his bones showed through remnants of flesh and fabric. Then he fell into unconsciousness from the pain and when he awakened, they asked him why he had refused to accept help. The aforementioned Leonid answered that he feared punishment since he thought they planned to kill him.

The Royal Highnesses subsequently visited him at the clinic. They brought him gifts and money for treatment, and also asked the reason for his hatred of them. Leonid answered that he did not experience hatred and that a sense of duty had drawn him to lobbing bombs. He saw any political authority and command as blatant evil and considered them worthy of destruction. The fact that the royal couple enjoyed widespread love was, in the patient's eyes, an aggravating circumstance, for it could give rise to wavering when considering an enemy who was subject to destruction.

PARFENY

I remember our meeting with Leonid, who had been de-footed. It was Dr. Leon, at the hospital, who uttered the word *defooted*. It seemed he heartily liked that term since he kept repeating it the whole time. At some point, it became clear to Ksenia and me that Dr. Leon was utterly drunk. I am not inclined to overestimate the doctor's guilt since Ksenia and I did, after all, show up unannounced. He repeated several times that if his patient had not been defooted, he would have seen the business through to the end and would have blown us up after all.

"I would have blown you up," Leonid spoke up, echoing.

"But now you're defooted, you won't blow them up," smiled Dr. Leon.

Leonid shrugged. Ksenia took his hand in her own:

"We issued a decree pardoning you."

A tear rolled down Leonid's cheek. Several tears flowed down the doctor's cheeks too:

"That's simply . . . By doing that, you have simply . . . defooted us all."

Leonid kept silent.

"Gestures of that sort…" Dr. Leon loudly blew his nose. "Now he won't bomb you for anything."

"I will," said Leonid.

That deplorable event was the opening of a series of assassination attempts on the Island. In former times, sometimes evildoers killed hated people, shooting at them from behind corners or, let us say, sprinkling some poison into a goblet. In addition to that, they were ruled by lively, albeit sinful, feelings. The attacks that began to overwhelm the Island in recent times lacked feeling: thought prevailed, vile and unfeeling thought.

Feeling and thought necessarily reside in harmony, in order that they may check one another. If one of those components is lost, you may await great misfortunes.

When on trial, one of the bombers said:

I am as cold as an automaton.

Where did this woe come from? How did it appear? Did it not come with those numerous mechanisms that entered our life, destroying Island people's customary gentleness? Bombers blew up a police colonel, an army general, an editor of the *Island Broadsheet* who supported belief in the powers that be, and also the director of the postal department that helped distribute newspapers. But the evildoers' most important goal was to kill Their Royal Highnesses, who personified all of the country's political power.

What was lamentable: it was required in *progressive* circles to call the evildoers not evildoers but fighters for a better life. Nobody, including the fighters previously mentioned, knew either what that life consisted of or (most importantly) what made the current life bad. Perhaps that was why the fighters stopped speaking about a better life and replaced it with a new life. Many people back then doubted that it would be better, but nobody doubted that it would be new.

Nine assassination attempts were made on the ruling couple. Bombs were tossed and bombs were placed but with time people also began shooting from distances near and far, something that was apparently not customary for bombers. After that, they began to be called fighters, though the choice of murder weapons broadened extraordinarily: rifles and pistols and knives and hatchets could be used, and yes, the bombs we previously mentioned too. Those were not excluded either.

Glory to the Creator that guardian angels followed after the fighters, selflessly disabling the bombs or blowing them up prematurely. Thanks to those angelic efforts, the hands of shooters began to shudder or grains of sand landed in their eyes. The fighters' inventiveness was inexhaustible and they sought ever more new methods for killing and that (and may progressive people not take this amiss) made them the true evildoers. Even so, this misfortune began to subside with time.

PARFENY

It is interesting how Brother Ilary writes about progress. The word had just come into fashion at the time and the chronicler avoids it when possible. He obviously does not like the word: it appeared on the Island with the first bombs.

I recall our conversation with Ilary. He said then that history's primary event was the incarnation of Christ. That had already occurred and so history generally had no more serious tasks.

"It is now the universal history of moving away from Christ," said Ilary.

"Moving away in all senses?" I asked, to clarify.

He nodded:

"Perhaps it is even like this: it is the history of universally moving away from Christ. Hope is now placed on personal history."

When Ilary said at another time that history had set off on a false course, Ksenia asked why he wrote.

"I am writing the history of an error," responded Brother Ilary.

Ksenia and I were recalling him today. He departed from our life forever. Small, redheaded, with a beard that did not grow well. That is what the enemies of progress looked like.

In the tenth year of Parfeny and Ksenia's coregency, a railroad was built on the Island. It was laid from North to South, connecting the two parts of our realm. The ruling couple invited me, a humble chronicler, to the opening and we made that journey engaged in traveling conversation. The route went through the Forest, where there had once been a battle between North and South.

And it occurred to me how simple it is these days to traverse this Forest. The Forest looks like a painting when viewed out the window, but during that distant war, the Forest threatened danger and death. How about that, it occurred to me, we have people whose ancestors hated one another riding in the same train and not even a trace of that hatred now remains. There is only the joy of being in motion together. The iron horse pulled our train carriages, engulfing us in smoke and steam. Its power summoned fear in those riding but there is also pride in the height of the human spirit, whose invention has united so many different people.

I quickly calculated that there had been no explosions for seven years and if we needed to unite around the steam engine to maintain order, then so be it. After all, everybody nowadays talks about *progress*. Maybe, contrary to expectations, it will also turn out that technological advancements will help to soften angry hearts and brighten muddled minds.

In the twelfth year of the reign of husband and wife Parfeny and Ksenia, a certain Maxim found work in the Royal Palace as a cabinetmaker. Maxim could chisel a tree into a chair without using nails or glue and the mastery of his chairs remains unsurpassed to this day.

Recent preferences for bentwood chairs not only fail to negate the beauty of Maxim's chairs but, to the contrary, make that beauty stand out even more. As for their durability, it would be excessive to speak of all they saw from Maxim himself: flying from one corner to another in a moment of fury and even the explosion he himself arranged.

Truth be told, however, he paid tribute to that craze by making bentwood chairs too. He learned well how to bend the material and perfectly mastered methods for making those wares, but none of that stifled his love for chairs constructed from a whole tree.

Unlike the bentwood chairs, Maxim's custom wares have survived. The cabinetmaker is no longer of this world but his creations still stand in the Palace halls and in the workshop where he made many marvelous things. The materials the master's assistants procured for him were marvelous too: various types of wood and stones and even the fossilized bones of animals that no longer walk the face of the earth.

The one thing they did not procure was the actual powder that was detonated. As was subsequently clarified, Maxim himself brought the powder to the Palace in small amounts. He was working at the time on carved panels in a hall located under the royal refectory.

After refusing assistance on the panels, cabinetmaker Maxim was not observed as he portioned out the powder into bags and set the bags themselves in places that were favorable for a destructive blast. Maxim timed the explosion for the royal lunch, which always took place at approximately the same time.

Ksenia felt under the weather on the day the scoundrel had set for the explosion. Unbeknownst to cabinetmaker Maxim, Their Royal Highnesses did not go to lunch on time. The explosion rang out when only servants were in the refectory. Twenty-six people perished. The murderer, smeared with blood, darted amidst the wreckage in the refectory. He foresaw discovering what should have remained of Parfeny and Ksenia among the pieces of arms and heads strewn with stucco but he found nothing.

The scoundrel set off at a run when he saw an approaching guard. If not for that, Maxim – spattered in blood and alabaster – would have been taken as a victim of the explosion rather than its perpetrator. He gave himself away by running off and the guard quickly captured him. The demolitionist denied nothing after learning that Their Highnesses had been saved; he lost all hope. By the end of the day he had confessed to everything and showed how he brought in and placed the powder.

According to Island laws, Maxim faced a royal trial. He awaited that trial over the course of seven weeks but did not make it. The day he was being taken to the trial, a crowd on the street seized the scoundrel from the guards. The accused was dead several moments later. Thus ended the life of Maxim, a person who received retribution for his sins in both earthly and heavenly life, whose abandoned talents are evidenced by the chairs and other pieces of furniture that have been preserved.

And so, looking at what happened to Maxim, I doubted that technical progress fosters the progress of human beings. The second exists independently of the first and, in all honesty, most likely does not exist. The steam engine makes travel more convenient but wayfarers themselves become no better.

KSENIA

Parfeny and I were supposed to pass judgement on that person. Few in our history have been sentenced to death, but that is what the Island's citizens demanded. No matter how repulsive Maxim was to us, we were still convinced that a person, as God's creation, cannot be deprived of life. We were not the ones who gave him this life so it was not for us to take it away.

On the other hand, twenty-six killed is monstrous in and of itself. Beyond that, each victim had numerous kinfolk who indefatigably and – this is important – loudly called for retribution. All that together made the public mood harsh. Parfeny and I did not know how to subdue that and, yes, to be candid, we did not especially aspire to it.

The decision came on its own. When the arrestee was being led to the courthouse, the crowd disarmed the escort on the street. Maxim was killed on the spot. His body – naked, for some reason – lay on the bloodied paving stones until nighttime. It was impossible to recognize the deceased: I say that because we saw him several times when he was alive. We gave him and the other servants Christmas gifts and even triple kissed him at Easter. He stood out from others because of a particular elegance and also a silver streak that beautifully divided his jet-black hair. We recognized

119

him, naked, by that streak of hair. He resembled a piece of bloodied meat.

We had to go to the scene because the crowd would not hand the body over to the guards. Even after we showed up, they continued kicking the body and the gray streak of hair limply floated up with each strike. There were many guards but they had made no attempt to take the body away by force. It became clear that there were few guards – only two – when the body had been a living person.

I asked the head of the guards why he had not foreseen an attack on the escort and had sent only two people with the arrestee. The head of the guards began to answer but a deafening whistle rang out and a locomotive began moving along an overpass. For some reason, the wisps of steam did not float up, they floated flatly down, dissipating at our feet, like the head guard's words.

He went on with his explanation after the locomotive passed but Parfeny gestured to him to stop. He quietly told me that the head of the guards had, quite the opposite, foreseen everything. The head guard had thought he was ridding us of a difficult choice. Perhaps that is how things were.

Looking at Maxim, I recalled how I had triple kissed with him. I recalled that because, unlike all the others whose cheeks I touched that day, his beard was surprisingly soft. Only his did not chafe my skin. I told Parfeny of that at the time and he smiled. Only after did I understand why he had smiled – and I too smiled. Though I later blushed. And went to confession the next day.

Parfeny walked up to what remained of Maxim and whispered something to him that nobody else heard. But standing next to him I heard: *What was the reason?* And I mentally asked the same thing. After the warm April night, the smell of candles, after those soft embraces – what was the reason? The dead Maxim could no longer answer that question, though I suspect he could not have answered when alive.

"What sort of time is this?" Parfeny asked me that evening. "They love and hate ideas. Not people."

"And it is unclear what can oppose that," I said. "Punishment? Other ideas?"

"Patience, I think."

"They await practical measures from us."

He placed his hands on my shoulders:

"Oddly enough, I think patience is the most practical measure."

In the fifteenth year of Parfeny and Ksenia's reign, the peasant Petr traveled around the Island's burgs and hamlets, showing his son Yevsevy at fairs and earning a living for the two of them. Petr had declared that he was going to show someone dog-headed to the venerable public, for Yevsevy's face was completely covered in hair.

Many at the fairs doubted, however, that Yevsevy was truly dog-headed. Despite the fact that there was abundant hair on his face, Yevsevy's ears were human, while the ears of Saint Christopher the Dog-Headed on icons were truly canine. In addition, although Yevsevy barked at the fair, he later changed over to human speech in a pub, rather crude speech to boot, and his fondness for an entire shtof of vodka indicated that he was no dog. Many people argued about that incident, not understanding if Yevsevy was an omen.

A second incident was inarguable and boded nothing good. A she-ass came out to the Main Square and uttered in a human voice:

Revolutions are the locomotives of history.

After thinking for a bit, she added:

We have nothing to lose but our chains.

Some saw a bad omen and a threat in that and thus proposed slaughtering the she-ass, but, per order of the prince and princess, the animal was sent to the circus, where she spoke only once. The speech was puzzling but less sinister:

Reason has always existed, but not always in a rational form.

The she-ass's utterances stopped there and only a roar sounded from her lips. The roar sounded unusual, somehow not even ass-like, and that roar clearly gave the sense of readiness for a fight.

In Parfeny and Ksenia's twentieth year, the *demonstrations* began, something previously unprecedented. Island residents clearly heard *demon* in the name of the event itself, so significant numbers of participants did not initially gather. It was obvious, however, that the word was filled with some sort of unearthly power since things gradually began to take flight. Or perhaps it was the opposite and things were headed toward a rapid descent – everything here depended on one's standpoint.

After realizing that a new world cannot be built by only detonating bombs, the fighters for a new life discovered that demonstrations had a far more explosive effect. Human nature rejects murder so few people had sympathized with their bombs. It was far more rational, reasoned the fighters, to devote themselves to human nature.

It is not simple to change a person's nature but it changes easily within people. It is enough to gather them together – they will be obedient. There are no individual forces of will within a crowd, there is only a common force of will, which can be manipulated.

That is what they think.

Demons organize demonstrations. That is what I think.

As time passed, people began gathering for demonstrations more frequently, nearly daily. The number who came increased too. Seeing that no one impeded them, the fighters began expressing themselves ever more harshly and holding demonstrations in places closer and closer to the Royal Palace. The authorities sat by, as if not noticing what was happening.

One day, stones began flying into the Palace and city watchmen were positioned around the building. On that same day, despite entreaties not to do so, Prince Parfeny went out to those who had gathered. Someone in the crowd hurled a stone and it hit the prince in the shoulder. The head of the guards ordered the hurler be seized. It did not take long to find the scoundrel since people from the crowd betrayed him. They had not expected that matters would escalate to hurling stones, although how could it be limited to simple conversations?

The guards wanted to continue restoring order but Parfeny stopped them. He entered the very thick of the crowd and asked what, exactly, concerned these people. Several voices rang out, demanding Parfeny leave the princely throne. When the prince asked them what sort of governance they would like to see and what they awaited from it, he received no intelligible answer.

They began telling him of drought months and their opposite – rainy months – and about forest fires and crop failures. And then Parfeny approached the men who had answered him and asked:

Do you know of some governance other than heavenly governance, that would rid the Island of the disasters you have enumerated?

And when the men who had spoken with Parfeny answered him, people in the crowd began smiling and later they even openly laughed, for everyone understood there had not yet been such governance on earth. The crowd then dispersed peacefully. The next day, however, it came to the Royal Palace again, in even greater numbers.

The crowd grew larger each time and the accusations were more severe. And the conversation no longer concerned drought. The royal couple were faulted for having allegedly plundered the State Treasury. No one smiled after that speech and stones again began flying through the Palace windows.

And then, little by little, it became obvious to all that the crowd had a ringleader by the name of Kasyan, nickname "Askance." Which described him well. And he was mostly bald, but more than anything he was mean. Kasyan did not throw stones but his speeches were heavier than stones because attendees' eyes filled with rage after hearing them.

Parfeny went out into the crowd on one of the most unsettled days. After listening to accusations of looting the Treasury and his own personal crookedness, he asked where these people had gotten their information. The crowd parted and made way for Kasyan to approach.

Newspapers on the Continent, Kasyan said in a reedy voice, are committed to transparency regarding information about what the powers-that-be on the Island have acquired. It has been mentioned there that the prince's property is so small as to be unbelievable. A person of such stature as, let us say, that prince cannot have so few possessions at his disposal. It can only be concluded that he is hiding information about his genuine prosperity in order that (who knows) the sources of his enrichment not be disclosed.

Ashen, the prince responded to Kasyan:

Yes, my property is not great since there have been many circumstances when I have needed to spend my own money on state necessities.

Askance looked around at those in attendance, in order to speak not for himself but as if for them:

So perhaps, O Prince, you will name those circumstances for us? And why did you not mention them earlier?

Because, Parfeny responded, it is best not to speak of certain things. But since my money has become a temptation for you, I will say it was spent in the days of droughts and floods, when the Island's public coffers were already empty. The Treasury kept a record of money spent and it will be divulged tomorrow.

The next day, the newspapers published an accounting of expenditures in days of woe, from which it followed that the prince's personal money was used for purchasing bread, building houses for those whose homes had burned, and numerous other goals that required the newspapers to use seventeen supplementary pages to enumerate.

This information plunged the fighters for a new life into despondency and resulted in, to use their favorite word, a bombshell. People discussed the information, were astounded by it, and love for the royal couple grew extraordinarily. Seeing that, the fighters resigned themselves to considering their cause lost. Imagine their surprise when the same number of people came to the next demonstration.

A new misfortune made itself known three months later. In the presence of all who had gathered, Kasyan accused the prince of adultery and violation of a young maiden, Lukeria, a juvenile who was also of feeble mind. This time, the Main Square seemed to be a boundless human sea. Not only stones flew out of the enraged crowd: several shots were heard too.

Despite the security detail's objection, the prince appeared again before the people. Parfeny entered the crowd and found himself surrounded on all sides because people would not let guards in after him. He thrice began to speak but Kasyan's people answered from the crowd with jeers and whistling. The people, however, awaited the prince's answer and forced the jeerers to be quiet.

Parfeny could hope for only one thing: the trust of those gathered around him. To hope, by right of the fact that he had never deceived them. When complete silence had set in, he said:

What you accuse me of is an untruth.

As he uttered that, Parfeny turned in order to go to the Palace and the crowd parted before him. People did not make a single sound as he walked. And that silence resembled a miracle. And the fact that they allowed him to leave seemed a miraculous rescue.

The next day, Lukeria was subjected to a medical examination. She turned out to be a virgin.

The demonstrations continued. In the sixth month of this troubled time, Parfeny went out to the crowd for the last time. He asked:

What do you await?

And the many thousands of people on the square answered as if in a unified voice:

Something new!

Parfeny bowed his head, signaling understanding.

Two days later, in the evening hours, Their Royal Highnesses met in the Royal Palace with representatives of the insurrectionists. They could already be called that because excesses had begun around the Palace, though the guards had not yet received a command to regain order. Those gathered at the Palace sat together all night and all day; people did not disperse from the square.

On the third day, late in the evening, Parfeny, Ksenia, Askance, and certain of his comrades-in-arms appeared on the front steps of the Palace. After waiting for quiet, Parfeny addressed the crowd:

People of the Island, you wanted something new. Since I heard no other voices, I consider that the will of the people and resign the authority that was vested in me. Following your representatives' proposal, henceforth Princess Ksenia will govern the Island.

When the noise that arose on the square had quieted, Ksenia bowed to those gathered. After a moment of silence, she said:

I accept this reign for the good of the Island.

Then Kasyan, who lacked the dignity of the royal couple next to him, said a few words. And his words were, like him, petty and quick. With an unexpected ardor he began assuring the crowd that a solution of this sort suited the insurgent people.

To others, it might have seemed that something new had come in the form of the old, but it was already clear then that this was not how things were, not at all. Many in the crowd wept. They were primarily those whose voices had not been heard, for they had uttered nothing, out of fear. They, however, were not alone in weeping.

The tears of those standing on the square flowed from love and sympathy for the prince, from the looming uncertainty, and for some reason, even from the word *suited*, which Kasyan had uttered. That word, like nothing else, spoke of the onset of something new.

Chapter the Fifteenth

KSENIA

A long-awaited calm set in during the first year of Princess Ksenia's reign. After Kasyan, also known as Askance, was unable to come to an agreement with his comrades-in-arms, it was obvious that he saw in Princess Ksenia something akin to his own rescue. To the great joy of many, the demonstrators no longer gathered. It was possible that the fighters for a new life had lost all their strength or it may simply have been that they feared a power struggle amongst themselves in the event of an immediate victory. In any case, everyone thought that calm would be temporary.

Ksenia proved herself a wise leader. She had intentionally stayed in her husband's shadow for many decades, but it had never been a secret that her opinions had become defining for Parfeny. And the fighters were wrong if they thought they had made a decisive step toward taking power by agreeing to the reign of a woman. They had made a step, perhaps more than one, in the opposite direction.

Soon after Ksenia's accession to the throne, it became clear to everyone that she was tougher than her husband. Ksenia made decisions more cautiously than Parfeny and sometimes it seemed that cautiousness was excessive but, after making those decisions once, she never renounced them and she watched that everything was unfailingly accomplished.

KSENIA

And so, there's what I turn out to be, but the fighters for a new life had not known. And chronicler Ilary had not known.

I saw how Parfeny smiled as he read those lines. He knew.

But I understood that everything would fall apart. That the day would arrive when nobody would listen to me, the tough one (that Ilary!), either, or my orders. Nobody needed to be a prophet to see that: history's motion had been divined, if only roughly. That motion could have been slowed but not stopped.

When we met with Kasyan that sad night, he talked a lot. There were several other characters with him, but he did most of the talking. He had a reedy voice, it sounded like this Russian melody... Yes, *Flight of the Bumblebee*. And he circled around us like a bumblebee too: small, nimble, askance. Significantly balding.

I don't know if bumblebees go bald, but baldness is what made Kasyan an absolute bumblebee. He spoke, Parfeny nodded, and it was unclear if he was agreeing with Askance or just lowering his head in time with that insane music. Parfeny was calm.

Parfeny and I had spent the entire previous night talking through what we should do. He thought that we had to give in to the crowd's demands in order to avoid bloodshed. I responded that the crowd had no demands, they were simply present and it was the gang that gathered the crowd that we needed to speak with.

"But that crowd is present for some reason," Parfeny objected. "That means it's their crowd. We'll come to an agreement with the people they send from the square."

I buried my head in his shoulder.

"But it's impossible to come to an agreement with them.

You give them your hand and they'll bite off a finger. Or vice versa. You know what I mean."

"That's why we'll offer them a finger. We'll see when we get there."

They did not actually bite off a hand. Judging by the glances that Askance tossed at his comrades-in-arms, I suddenly realized that they were now his main enemies. He looked at them, putting it mildly, with a sideways glance. He agreed to my leadership surprisingly easily – he was even the one who proposed it!

We discussed scads of other details and he continued circling around us. He was laughable. And I felt his un-believable energy and understood that this insect's bites were very painful, whether you were with him or against him. The fighters for a new life understood that too.

A new life. When I heard that phrase, I was over-whelmed with offense for our current life, which is not so bad at all. The present loses out to the future just as reality loses to fantasy. And persuasion is pointless here: the future possesses unlimited resources. Only later can it be compared to the present, though then there's no longer any point. It's too late.

PARFENY

Yesterday we had an unusual visitor: Jean-Marie Leclerc, the famous French film director. We've become some-what interested in film in recent years and we like Leclerc. Especially his *Man without a Biography*. It's the story of a spy who's always under deep cover and has to learn his own new biography each time.

Imagine this: he could name any detail of his non-existent past – his father's eye color, sister's age, or the corner where the grand piano stood in the living room. That was someone's real life, in flawlessly precise details that he attached to himself. He had a phenomenal memory and could recall thousands of details.

That memory of his played a mean joke on him. He blew his cover when he forgot his own biography. He remembered all the details and events he'd learned by heart, just like before, but everything had blended in his head like milk and coffee. He had to resign and take an early retirement. Secluded in a suburban house, he recollected his life, which multiplied many times until the end of his days.

Now the funniest part: Jean-Marie is planning to make a biographical film about Ksenia and me. He called it a "biopic." The union of two words: *biographical* and *picture*, biopic. We might have bid him farewell for just the word ... if he hadn't been Leclerc.

He was apparently inspired by *A History of the Island*. Leclerc's thought is that the film could be called *Parfeny and Ksenia*. Without even conferring, Ksenia and I quietly but firmly said *no*. And then Leclerc fell to his knees in front of us.

That was unbearable. The great Leclerc in front of us on his knees, like one of our servants in the long-gone Middle Ages. Ksenia and I told Leclerc:

"We'll think about it."

And then this person started grabbing at our legs, trying to win our *yes*. That *yes* finally sounded from me because Ksenia, as we now know, is tougher.

Leclerc liked that (lovely alliteration). He shouted that no director in the world ever had consultants like us for a historical film about the Middle Ages.

Us as consultants? That was the next surprise Leclerc had saved for us. You don't cry about your hair after your head's been cut off, so we agreed to that too. And became consultants.

Since the details were presented to us using the salami principle, we only found out at the end of the conversation that they'd already started work on the film. It turned out that the director and the crew were going to start shooting it in a week.

We asked leading questions about the screenplay. Screenplay? Leclerc rocked back and forth, as if he were planning to fall at our feet again, but something held him back. He didn't have any screenplay, in the usual sense of the term. Yes, he had preparatory materials but nothing more. That's how he'd made all his films.

I asked Leclerc how he works without a script. Very simple. He drinks coffee with the actors when he arrives on the set. Tells each how to move and what to say.

"Creativity should begin and end on the set. Period," said the director, slapping himself on the thigh.

Yes, one more thing. When he was standing in the doorway, Leclerc seemed to recall something. Lieutenant Columbo's last question. Just one more thing: Would we agree to come to Paris for consultations? We would receive (he thought for an instant searching for the right words) the royal treatment.

This was the only scene in the great director's production that we didn't respond to. We'll think about it. It's hard to decide immediately. At our age ... At the word *age*, Leclerc burst out laughing and that was, I think, the only deviation from the script that, according to what our guest said, he doesn't have. He was embarrassed, embraced us as we saw him out, and said:

"What are you talking about, at your age?"

The seventh year of Ksenia's rule marked the completion of construction of the Library, which is similar to the Palace in terms of beauty and grandeur. The Library ended up even taller than the Palace, making it the tallest building in the City. Statues of great people from the past were installed at the base of the Library's columns so that their names would not be forgotten: Plato, Aristotle, Herodotus, Homer, and Agafon the Forward-Looking.

Did Agafon foresee such an honor? From his high spot he saw those who had gathered, as if verifying that his predictions were being carried out. Books were delivered to the Library under his unblinking gaze. Some books were purchased on the Mainland, some were donated by Island residents. The Monastery handed over a large number of manuscripts but Agafon's prophecy was not among them, something that I think would not have surprised Agafon very much.

On the day the Library opened, a huge line formed for library cards. The line ended up being so long that it was obvious one day would not be enough for cards. Even a week would not do. On that first day, as many people as could fit in the Library's Large Hall received cards.

Card holders sat all evening, reading the books that had come to them. Many who were not accustomed to reading moved their lips and a few traced the lines with a finger since they did not know how to read at all. They went line by line and smiled, joyful to be involved with books and pouring out tears, regretting their illiteracy and swearing that evening to learn to read.

The City's most venerable citizens were offered the opportunity to bring books home but they did not use it, for who would see them reading there? They, like the rest, liked the Library's cultured quiet, the rustling of turning pages, and the smell of old folios. With time, readers began choosing books for themselves to fit their hearts' desires, though there was still a book shortage. People continued stocking up on books from the Mainland, and this thirst for new books and knowledge was a sign that the Island was moving closer to universal literacy.

In the ninth year of pious Ksenia's reign, a tram line was launched in the City. Iron rails had been laid on the streets and electrical lines were strung up the year before. The tram had been brought from the Mainland, since nothing of the sort was produced on the Island. Seven tramcars (matching the number of liberal arts) were purchased and the Main Square in front of the Library became their hub – that was a very promising starting point.

All seven tramcars were of different colors and they departed the hub in the order of the colors of the rainbow. Their last stop was the city gate, which had long been unlocked since it was now located almost at the City's center and the walls that met at the gate had been so dilapidated that they were finally taken down. Each tramcar had a pedal for its bell and the bells rang constantly. That happened until every City resident had at least one opportunity to ring the bell.

Many people loved what was called "riding the imperial": riding on the tram's roof. The height and the fresh air made their heads spin but the opportunity to look into second-story windows only increased their passion for riding that way. The imperial's benches stood along the sides of the tramcar and the riders there sat back-to-back. They could naturally see the windows but curiosity about second-floor windows dwindled over time since the buildings had first floors, too, and one could peer into those windows without clambering up to the imperial.

Others now rode to work on the tram and thus needed to leave the house much earlier since the tram route did not necessarily lie close to their workplaces. After riding to an end stop, they exited the tram and hailed a cart or simply walked to wherever they needed to begin their workday.

The tramline generated a special respect among residents due to their incomprehension of how the contraption moved. That respect deepened because the tram had no chance of turning where there were no rails.

The impossibility of turning reminded Island residents of the famous story about the Centaur, who was only able to move in a straight line. Everyone in the City knew that the Centaur had been led to Solomon via Jerusalem and buildings along his path needed to be torn down: that is how straight the Centaur's path was and that is how impossible it was for him to turn. When it became necessary to tear down a poor widow's house, she tearfully appealed to the Centaur, asking him to bypass her home. And the Centaur took pity on her, bypassing her home at the expense of a broken rib.

Worthy of respect are those who do not turn from their path, though their merits fade if compared to those who sacrifice for the sake of their neighbor. This tragic but joyful story settled like a reflection on the tramcars as their motion around the City simultaneously reminded everyone of true valor and mercy.

In those years, the demonstrations had nearly stopped, so no more explosions were heard and a long-awaited peace came over the entire City and Island. The Library and the tram so caught Island residents' fancy that the fight for a new life seemed less captivating than the rustling of books being read and the tram's clanging.

The self-propelled tramcar aroused delight and incomprehension for a long time. One might recall that the train moved on its own too, but it was large, a locomotive pulled it, and for some reason that was far less exciting for the imagination. The tram was on its own. It seemed to contain all its power within: it did not produce steam and the electrical wires from which it received its vital currents were somehow mysterious and thoroughly inexplicable.

Many who went to the Library dreamt of figuring out that astonishing vehicle's secret. And so the tram and the Library became somehow indissolubly linked, the sole path to a bright future that was far calmer and more venerable than the path proposed by the fighters for a new life. People had begun to forget about them. Kasyan and his comrades-in-arms, after all, could propose nothing similar.

In Ksenia's eleventh year, a seafarer and a tiller of the land met in the city port. They had not sought a joint discussion but their meeting somehow came about, perhaps because what better place is there for a discussion than an island port? One word led to another and it was revealed that the seafarer's father had drowned during a storm. A while later it became clear that his grandfather also died sailing the seas. And then the tiller of the land said:

Believe me, O navigator, that if I were you, I would never have gone out to sea.

The seafarer asked the tiller of the land how his father's life ended.

He died in his own bed, answered the tiller of the land. He died surrounded by his progeny and members of his household. Answering the question of how his grandfather died, the tiller of the land said he also died in his bed. And then the seafarer told him:

Then know, brother, that if I were you, I would never lie down in my bed.

History has not recorded their names since in a port one can run across many people whose names the memory is incapable of retaining. But their words, which are more important than their names, remain. And those words lose neither their power nor their beauty due to the namelessness of those who uttered them. Words require no names.

Certain wanderers have said that conversation took place not on the Island but on the Mainland. Others maintain that it never happened, in the actual sense, and that a mysterious preacher allegedly thought it up. None of that, however, applies much to words: they live their own life, appearing where they are needed and emanating from the lips of various people. There are no ownership rights for words, thus no one possesses them.

What someone says often transforms into common property so that others' words become our own. It even happens that it is not people who give rise to words but the opposite, so it would not be surprising if a seafarer and a tiller of the land came together simultaneously in several ports and the conversation noted above began to flow between them.

In the twelfth year of Ksenia's rule, the University was opened. Opening the University was unavoidable, given the craving for knowledge that had come about because of the Library, the tram, and even earlier, the train. Although primarily young people went to the University, others did as well. Mature men who were street-smart from experience and invested with power also attended lectures.

Kasyan and his cronies came out in favor of women's right to education, and the most impatient fighters for a new life decided to detonate something highly explosive in order to support women in their aspirations for enlightenment. Meanwhile, seeing women's affinity for science, the powers-that-be at the University made the University accessible to women.

Fearing they were late with their intervention, the fighters hastened to detonate the bombs they had already prepared but, unfortunately for them, the quantity of victims was not great.

Nothing good, they said, comes of haste.

And may that, they said, be our lesson.

Since the matter concerned the question of women's rights, these bombers were women but then the villains' ringleaders forgot why the bombs were exploding in the first place and decided that henceforth only men should detonate the explosions.

This particular failure, they said, was the best evidence that women need education.

The University's first professors arrived from the Mainland on a steamship. A huge crowd greeted the professorial steamship when it docked at the Island. Domestic history was among the social sciences offered and I, the sinner Ilary, was included in the instructors' ranks, which filled me with pride for I had become a professor.

The overseas professors initially looked upon me with bewilderment since it seemed dubious to them that there could even be an opportunity for history to exist on the Island. They changed their minds after becoming acquainted with the disparate historical notes found in various parts of our land, as well as with this chronicle devoted to the Island's general history.

That, however, did not hold them back from quibbles and advice regarding *A History of the Island*. The description of years gone by and the chroniclers' conclusions seemed uncontemporary to the professors and they called the chronicle's language "antediluvian." The aforementioned characteristics apparently only deepened with the years and that came into irreconcilable contradiction with progress, which was gathering speed.

138

The matter concluded on a day that was far from wonderful, when professors at a session of the Island Historical Society demanded the history be rewritten in accordance with contemporary scientific information and the overall course of progress. I, feeble-minded Ilary, refused to rewrite history, declaring that this was how it had been passed down to us by our ancestors and how it would remain, unchanged, for the ages.

You are an obscurant, the professors told me. Engage in your backward history as you see fit. We will write a new one. And please do not think that your history is different from ours, for everything is subject to universal laws that are evidently unknown to you.

At their insistence, they held a debate right then and there, so I began answering their questions, using my rather small strengths.

What is history, the professors asked me.

History, I answered, is a description of the struggle of Good and Evil, a struggle led by human hands.

What, in your opinion, can be considered a historic event?

Without pausing for a moment, I said:

Any victory of one force over the other can be a historical event since the ratio of those victories and losses determines a people's spiritual condition.

These two theses that you have presented, they responded, underlie your fundamental delusions, since history describes not the struggle of Good and Evil but an uninterrupted chain of causes and effects. A historic event is an event that changes the course of history. Brother Ilary, kindly work on forming cause-and-effect chains, otherwise we shall ban you from teaching at the University.

I was sorry to upset my colleagues but I stated to them, imbued with a spirit of meekness and humility, that it was pointless for me to create the chains they had mentioned since they are built only

139

of links known to us, whereas most actual links are concealed from everyone.

Is that not why, I asked, we possess a multitude of histories of the same period and they contradict one another? And you yourselves, respected colleagues, build no chains. Someone following your method, which I shall call magnetic, gathers links for prepared chains. I shall permit myself to note that this is not very complex if one has good knowledge of the material.

You are an interesting product of the Middle Ages, the professors told me, but your influence on malleable minds is intolerable. And you are thus being removed from the University.

Princess Ksenia rose to aid me, extending her ruling right hand over me and compelling my venerable opponents to come to terms with my presence. This is unsurprising since she and her pious spouse are also products of the Middle Ages so how could she not stand up for me?

Without saying a word to anyone, I gathered up my belongings and left for the Monastery late that night.

The royal couple attempted to reconcile the professors and me by bringing the opposing sides together at their residence in the Palace. In order not to continue the useless arguments, I immediately said that I refused to make chains of causes and effects, given that those who construct them work according to their own individual inclinations and tasks.

Where in those chains, I asked, is the struggle of Good and Evil that is the driving force of history?

I said:

I, sinful Ilary, am resigning from the University of my own free will and am returning to the Monastery in order to continue describing history in the proper way.

I explained that this endeavor to which I have been devoted for a lengthy time is more characteristic of me. That the monk's vestments fit me better than a professorial robe. I begged for Their Royal Highnesses' blessing to continue with history and bowed to them from the waist after receiving it.

The prince and princess embraced me and said:

O beloved Brother Ilary, continue to engage in history according to your heart's content and without chains of cause and effect. Good and Evil differ from causes and effects in that they are more obvious.

Before leaving, I reminded those in attendance about Agafon the Forward-Looking's prophecy, saying that my only advice to the professors would be to seek it because its discovery would explain much of history.

The professors smiled and several even laughed, but Prince Parfeny ordered them to cease their laughing. As I walked through the room, I heard someone's voice saying that old history was leaving in my person and that they, the professors, considered it their duty to create a new history.

After turning my face toward the voice, I answered that history never leaves, and then I caught the edge of my vestments on a table and could hear the fabric tearing. *This, my vestment, is rent*, flashed through my head, portending nothing good.

KSENIA

We are in Paris. Need I explain that Jean-Marie talked us into it? I think persuasion is his main gift.

In reality, there was no need to persuade us: we very much wanted to go to Paris. Somehow, we'd never made it to Paris – we'd only ever had a couple of trips to the mainland, for negotiations. We didn't travel much at all before, that's what the times were like. We'd read about Paris, then seen it on postcards and, later, on television. It lived in our consciousness like some wonderful dream, but it wasn't completely clear that a city like this actually existed.

It exists. We're sitting in a café on the Grands Boulevards. On the terrace, facing the boulevard; these are spectator seats.

People take photographs of us. Left to right: Monsieur Bénard, who's looking after us, Parfeny, and I. Monsieur Bénard is putting his life on the line for us, that's what Leclerc told him in front of everyone. Monsieur Bénard asks us to call him Dominique.

The May sun makes its way through the plane trees so its glimmering patches of light quiver on our faces. The edges of an awning flap somewhere overhead. A light, clothy sound. Clothy and burgundy-colored. It's mixed with gold, it's a banner that crosses the entire boulevard, advertising the treasures of Tutankhamun.

Dominique ordered coffee and croissants for us. Water. I requested paper and a pen too. They're having a conversation; I'm writing. I'll die of emotional overload if I don't write. From time to time, my gaze shifts to pedestrians. They're in no hurry.

The ideal rhythm doesn't hurry but it lacks delays. Only when we are sitting can we keep up that rhythm. The time has passed when we could walk along a sidewalk without hurrying. That's too bad. We should probably have left the Island for France and begun to walk as they do, a knapsack over the shoulder, offhandedly tossing back a lock of hair, smiling at our thoughts. People walk differently on the Island.

Several people asked for our autographs: everybody here knows about our visit. Even so, there's no excitement on display. Our age surprises them; antiquity generally surprises them. I find their polite interest appealing. It's as if we're part of what Paris offers in May, something from Tutankhamun's domain.

I was recalling Ilary and his firm opposition to the professors. Yesterday at the hotel we read his quirky story about that out loud before bed. We wept.

Ilary died over seventy years ago. He never saw Paris. That's a strange, even hilarious thought, one that could only cross my mind here. I wonder if this would have affected that wonderful style of his? I don't think so.

It feels lonely without him.

In the eighteenth year of pious Ksenia's rule, the demonstrations resumed. Neither the Library nor the University nor even the tram could improve the public's disposition, though that might have initially seemed possible. The struggle for a new life was continuing, although that mysterious life was now more frequently called *better*. One word somehow replaced another, unnoticed, but if anyone were to ask a person on the street why new was better, the person would not have answered.

The passion for change united everyone, from factory workers to university professors. More and more people attended demonstrations, and if the guards were previously able to stand up to the human force, now they did not even attempt to do so. Princess Ksenia turned out to be caught in a trap. Visiting the Monastery in those sorrowful days, she told me:

If I order the troops to drive the crowd away from the Palace, then a war will start. If I do not act, it will all end in a coup.

Kasyan and the fighters awaited decisive actions from the authorities. They were hastening those actions by throwing stones through windows at the Palace and many other buildings that housed the Island's government. Everything that happened eighteen years earlier was repeating with but one difference: the events had a greater scope and the actions were fiercer.

Geronty, the Island's bishop, came to one of the demonstrations that took place at the city gate. Decrepit in body but strong of soul, the bishop stood on a high, flat rock by the gate and addressed the crowd.

He said:

Hatred in this country has passed all conceivable limits.

The people, who were initially not listening to the bishop and had even whistled at him, soon began to quieten.

He also said:

Believe me, my children, that nothing good can be built on hatred, for hatred is as unstable as sand and everything standing upon it will crumble.

And his voice strengthened with every minute and the people's sympathy for what he said strengthened too, because everyone understood the correctness of Geronty's words. It seemed that the bishop standing on the rock was closing the gate to a place whence there was now no return. Of course there was only the appearance of that since the city walls no longer existed and all that remained of the gate was a heap of rocks. Many people, however, distinctly saw how the gate – whose huge panels again hung on hinges – had slowly begun to close, following the motion of the bishop's arm.

The bishop recalled the cautionary tale of how four beasts with good intentions took up musical instruments and decided to play

144

as a quartet. Since the story was new and no one on the Island had heard it, the attendees were rapt. The bishop told of the beasts' unsuccessful attempts to create music and he even made faces, depicting how each of them tried to play. At some point, the rock he was standing on shifted and Geronty began slowly moving as he showed the beasts' motions. The beasts changed places in the hope that this would create the long-awaited music.

People in the crowd began laughing and their laughter was kind. They did not yet know where the bishop's story was leading but they liked the story for what it was. After blowing into an imaginary horn at the conclusion, Geronty suddenly grew gloomy. The crowd felt dispirited, too, after expecting the performance to continue.

Moving around in an expanse leads to nothing, said the bishop. Especially when creating music is concerned. Each must learn to play his own instrument.

After a pause, he added:

Life will not become better because you are on the street, milling around on the cobblestones. I call on you to disperse immediately, for each of you to go about your business. God blesses those matters. Only for milling around in crowds is there no Godly blessing, because the result of those wanderings is division and fratricide.

At those words, someone cast a stone at the bishop. The throw was not especially precise and the stone whistled past his temple. Geronty involuntarily took a step forward, stumbled, and fell from the rock.

He did not perish. His eyes were closed when they lifted him up but life still glimmered within him. The bishop was carried through the crowd. At the front there strode a person with the bishop's miter in his hands and the crowd parted before him, as the sea before Moses. Geronty's uncovered head swayed in time with the motion and his gray hair became more crimson with each moment. The

145

bishop was carried into a tram that had driven up. The self-propelled vehicle made no stops as it rushed toward the Library, not far from where the City's medical clinic had recently opened.

The person who tossed the stone was caught. Several men who looked to be factory workers held him. The eyes of the captured man were filled with horror. Everyone froze for a moment, standing in wordless silence. Then the captured man unexpectedly tore his arm away and began screaming. His scream was devoid of words but it disturbed that fragile silence that held the scoundrel's hope. He was knocked to the ground and people began kicking him. There, on the bloodstained cobblestones, he parted with his life, which had never warmed anyone. People say they saw Kasyan and his comrades nearby. But they did not interfere.

A prayer service was held the next day, asking that health be bestowed to Geronty; the Monastery could not hold all those praying for the bishop. The prayer services became daily. On one of those days, Bishop Geronty regained consciousness, giving hope for his recovery. With the help of the monks serving him, he sat on his bed and said that he forgave the man who threw the stone, but then he lost consciousness again.

After being laid up for another week, the bishop opened his eyes again and this time he did not close them for the rest of the day. He told those around him that he observed the struggle of Life and Death during all the days he spent ill, and he said that Life told him to forgive the scoundrel because that would give Life new strength to fight. The bishop experienced a certain relief after uttering words of forgiveness. After spending another week in bed, he felt able to breathe freely and realized that Life had defeated Death.

Upon hearing that, Kasyan and his associates called for a new demonstration in memory of the man who threw the stone. They called him a victim of the fight for the future because (said Kasyan) the bishop was alive but the killed man was dead. Given that one is alive and one is dead, can (asked Kasyan) the one who is alive be considered a victim? Kasyan's speech was florid and not everyone understood it, but people gathered for the demonstration because the speech was actually about the dead person. It is known, after all, that people in our land feel particular respect for the dead.

It came to light at this large assembly that the deceased's name was Mikhei. Details of Mikhei's grievous life path also became known: he was orphaned early in life and a paternal aunt by the name of Domna beat him. Witnesses turned up saying Domna had beaten him on the head with a cast-iron pot, which slowed Mikhei's reasoning considerably, although it had never been quick.

Kasyan stood before the attendees and called Domna's heavy hand the hand of a rotten regime. In developing that visual image, Kasyan's comrade-in-arms Markel likened the cast-iron pot to a weapon in the hand of the aforementioned regime and called for seizing the Arsenal.

Touched by the slain man's fate, the crowd set off toward the Arsenal. Several of the factory workers whose blows had cut off Mikhei's life journey walked at the front of the procession. They regretted not having known of Domna's actions but even more so not knowing the sort of regime standing behind her. After meeting resistance from the guards, the crowd moved into attack mode but was quickly repelled.

Addressing the crowd, Kasyan explained that the rotten regime's hand was still firm, thus it was best not to end up beneath it. He led people away to neighboring streets, making it possible to hope that everything had worked out for the best this time too. The crowd stood on the streets all night and was unusually quiet.

Just before dawn, Kasyan and Markel chose the strongest men and again led them to the Arsenal. Fatigued by the confrontation during the day, the guards had unintentionally fallen asleep. Their sleep could also be explained by a lack of fear: no one from the guard imagined an attack on sleeping men during the hour of their best dreams.

After a brief explanation of tasks, Kasyan summoned his comrades-in-arms to storm the Arsenal, while he himself took shelter in a nearby alleyway. The comrades-in-arms were taken aback, since they thought he would go with them and lead the storming. Kasyan explained to them that they were the hands of the uprising but he was its head. The head should be in safety. After explaining that, he reminded them that Mikhei's unprotected head had been beaten. Nobody could argue with that.

The Arsenal was taken surprisingly quickly. Submerged in sleep, the guards did not put up a worthy resistance and were disarmed. Learning of that, Kasyan came out of his alleyway and took command once again, uniting head and hands.

The first thing that came into that mind of his was to bring the crowd back to the Arsenal and distribute weapons. The insurrectionists opened crate after crate of weapons and handed rifles to toiling workers in an endless line – people all over the City converged when they learned about the distribution of rifles. By noon, the City was armed. The authorities maintained their silence.

After ordering eleven guard officers to walk ahead of him, Kasyan brought them to the square in front of the Arsenal. He also appointed escorts to accompany them. These were not even his comrades-in-arms but ordinary people who had arrived during the night. After placing the officers in front of the roaring crowd, he told them not to even think about fleeing and ordered the escorts to hold them at gunpoint. A weapon is bewitching, so the escorts readily fulfilled the order. Joy gleamed in the escorts' eyes because of their involvement in a historic event.

Stepping a decent distance from the arrested, Kasyan addressed the crowd with a fiery speech. After listing the bloodthirsty regime's crimes and reminding his listeners of the first victim in the struggle for freedom, Kasyan called the officers "shadows of the past" and the crowd standing before him "lights of the future." He took a breath, looked at the escorts, and quickly said:

Fire!

Almost all the escorts shot due to the unexpectedness. About five of the officers were killed instantly; the others writhed on the ground, screaming. And then Kasyan ordered they be finished off. The horrified escorts threw down their weapons and melted into the crowd, where people stood speechless, armed, and stunned by the cries of the wounded. Nobody, including those who had shot, understood what had happened.

Fear gripped Kasyan because he sensed the waves of indignation that had set off along the human sea. He did not know what might replace that silence if it were to continue several more instants. And so he began to shout orders that people loyal to him finally finish off the wounded. After that was over and full silence set in, a shout rang out from the crowd:

What for?

Instinct hinted to Kasyan that he would be victorious if he were to maintain calm as he spoke and so he answered quietly:

Not *what for* but *for what*. He looked over the crowd. For them to stop resisting us. So they do not even dare to think of it!

By evening, news came that the city garrison had rebelled and gone over to the insurrectionists. When Kasyan was notified that fraternization was taking place between the rebels and the city population, he went to the garrison and took command. The fraternizers were drunk because they routed the royal wine cellar while celebrating the dawn of freedom. Senior officers were found in the basement, tied up. At Kasyan's order, they were also executed.

At that same time, however, troops loyal to the government were already advancing toward the City. The garrison that had gone over to the insurrectionists moved out to greet them at the ring road, as did a detachment of the armed population that had expressed the wish to fight. By the next morning, both units of troops stood facing one another.

KSENIA

That night the government gathered at the palace. Klavdian, the Island's field marshal, was also invited. We knew about everything that was happening but did not interfere, lest it worsen an already desperate situation.

The field marshal told us that troops loyal to me would reach the city limits by the end of the night. He lit his pipe and added that these were his best detachments and that they would handle any problems, be they armed citizens or the garrison that had betrayed the army. The field marshal assured those present that these were well-trained troops, unlike the garrison, where the primary duty was to march in parades.

The field marshal's velvety voice and, particularly, the smoke rings slowly rising from his pipe, instilled confidence.

"Just give the command, Your Highness, and order will be restored."

I was inclined to give that command, but Parfeny said a few words.

"Order will be restored. For today. But what about to-morrow, the day after tomorrow, every day? I think we must come to an agreement with the mutineers."

"The mutineers will perceive negotiations as our defeat," said Klavdian.

"But suppressing the insurrectionists will not be our victory," Parfeny objected. "The population is armed and aggressive and we cannot keep a platoon on every street."

What Parfeny said irked me.

"But it's a mutiny! You're proposing to utterly disregard the law in order to oblige criminals. Then why is there a law? And why, one might ask, is there a government?"

Parfeny paled and I began to feel sorry for him. He always went pale when he was agitated. He looked at the floor. He said:

"There are situations when the government is powerless to defend the law. In those situations, the government can only do one thing: step aside and avoid unnecessary blood-shed. Mutiny is not in a country, it is in souls, and an army cannot prevail there."

The field marshal knocked the ashes from his pipe into the fireplace.

"Eh, Your Highness," he bowed to Parfeny. "That's all philosophy." He turned to me. "Give me a command and I will subdue those souls. Or send them to hell."

"You are the one who decides here," Parfeny told me. "My advice is to let those people live as they are so inclined."

I was not looking at Parfeny but I felt his gaze upon me.

"I am the one here who decides. And you will hear my decision tomorrow."

Everyone left and I remained alone. Never before had I made decisions without Parfeny.

And my heart sank. And I began to weep.

151

In the morning, Kasyan and his comrades-in-arms were invited to the Palace. The meeting did not remind anybody of the one that had taken place eighteen years earlier. This time, Kasyan acquitted himself as the person in charge. He announced that the people demanded a republic.

Everybody knew the people had demanded no such thing since they did not know that word and were simply listless. As was soon explained, Kasyan did not need a republic either: he longed only for the regime to fall, in order that he himself might pick it up later, after it fell. Kasyan announced that general elections were needed and he heard no objections.

An hour later, he appeared on the Main Square and clambered up on the tram's imperial. He proclaimed that elections were looming and that from now on, each person was free to vote for whomever they saw fit. The crowd greeted that news with jubilation and those awaiting a better life tossed their peaked caps in the air as others even shot, also into the air.

But the crowd suddenly went silent once Bishop Geronty had mounted the imperial.

I think he wants to be elected, Kasyan shouted to the crowd. The crowd came to life.

After making the sign of the cross over the human sea, Geronty said:

No, I do not want people to elect me. That is because I remember one certain story about beasts. You know how I love stories about beasts.

The bishop began telling about a crow and I, standing there, thought I had already heard the beginning of this story somewhere. The carefree bird was sitting on a spruce tree, holding cheese in its beak. Due to certain circumstances, there was a fox down below, under the spruce.

Tell me, my sister, the fox said to the crow, are you planning to vote for a new life? The crow kept silent. Geronty's gray hair fluttered in the wind.

I thought, said the fox, that you would give me wise advice so I might make the right choice. The crow was obviously in no hurry to share wisdom.

Your enlightened opinion is very important to me, the fox sang out in Geronty's voice. The fox looked up at the crow, who remained silent. The bishop placed a cross to his lips and kept silent himself for a moment, showing what it – genuine silence – is.

It is just that you, O crow, have no answer, said the fox. Which is why you cannot say if you will vote for a new life. No, cawed the crow, I will not vote for a new life.

At those words, the cheese fell out of the crow's beak and ended up in the sly fox's paws. The crow was sad. The crow sat in its spruce tree and thought about what had happened. The crow regretted losing the cheese and was attempting to understand its mistake. It repeated the same question over and over: And what if I had said *yes*?

The crowd responded with laughter because it found the crow's stupidity funny. But Bishop Geronty was not laughing.

He asked:

Do you think that only crows are that stupid? No, the same thing happens with people. Especially when they turn into crows.

A shot rang out from the crowd. Geronty grasped a railing, and slowly slid to the imperial's plank floor. Kasyan took out a handkerchief and wiped away the drops of the bishop's blood that had dotted his own forehead. The shooting and the commotion that broke out roused Kasyan to hurriedly leave the imperial. The tram pulled away, carrying off Geronty's dead body.

The next day, an election day was named before a vast assembly of people. Residents of the Island, Kasyan obviously among them, were nominated as candidates. It lay ahead to elect the most worthy.

A short time later, however, it became clear that Kasyan was not among the most worthy. There was no doubt that the voters did not consider him thus. Downhearted at the public lack of gratitude, the night before the elections, Kasyan and some armed people broke into the Palace and took the royal couple into custody. No one defended Parfeny and Ksenia.

In the morning, Kasyan declared himself the Island's sole ruler.

PARFENY

Our wonderful Ilary died that day: his heart stopped. I think it seemed to him that history had taken a wrong turn. Detoured into some sort of thicket. He did not want to accompany it there.

The chronicle was passed on to Brother Galaktion, Ilary's student, for keeping.

KASYAN

I Galaktion, unlearned and crude of intellect, attest:

In the first year of the Great Island Revolution, big changes commenced on the Island. They could have been even larger if Kasyan had managed to execute the royal couple as he dreamt.

In his first address to the Island's citizens, he announced the triumph of what is new and then immediately reverted to the old. Without naming names, Kasyan informed Island residents that the bony hands of the past, which should be chopped off, were reaching for a newborn life.

Those listening to him began to worry because they quickly guessed who Kasyan had in mind. As they celebrated the arrival of what was new, Island residents remembered that those hands were not so bony. They did not argue with the assertion that the radiant future was better than the gloomy past but they were not prepared to part with Their Royal Highnesses, whom they loved.

Seeing that everyone was agitated, Kasyan announced that he did not intend to execute the royals and that the bony hands were only an abstraction. Owing to the ancient age of the couple in question, he proposed sparing their lives, in the capacity of museum exhibits, by evicting them from the Palace and giving them a service room at the Museum of Island History.

The new administration immediately published decrees.

First. The Royal Palace as well as the residences of the Island aristocracy were handed over to the fighters for a bright future.

Second. A monument recognizing victims of the Revolution, represented by the murdered Mikhei, must be installed as soon as possible.

Third. The Monastery was confiscated for use by the state, which had acquired a new faith: faith in the Future. The Monastery's Church of the Transfiguration was renamed the Church of the Bright Future.

Fourth. A new era was introduced in the realm of chronology. The count of years now begins with the year of the Great Island Revolution.

Fifth. The Island's revolutionary leadership declared war on France and appealed to all true patriots to rally around said leadership.

A signature stood beneath all the decrees: *His Brightest Futurity Kasyan*

PARFENY

We're sitting in the Luxembourg Gardens with our legs wrapped in blankets. Ksenia's eyes are closed under rays of the spring Paris sun.

The funniest thing is that this war is apparently continuing even now. A full-fledged Hundred-Year War: it seems they forgot to reverse the decree. Happily, very few in Paris know about these military operations.

"I wonder why Kasyan declared war then," says Ksenia.

"So people would rally around him."

Ksenia smiles but doesn't open her eyes.

"But why France?"

"Because France is far away."

Bicyclists ride past us (the sound of compressed sugar) on fine gravel. They have all sorts of nonmilitary things on their racks: bags, packages from a nearby supermarket, pots with flowers, thermoses. A poodle with a bow tied on its head.

Of course His Brightest Futurity allowed a colossal blunder with us. As the soldiers guarding us told it, at first there had been discussion of a fatal fall down the stairs for us. Two of us walking together, two of us slipping and killing ourselves. What, from Kasyan's point of view, could be more natural? The stairs in the basement were stone and slippery. Walking by twos on the stairway is dangerous . . .

Why did he not carry his plan to completion? I think that his fixation on theater – and, to a greater extent, on France – let him down. The genetic memory of the century when people spoke French on the Island. Kasyan did not abandon his dreams of our execution but he saw the guillotine and the rolling head . . . and he wanted no less. There was a trace of Frenchness in all of his actions. I think that his love for France – along with France's distance – was to blame for the war he declared.

People say that Kasyan went to Paris in his early youth, to conquer the city. But his squeaky voice simply drowned in the city noise. Now he was declaring a second attempt at conquering and it was even less likely to succeed than the first.

If not for France, they would have done us in during the first night in the basement, with no pretensions at all for the novelty of the guillotine. And besides, people stood up for us on the square, people who retain something human under any circumstances.

The sun hides behind the clouds and now it's growing cooler. Dominique offers to bring our car right into the

157

garden; he has permission. We decline that honor and walk to the exit under our own power. Along the way, we run into women collecting autographs but Dominique shows them a preemptive gesture that says *non, madame*. A spare but definitive motion. I think Kasyan would have paid dearly for that sort of ability, but one must be born in Paris for that.

Dominique wants to settle us into the car by the Luxembourg Gardens gate but we (the second labor of Hercules) say we'll walk to the hotel. A gesture blending surprise and delight. As the Panthéon comes into view, our refined friend says it would have befit our rank to have housed us there rather than at the hotel. I tilt my head in gratitude:

"The company is excellent there."

"It is only too bad that they are all deceased," Ksenia smiles.

Dominique blushes.

"Forgive me."

He had not considered that circumstance.

Speaking of which, our Church of the Bright Future is a distant relative of the Panthéon, where revolutionaries initially lay. Though yes, they were later removed.

Ours were removed too.

His Brightest Futurity declared himself Chairman of the Island and Atanas, his comrade-in-arms – who had been assigned a most important post, as Minister of History and the Bright Future – was appointed his deputy. Since the Revolution had resulted in the bright future becoming the present to some degree, he proposed during the government's first session that the present be included in his sphere of responsibilities too.

Kasyan cut off the minister's speech and pointed out that only he was working on the present. After agreeing that the bright future had arrived, the chairman of the Island expressed confidence that this future could become even brighter and that the minister would have plenty to work on there. It is said that Atanas blushed but dared not enter into debate with the chairman.

After arriving at the Monastery with the goal of transferring it to the government, Atanas requested that *A History of the Island* be brought to him for a quick perusal. The history did not satisfy the minister, particularly the part describing the one-hundred-fifty-year dominion of the Apagonians.

A great people cannot have this sort of history, said Atanas. In other words, a people with a history like that cannot be great even if the people itself is obviously great. What follows from that?

I, a sinning man, did not know.

Atanas placed a hand on the manuscript.

And so it follows that history must be brought into accordance with the greatness of the people.

When I took the liberty of pointing out to him that our history was granted to us by God, he answered that God no longer exists in the previous sense. I asked Atanas what God is in the new sense and he answered:

The bright future.

A week later, the Supreme Council, which was dedicated to the past and the future, gathered at the Palace and I was brought in too. Island Chairman Kasyan was first to speak and he alerted the attendees to the fact that *in the life of every people there exist past, present, and future.* Unable to cope with that delight, a Supreme

Council member demanded that those words be included in a history textbook and that all further historical compositions open with them.

Chairman Kasyan initially wanted to question that proposal, pointing out that he had expressed more impressive opinions that he could bring to the public before too long but the Supreme Council considered it compulsory to immortalize all the chairman's thoughts in order that not a single one be lost to posterity. Seeing the council's steadfastness, Kasyan was forced to agree.

Inspired by the attention of his comrades-in-arms, the chairman gave them the gift of a more impressive statement that caused a new eruption of approval: *History should not only express the past.* According to Kasyan's thinking, historians henceforth should describe the future, too, since it will end up becoming the past. He called for making the future a special section of history.

In expanding on the chairman's statement, Atanas proposed calling the section about the future *prophecy.* Here, however, a harsh rebuke awaited him.

The essence of prophecy, said Kasyan, is not scientific and *we are engaging in scientific foresight, which is the sole correct foresight because it is true.*

Historians were instructed to dedicate themselves to scientific foresight of the future without enamoring themselves too much with the past or even the present, which lies too close to the past. I, the utterly sinful Galaktion, was ordered to remain the keeper of the past and correct it from time to time to the extent that would be gainful for the present. I, who repented for the burning of history, will atone for my sin by continuing to work secretly on the history of the present, which is flowing into the past, unnoticed.

The council deemed Atanas's instructions to destroy the entries related to the Apagonian dominion to be correct and historically expedient. Any mentions of that period were forbidden and such mentions would henceforth be deemed a state crime.

After all the aforementioned changes had taken place, I, a true student of the deceased Ilary, felt a lump rise in my throat when thinking of the university professors. Further events showed that I was wrong to worry about those researchers. They would soon publish a memorandum stating that the role of the past in history is exaggerated and the meaning of the future minimized.

Responsibility for that state of affairs was placed upon Ilary, who maintained that history was dolefully receding from its zenith. The professors, to the contrary, thought history's zenith lay ahead. Their scientific thought agreed with Kasyan's doctrine on that point. In the spirit of the referenced doctrine, the professors announced the creation of a new discipline: *scientific foresight*, which described, based on cause-and-effect chains, events that were certain to come about.

This did not mean that all the scholars thought identically. The famous professor Fouquet, who had come to the Island from France, outspokenly announced that history studies the past, utopia studies the future. That person declined to recognize foresight as a scholarly endeavor.

In defending foresight as scholarship, the professors told him that the aforementioned was founded upon two equally significant points: the beginning of a new epoch and its end. The beginning was the Revolution, the end *Perfect Harmony*. When provided with those two points, it was enough to join them with a line: looming events then appeared with even more clarity than did past events. The professors called that magic line *the line of development*.

Wracked with doubts, the French professor demanded they furnish scientific proof of the inevitability of Perfect Harmony and promised that he, Fouquet, would support that theory upon receiving proof.

The professors' answer was scientifically concise and spoke of one lone piece of proof that they termed devastating: Kasyan's brilliant doctrine confirmed the onset of Achieved Harmony.

No objections followed, meaning the professors' answer obviously made the strongest possible impression on the French professor. Calling their proof "devastating" forced Monsieur Fouquet to secretly charter a boat and set off for the Mainland under cover of darkness. Island newspapers reported the next day that Professor Fouquet was overwhelmed by an airtight argument and thus fled.

He expressed his attitude toward Kasyan's brilliance after reaching French shores. Fearing that my continuation of the chronicle could fall into the wrong hands, I will not consider repeating what he said, which I heard on a French radio broadcast. I will say only that Fouquet was holding up surprisingly cheerfully for a person who had been overwhelmed.

Atanas, Minister of History and the Bright Future, attempted to develop Kasyan's doctrine. I am referring to a university course, *The Flow of Time*, which Atanas introduced at a session of the Island Academy of Sciences and called "revolutionary." The essence of Atanas's proposal boiled down to a summary of a series of events, opening with Achieved Harmony and gradually moving toward the beginning, which he considered the Stone Age. Under that configuration, the course was based on and began with the future. Only later did the past appear, albeit to a far smaller extent.

Kasyan himself immediately condemned the presentation. His Brightest Futurity interrupted Atanas and directed the Academy's attention to the fact that, according to Atanas, the flow of time had been directed backward. Kasyan called the minister's views unscientific and accused him of imposing Fouquet's ideas as well as having a secret desire to send the Island's development into the Stone Age.

Atanas meekly objected that his observations had nothing in common with Fouquet's fabrications since his own views recognized the existence of Achieved Harmony. But His Brightest Futurity refuted the minister in (as they say) two words by defining Atanas's views as *regurgitated Fouquetism*. Atanas, who was still holding the papers with his presentation, nearly did regurgitate from the unexpectedness, passively confirming Kasyan's correctness. His Brightest Futurity extended his hand in the minister's direction, warning those in attendance that what the apostate Atanas said might still cause hiccups for Island science from time to time.

After that revelation, everyone expected Atanas's immediate fall, though it did not follow. Following that session, His Brightest Futurity displayed latitude and a lack of grudges and invited Atanas to make a joint visit to a cultural event planned at the Menagerie. The minister considered that a good sign and was elated.

Kasyan returned alone from the Menagerie. The morning papers came out with a funeral notice framed in black about the untimely demise of the Minister of History and the Bright Future. The newspapers mentioned no details, limiting the material to dry statements saying the minister had been eaten by a crocodile.

Despite the deceased's apostasy, Kasyan announced a national period of mourning and ordered that a solemn funeral be planned. Since nothing remained of Atanas, the coffin contained the crocodile that had eaten him: the reptile was destroyed instantly after devouring the minister. Kasyan shed many a tear for his comrade while tossing a clump of soil on his grave.

He said:

Anyone who thinks that we are burying Atanas is mistaken.

Kasyan's eyes scanned the crowd before continuing:

We are burying an epoch.

Discussion of questions about the past and the future was considered closed. The Island was moving along a *line of development* from the Revolution to Achieved Harmony.

KSENIA

We've been in Paris for a week now. Yesterday I asked Jean-Marie when we'll begin helping him. He started laughing and said that just our presence here is a huge help. I find that answer surprising. We haven't read a screenplay because there isn't one, but why aren't they inviting us to the studio? Maybe there's no studio either?

I couldn't hold back and asked our director about that. He started laughing again. He's always laughing, that Jean-Marie. He said we'll go to the studio tomorrow. It's in one of the Paris suburbs.

Dominique came for us early in the morning and gave us a tour along the way. It was a pointless effort in my case since I don't remember a thing. I was more interested in simply looking at the streets and using my imagination. I nodded in time with Dominique's story. I wasn't listening to him.

When we arrived at the studio, they seated us in an electric car. Jean-Marie was at the wheel. We drove past medieval castles, buildings destroyed by bombing, and even an African village. We recognized our set from afar, by the royal palace.

People in medieval Island clothes are drinking coffee. There's the perceptible smell of a stable: horses are harnessed to carts and horses await their riders. We're invited to the director's table and offered coffee. Jean-Marie introduces us.

Applause. Then those present greet us in turn and we shake their hands.

The last to approach is a boy who's about eight years old. His hair has been stuffed under his hat. Based on the lock of hair that's sticking out artistically, it's clear that he's fair-haired.

"That's you," the director tells Parfeny. "And his name's also Parfeny."

During filming, all Jean-Marie's actors use their characters' names, even in their regular life. I'd read about that. Completely putting themselves in the role.

Parfeny offers his hand to the boy.

"How old are you?"

"I'll turn eight soon. What about you?"

"Three hundred forty-seven."

"So that means you've already retired?"

Parfeny pats his cheek. The boy presses his cheek to his shoulder and Parfeny withdraws his hand.

"He's surprisingly organic," Jean-Marie explains to us.

Parfeny smiles at his namesake.

"Do you want to be an actor?"

"Yes ... Or a prince. But that's hard ..."

"No it's not. All we'd have to do is adopt you."

The boy nods pensively; his gaze is serene. Parfeny's eyes tear up in the wind. I didn't have a child for him and I think that was wrong.

When they start filming, little Parfeny walks out of the palace with a piece of smoldering charcoal in his hands. He walks up to a wall and draws a funny face there. The mouth is slightly crooked and the boy attempts to erase the end of a line. Nothing helps and the corner of the mouth ends up smudged over half the face. He tosses the charcoal and scratches his nose as he looks at his work. His nose has ash on it.

Little Parfeny walks across the city square. The camera soaring over him follows as his arm slides along the wooden side of a cart. Touches the horse's bridle. The horse tilts its head toward the boy and he strokes it. The assistant lets a kitten out of a carrier and it takes a few steps to the side. The boy continues patting the horse.

"Kitten," Jean-Marie reminds him, through the megaphone.

Parfeny junior picks up the kitten, and rubs his ashy nose against the kitten's nose. Holding the kitten, he goes back to the horse and lifts the kitten up to the horse's muzzle. The kitten arches from fear. The horse thinks a bit, then its long tongue licks the kitten's fur.

"For some reason we didn't have cats at that time," says Parfeny, "but I understand that's not important."

"It's not important," Jean-Marie confirms, not looking away from the set.

A merchant appears by the horse, takes it by the bridle, and leads it away. An instant before that, an assistant had deftly placed a nut on the plank roadway; one of the cart's wheels runs over it with a crunch. The camera focuses dolefully on the crushed nut.

The exit from the palace is filmed in four takes. Four times the boy draws on the wall, which turns out to be clean four times, four times he absent-mindedly walks along the city square and touches the horse's bridle. The kitten plays out fear and the horse licks the kitten with its previous pensiveness. The cart begins moving, running over a nut in its path that is thrice revived. From time to time, the director tosses quick glances at Parfeny:

"The endless repetition of life. Do you feel like you're a phoenix?"

Parfeny smiles:

"More like a barrel organ."

In the fourth year of the Great Island Revolution, a monument was raised in front of the Palace, honoring the uprising's victims. Mikhei's image was immortalized in bronze. The hero who departed prematurely was chiseled in a double-breasted suit, something he did not wear in life. People said the sculptor initially wanted to put a naked Mikhei on the Main Square but Kasyan ordered that the hero be dressed.

Mikhei was standing on his right foot, as if preparing for flight, his left foot already breaking away from earth as his right hand stretched upward, holding a star. Behind him on the pedestal, a dwarfish Domna was clambering up, holding a pot of extraordinary size as she embodied the cursed past. To further embody the past, the sculptors set crocodiles free at the base of the monument alongside Domna. Their wide-open jaws threatened to swallow anyone believing in the bright future.

The idea of depicting the crocodiles belonged to Kasyan too. In that idea one might have seen the artistic embodiment of the fate of the Minister of History and the Bright Future if not for the fact that the monument was poured before his tragic demise. One can only surmise that the chairman of the Island knew of Atanas's fate due to scientific foresight.

In the fifth year of the Great Island Revolution, Chairman Kasyan purchased an automobile known as a *Rolls-Royce*. By that time, Island residents had already grown accustomed to vehicular traffic and autos of various makes traveled along our roads. This was, however, the first time that the wheel of a Rolls-Royce touched our hospitable soil, for the cost of this automobile exceeded all rational limits. In speaking of rational limits, I am forced to note that I have never purchased cars of this sort so I can only vaguely judge the degree of rationality since when all is said and done, what do we here on the Island know about Rolls-Royces? All that is known is that for an important government purchase to be made, of course other, less significant, expenses needed to be reduced. Nothing was announced about reductions but they were certainly felt in hospitals, schools, and libraries.

In the sixth revolutionary year, mural painting began in the Church of the Bright Future. Work on a fresco depicting the chairman of the Island was ongoing in the altar. On the right-hand side, they drew an image of Mikhei with Domna stealthily approaching him, and Atanas was to appear to the left with an enraged crocodile.

Markel, who had become Kasyan's right hand man, was appointed to take charge of the mural. It is no surprise that the church's narthex housed a likeness of horseback rider Markel piercing a crocodile with a spear since it was Markel who destroyed the reptile that swallowed the minister.

The chairman of the Island visited one day, to have a look at the murals. After inspecting the church's three main frescoes, he returned to the narthex and asked Markel how the horse happened to be in the crocodile's enclosure. Markel answered that there were undoubtedly horses at the Menagerie and he had used one of them for his victory over the reptile.

Kasyan, who thought Markel wished to surpass him in terms of glory, called over the Minister of Culture and Menageries, who was also present at the viewing, and asked if it was true that there were horses at the Menagerie. The minister, a cautious person who valued moderation in life, answered that horses were present in the establishment entrusted to him, although in extremely insignificant numbers. After noticing Kasyan's unkind glance, he added that even that small number consisted exclusively of ponies.

Well then, uttered His Brightest Futurity, then we shall portray our friend Markel sitting on a pony because *in art we value realism above all.*

Kasyan's secretary urgently jotted down that pronouncement. In continuing his artistic interpretation of the fresco, Kasyan added that only a pony could have fit in the crocodile's enclosure so the icon painters could not possibly have endeavored to depict a warhorse. The secretary sent Kasyan's words regarding realism via courier to the editorial board of the *Dictionary of Creative Catchphrases*. After thinking a bit, he sent a note, too, saying that only a pony could fit in the crocodile's enclosure. And he had not erred: the combination of realism and mysteriousness ensured widespread fame for that phrase.

Before leaving, the chairman of the Island also met with the Guards of the Future, who had replaced the monks expelled from the Monastery. After hearing their report about the activity of the newly formed institution, Kasyan unexpectedly asked the Supreme Guard:

How am I fated to die?

Everyone lowered their eyes at those words but Markel said:

You are immortal, Your Brightest Futurity; you simply cannot die.

Kasyan repeated, as if he had not heard what Markel said:

I am asking: How am I fated to die?

And then the Supreme Guard of the Future answered:

Your Brightest Futurity, it lies ahead for you to meet your demise from your Rolls-Royce.

Kasyan said nothing; he just exited the church in silence, surrounded by his entourage.

Several days later, the chairman's Rolls-Royce was banished to the Palace garage. There were orders to care for the automobile most painstakingly. Its component parts were to be greased with oil and, after filling the tanks with the best gasoline, they were to arrange daily car rides on the highway, in order that the Rolls-Royce's gears not be subjected to rust and ruin. A *Hispano-Suiza* automobile was procured for the chairman. Perhaps it was not as luxurious as a Rolls-Royce, but its merits were no insult to the leader.

It was in that car that the Island chairman visited the University. The former history professors, now specialists on scientific foresight, who had already been nicknamed *foreseers*, told His Brightest Futurity about their work. They reported to the chairman that never before had their research taken on such a creative nature. That was the unvarnished truth.

They had built cause-and-effect chains based on scientific foresight regarding events that had not yet happened. The foreseers argued bitterly amongst themselves, for each researcher built his own chain where some invented events gave rise to others and non-existent reasons led to similar effects.

Each presented his chain and proved that everything in it could occur that way. Kasyan's quotes were displayed too, as were poems and even pantomimes. This made the discussion gripping and attracted many people. It turned out the only thing that united all points of view was the conclusion that the future will be bright. The theory that won as a result of discussion was supplemented by the successful positions of other theories and then the fruit of the scholars' collective wisdom was presented to society.

After listening to the discussion for a time, Kasyan asked the debaters:

What is a constant?

That question confounded all the researchers except the dean, who deemed:

Your Brightest Futurity, you are the constant.

Blushing from pleasure, the chairman wondered if the University had any requests. The answer came in the form of a request to allow the question about a constant to be placed on the University's pediment. Permission was granted.

When summing up the meeting, Kasyan admitted that he learned the word *constant* along the way to the University, paging through a mathematics textbook. The question arose because he did not know the meaning of the word he read. The dean had his wits about him, too, and announced that, given the chairman's characteristic wisdom, it was very easy for the chairman not to notice the depth of his own question. After thinking a bit, Kasyan nodded and announced that he had a similar story regarding the word *leitmotiv*.

Despite the cordiality of the meeting and a new area of research in the search for constants, the professors' happiness was incomplete. They had expected the dean would ask for salary increases but the request turned out to be different.

Salary is not a constant, the dean later told the professors, and it, too, will increase at some time.

Three days hence, these gold letters met everyone entering the University:

WHAT IS A CONSTANT?
HIS BRIGHTEST FUTURITY KASYAN

171

Placed as it was, the inscription did not clarify if Kasyan's name indicated his authorship of the statement or if he was the answer to the question.

In the eighth year of the Revolution, Kasyan remembered his Rolls-Royce. And he asked about the condition of the automobile he so valued. And the answer was: The Rolls-Royce had been badly damaged during one of the drives. And then the saddened chairman wanted to see the wreckage of his auto, so he set off for the Palace garage.

Kasyan's eyes filled with tears at the sight of a pile of crumpled metal and Markel, who accompanied Kasyan, ordered that everyone leave, to allow His Brightest Futurity the opportunity to bid farewell to his Rolls-Royce. Markel himself sacrificed and remained with the chairman, who needed moral support.

The farewell went on for some time, but that seemed natural since everyone knew how attached His Brightest Futurity was to his automobile. But when the garage doors opened, those who entered discovered that the chairman was dead. We know of what happened behind closed doors only from what Markel said.

Kasyan placed his foot on the crumpled hood and said, laughing through his tears:

Everything the Guards of the Future foretold was a lie.

He said:

But could I receive my death from this automobile?

At those words, a snake crawled out from behind the hood, wound itself around His Brightest Futurity's neck, and struck his ear.

Markel, my dear comrade-in-arms, screamed Kasyan as if he had been stung. I can no longer hear you. If you hear me, I am telling you that my hours are numbered and I will state my thoughts briefly, out of necessity. I am convinced that there is truly nobody more worthy, honest, and rational than you.

According to the teller, at this point the chairman could not hold back and so gave a detailed description of Markel's valorousness anyway, although Markel (thanks to his modest nature) did not consider divulging it. After listing Markel's merits, Kasyan purportedly placed his hand on Markel's shoulder and said:

For the aforementioned reasons, I appoint you my successor and leave our beloved Island to you.

According to Markel, the chairman collapsed, as if dead, as he uttered these parting words.

Blood, a great deal of blood, truly was flowing from Kasyan's ear. Those who entered whispered amongst themselves that snake bites are not usually so bloody. Hearing that, Markel objected that this happened to be an automobile snake, the most poisonous kind of snake, which lives, as everyone knows, under the hood.

In answering a question from the Minister of Culture and Menageries about how the snake managed to reach the chairman's ear, Markel's eyes flashed as he said he knew other snakes who had made their way to that same ear and infused it with their poison.

The matter was easily explained: it turned out that when His Brightest Futurity heard the snake rustling around under the hood, he leaned, exposing that particular ear for the attack. As for snakes biting senior officials, the Dean of the University later announced that incidents of the sort were not a historical rarity.

Nationwide mourning was announced for the Island. Special newspaper editions stated that Markel had been proclaimed the Island's new chairman, in accordance with the departed chairman's wishes. That announcement obviously seemed to carry double meaning for some because in later references to the chairman's wishes, the word "departed" had been removed.

MARKEL

In the ninth year of the Great Island Revolution, a People's Council was established, and the Island's most worthy men and women were its members. In order not to expend valuable money that the government increasingly lacked, it was decided they would be elected in a simplified manner, by means of on-the-street polling.

The lack of money had in fact given rise to the thought of creating the council, in order that the people's dissatisfaction not focus on the supreme leader – it would instead be dispersed more evenly, in various directions. The council possessed unlimited rights for approving ukases from the chairman of the Island.

People had had time in recent years to forget the war with France, but Markel reminded the population that war is war and nobody had called this one off. It was the war that proved to be the reason for the Treasury's definitive impoverishment. When the impoverishment process concluded and the previous regime's money was gone, Chairman Markel had a cheerful thought: print new money. That was his first ukase and it was approved by the newly formed council.

Into a new life with new money, proclaimed Markel, who, deep down inside his soul, also wanted to beget catchphrases. This was unexpected since the public had grown accustomed to thinking all eternal sayings belonged to Kasyan. Markel's words remained unnoticed and did not take wing as catchphrases, instead hanging briefly in the air and then gliding down to earth.

Kasyan's portrait was printed on the new money along with something he said: *Money possesses purchasing power.* Kasyan was immortalized on the banknotes so the new monetary unit was called the kasyan. One kasyan equaled one hundred French francs.

Kasyans were printed on good paper and they turned out to be reliable money in the sense that they didn't malfunction and the picture of the perished chairman only gained color from copious contact. As far as his catchphrases went, certain complications emerged there because the money lost its purchasing power with indescribable speed. Island residents' salaries increased but the kasyan purchased less and less for them.

A short time later, the exchange rate for the kasyan and the franc was a thousand, though not in favor of the kasyan. Over the course of a year, the rate reached a million and salaries on the Island were thus calculated in the millions. This particular circumstance allowed Chairman Markel to call our state *The Island of Millionaires.*

In the fifteenth year of the Revolution, a monument to Kasyan was unveiled in front of a large gathering of people near the Arsenal. The sculpture *Laocoön* – which Markel once saw in a photograph – was used as a model. The chairman of the Island ordered that his predecessor be chiseled in marble but with only one snake and no sons. Kasyan's mouth was open. The sculpture portrayed the moments when the reptile was wound around Kasyan and he named his successor and was forced to quickly name the successor's primary virtues.

Markel did not limit himself to sculpture and so turned his attention to painting too. He came to the Church of the Bright Future and ordered the creation of one more fresco, dedicated to Kasyan. With that goal in mind, he made a very important artistic decision regarding the use of existing frescos.

In a scene of the serpent's temptation, the chairman ordered that Adam be dressed in a modest cheviot suit and that his head be drawn as Kasyan's. Markel himself was to be depicted instead of Eve, carrying a cane and wearing a formal suit and top hat. Chairman Markel fostered a weakness for such things after growing up in a village with typical oiled boots and loose-fitting coats. The wreckage of the Rolls-Royce, piled under the fateful apple tree, was intended as a backdrop for the two historical figures. The depiction shaped up to be highly successful since the serpent crawled from the wreckage into the tree. According to Markel, that was all very reminiscent of the events in the garage.

In addition, Markel's head was substituted for Saint George's in the fresco *Saint George and the Dragon* and the dragon became a crocodile. This was a long-time dream of Markel's. He ordered that the fresco with the pony simply be painted over.

KSENIA

We spent the first half of the day at the studio, where they were filming the knife-game episode. As is common knowledge, Princess Glikeria executed the boy who tossed the knife at Parfeny. So Jean-Marie preferred not to use that scene.

"A chopped-off head that says the murderer's name, well, I think you understand..." Leclerc winked at me, very subtly. "We'll stay out of harm's way on that one."

"We will," I agreed, to be polite.

Nevertheless, after filming, I asked Jean-Marie why the talking head didn't suit him.

Jean-Marie pulled at his ear.

"You see... It's not that I'm such a champion of realism, but since we're filming a biopic we need to follow certain genre norms."

When he saw my smile, he added:

"You know, I can even allow that the head spoke but we're keeping the commonly accepted notions of reality in mind. Reality isn't what was but what could have been, from the perspective of probability."

From that perspective, Parfeny and I are located outside the bounds of reality. Or maybe we don't really exist? Sometimes it seems we died long ago.

By the way, about realism. Kasyan spoke about that once, when he came to the Island Gallery. He talked about how impressionist paintings don't resemble reality. He repeated all that later, when he started selling off the Impressionists. But I wonder if he would have sold them off if they had resembled reality.

It has always surprised me that realism felt so kindred for the revolutionaries. That was especially surprising because the bright future they daydreamed about did not correspond to reality at all. After Kasyan's death, someone unearthed his statement that *reality should be real* – that eternal phrase determined the authorities' attitude toward art.

It's as if Kasyan had a presentiment of his own phantasmagorical demise and thus blazed a trail in art for realism and found a wise word for any kind of art. He recommended that painters copy photographs more frequently and that writers rewrite texts possessing a high degree of veracity: meeting minutes, for example. Top artists' paintings were soon indistinguishable from photographs and I won't even bother speaking about literature since everyone's familiar with those texts.

Kasyan's pathological lack of taste initially seemed like a bad joke, but it later took on more and more serious qualities. This was no laughing matter if only because the victorious bright future was doing its utmost to create a new religion.

Everything that happened clearly carried a slight smell of sulfur. The fact that Kasyan's petty demon took the Pantocrator's place in the Church of the Transformation confirmed the old thought that the devil is God's ape. We laughed as long as we could laugh but our laugh inconspicuously transformed into a howl.

Back in his day, Ilary wrote about history as the struggle of good and evil. In those times it seemed as if evil had definitively triumphed, but now a monstrous *antihistory* is establishing itself, repeating events of previous history in broad strokes. Everything we had occasion to experience in those years – the establishment of a new religion, the division between North and South – looked like an old film negative. Black had become white and vice versa. Unreal had become real.

PARFENY

I didn't notice when they started filming. There I am, a little boy, playing with knives. A close-up of my face. I broodingly pick my nose. From Jean-Marie's point of view, that's what a typical child should do. A child who's hurling knives, at any rate. The contrast of the immature childish consciousness and such an unchildish game … there it is, quirky antiquity. We don't need those Middle Ages: that's what the director's voice and facial expression say.

Ksenia calls out to me from the coast. I turn and that saves me from certain death. The knife pierces my forearm. I

ask Leclerc if Ksenia's shriek will be in the film. If weighed on
the scales of realism, the shriek, of course, could be omitted:
a little girl's cry near the sea, almost a day's horseback ride
from the capital. Basically, people don't shout over that
distance.

Jean-Marie smiles. Of course that episode will be in
the film. What's surprising there? It's an ordinary telepathic
occurrence. The shriek itself will be filmed on the Tuscan
coastline. Jean-Marie asks me about specific details that, in his
opinion, the film is still lacking. Do I have anything to add?

Probably yes. There's a decaying autumn leaf on the
grass. Its smell is intoxicating. I pick up the oak leaf and bring
it to my nose. Close my eyes. Whisper: the leaf is old. Ever
since then, everything old has been connected to that leaf.
There are acorns there, too, under the oak. Smooth. And
old; they crunch underfoot.

A monk walks past. He's walking tall and his head is
directed at me. Seeing me whispering, he asks:

"Are you praying?"

"It's leaves," I say, "they're old. But they used to be fresh."

Without stopping, the monk says:

"Fear not, O child, when stepping on autumn leaves, for
they have already died."

"And will I die?" I ask.

"I should say so."

The monk continued walking and his head kept turning
back even more.

"To do a one-eighty?" asks Jean-Marie. "It's an effective
sequence and we have no right to omit it."

They announce a break. As we eat lunch, the assistants
bring fallen leaves and scatter them around the set.

Jean- Marie attentively watches the work with the leaves as he cuts his steak. His knife knocks against the plate with a glassy sound.

"There's no naturalness to that," he tells the assistants, bringing a toothpick to his mouth. "Or perhaps better stated, no carelessness. Leaves, after all, fall as they wish, right?"

He's looking at me. I nod, confirming that yes, that's characteristic of leaves.

After lunch, the director stands Parfeny the younger under an oak tree and looks critically at the actor playing the monk:

"Are you able to turn your head a hundred and eighty degrees?"

He shakes his head in the negative. He obviously cannot go beyond ninety degrees.

"So what can you do?"

Another break is announced, during which time they bring in a real monk. The new arrival easily demonstrates the necessary quality: after forty years in a monastery, his field of view is broad and he can do other things too.

Parfeny the younger picks up an oak leaf. Everything comes out right in the first take. After the final *cut*, the boy asks:

"So will I die too?"

"I already said you'll die," answers the monk.

"But I thought you said that to the guy I'm playing."

The monk answers without turning his head:

"I'd say that to anyone."

Over the years, the bright future that the Revolution brought to the Island became ever less bright. Voices had even begun to resound, saying the bright future had remained in the past. Chairman Markel reproached them as voices of insanity, pointing out that the future cannot possibly be located in the past.

Meanwhile, food supplies were beginning to come to an end on the Island and His Brightest Futurity Markel issued an order to requisition peasants' surplus foodstuffs. As someone possessing a firsthand familiarity with peasant life, Markel pointed out spots where the sought surplus might be hidden. Armed detachments went from village to village requisitioning what they deemed surplus.

In the eighteenth year of the Great Revolution clouds suddenly began thickening in the clear sky over the Island. They did not spill a single drop of rain and did not blaze with a single bolt of lightning but rather took on the form of an old woman with a scythe.

Markel made a speech offering a scientific explanation, saying this was an atmospheric phenomenon created by motion in the air masses. The atmospheric phenomenon, however, did not disperse and during the third day that it hung over the Island an aeroplane was sent into the sky. After flying around the phenomenon several times, it rose to the phenomenon's highest point, the tip of the scythe. And as the Island's entire population observed the struggle between technology and an omen, everyone clearly saw a bright flash glisten on that tip. The aeroplane shook and began losing altitude. Then the aircraft went into a tailspin, corkscrewed, and rapidly began nearing earth. When it came in contact with the surface of a cornfield, houses began shaking across the entire Island and the recently painted head of Chairman Markel fell from a fresco in the Church of the Bright Future. The tolling of an unseen bell reverberated from somewhere near the sea, sounding as if it was coming from under water. A few instants later, everything calmed and the old woman's ghost dispersed in the sky and everyone understood that portended famine. As for the chairman's fallen head, that was seen as an omen of changes in his fate. Not changes for the better.

Astonished by people's unscientific views, Chairman Markel rushed to make an appearance with a calming statement. He announced that the aviator was to blame for what happened after touching the cloud's scythe – flying toward a sharp object is categorically forbidden. Despite accordance with recent scientific data, Markel's announcement was powerless in terms of restoring the calm. The peasants' selling of foodstuffs ceased completely and the old woman's heavenly scythe whistled as it began falling on house after house.

Another calamity that befell those houses were the *special brigades* that the Island's leadership had begun sending to burgs and villages just outside the capital. Their specialty was essentially shooting those who did not wish to part with their surplus foodstuffs. A bullet was the answer to explanations that a surplus had turned into a lack long ago. As His Brightest Futurity Markel said, *The time for discussions has passed*. The time for discussions had passed, repeated the machine guns and that became the catchiest of the new chairman's phrases.

In the twentieth year of the Revolution on the Island, a Labor Camp was established. It was primarily filled with peasants whose surplus foodstuffs had been seized. To Chairman Markel, this was seen as a display of mercy, for what could peasants do in their villages without foodstuffs? For him, with peasant origins, the answer was obvious. Nothing.

The Camp was located in the part of the Island where the Forest approaches the sea. The forced migrants' task there was to fell timber and send it by sea to the Mainland. When the thought of a

Camp occurred to Markel, four thousand peasants were sent into
the Forest. There were difficulties finding housing in the Forest,
though, because housing in those parts was limited to foresters'
small huts. On site, it became obvious that there were not enough
of those huts for four thousand arrivals, just as the food stocks the
foresters left in their huts were insufficient.

When the Camp's warden reported that to the chairman of the
Island, the latter became indignant. He said:

The God of the dark past, whom we annulled, fed five thousand
people with five loaves.

He said:

And so do you really think, after achieving the bright future, you
can't feed that amount of bread to only four thousand?

I can, answered the warden, I'm just afraid that the voracious will
not be sated by that because I am not God.

Chairman Markel then reminded him that there were plenty of
wild animals in the Forest, just as there were berries and mushrooms,
as well as moss and tree bark. There was, finally, also grass, which the
Island's people had consumed from time immemorial.

The warden marveled at the chairman's wisdom, lauded it, and
left for home. Since the thought about the Camp had come to
Markel in December, mushrooms, berries, and grass for food had
to be temporarily excluded, though the chairman did not take the
Forest's pinecones and acorns into account.

The arrivals had to overwinter in dugout shelters they hollowed
out themselves. In April it was ascertained that the number of
people in the Camp had decreased to five hundred. Upon learning
that, the warden sighed in relief since, as he said, there is a difference
between feeding four thousand or five hundred. In May, however,
four thousand more were brought in. But the warden was not
demoralized, figuring that his acquired experience should help.

In the twenty-third year of the Revolution, other clouds began thickening over the country. They developed in the southern part of the Island, which still cherished the memory of the long-ago war. People remembered not so much the war as the hunger that accompanied it, for those stories had been passed from generation to generation. Deaths of the tormented and the suffering of the survivors had etched themselves on family lore and memories for the ages.

Those memories gripped residents of the South like a vise and so people began banding together in detachments and preparing for a military campaign on the capital. On public squares they swore not to allow a repetition of what happened several centuries ago. They renounced, to an equal degree, the dark past and the bright future, proposing to focus on the present.

Sitting in the Palace, Chairman Markel quickly guessed where this focus was leading and so he dispatched special brigades to the southern part of the Island. It was decided to send them by rail. The convenience and speed of railroad transportation, however, did not cancel out the primary obstacle that had already arisen along the attackers' route: the Forest.

The trains were not built for operating in reverse. That function could have turned out to be a saving grace for the riders when the very first train was stopped while passing through the Forest. Markel could only guess what happened in the Forest since none of those he sent returned alive.

He then gathered residents of the North and announced that all the foodstuffs that had been requisitioned from them had been sent to the South. He also said that was, allegedly, a condition for southerners to remain in the same unified state as the northerners. That is what Markel said, but there was great doubt that it was true since southerners had contemplated nothing of the sort.

By our current time, the two parts of the Island had become so intertwined that the very thought of separating them was, to borrow an expression from the late Kasyan, thought unthinkable. But Markel said what he said and his words, catchphrases that they were, took wing, headed to the Island's South, and forced people to contemplate – and it was in that mournful sense that his words took flight. They became a phoenix that burned the entire South and gave rise to great troubles.

PARFENY

We flew to Tuscany with the crew for the film shoot. That little corner of Italy reminds me of the Island's southern shore to a surprising degree. Ksenia and I are staying in a villa provided to us by a Russian philanthropist and friend of Jean-Marie who is also one of the film's sponsors. Jean-Marie is staying there too; the other members of the crew have accommodations at nearby hotels.

The villa stands on a gently sloping hill surrounded by groves. Her Botanical Highness Ksenia identifies trees during a walk: stone pine, beech, acacia, stone oak. Jean-Marie watches her in amazement. He takes out his phone and asks us to stand under one of the trees.

We choose an acacia. We are already the acacia's twins: wrinkles, joints, hooklike fingers. The acacia, as bow-legged as we are, goes down to the sea, pretending that's her destination. It's important that Jean-Marie not confuse us with her. He steps behind some sort of shrub, searching for a place from which to take the photo. He crouches. And we continue standing under the acacia. The degree of woodenness in us is close to critical. It's a take.

After lunch, I sit in the living room. Display cabinets hold collections of local archeological finds: blackened coins with a turquoise patina, rings, silver buttons of unbelievable dimensions. We're witnesses of a time when buttons fastened with great difficulty. We feel like those buttons ourselves: we could be lying in one of these displays.

I sit, paging through the chronicle compiled mostly by people we knew. They searched history for good and evil. I delight in their capricious speech. The chroniclers preserved it but Ksenia and I did not: we've developed along with the times. Or become enveloped by them? Either way, we have become like our time, taking on its forms and speech.

The chroniclers were not entitled to change anything: to contemplate a river, one must sit on its bank. Modern-day historians do not understand that, they float along with the river. They walk in step with time. To describe something flowing, one requires a static point, somewhere at the intersection of good and evil. That pair has changed into different clothes but their essence remains unchanged.

I feel myself nodding off and so head for the bedroom. I look for a long time at Ksenia, who's sleeping. What will I do if she's the first of us to go?

The southerners created their army in mere weeks and armed it by breaking into arsenals. During those same weeks, Chairman Markel made speeches to the hungry population in the North, describing the qualities and quantities of foodstuffs stored in the South. According to Markel, the shabbiest southern shop there now held more edibles than the entire suffering North. Despite not corresponding to reality overall, those speeches contained a grain of truth since the very last supplies could not be taken away from the South and the special brigades did not have time to reach them.

His copious and inflammatory words about foodstuffs did their part. Northerners began signing up in droves as volunteers, greatly expanding the government's army, which was not so small to begin with. A short time later, that army set off for the South.

The troops were in no hurry. The commander in chief, as Markel had appointed himself, understood he could not afford to lose, since that would be the end of everything. He did understand that he could not allow victory either since victory would end the war that Markel had unleashed with such effort, a war that ensured his boundless power. An end to the war would also reveal to the fighters that there were no foodstuffs in the South either.

The most grievous part of Markel's situation was that he could not remain in the capital where thousands of armed people might turn their weapons against him at any moment. The point of the military campaign consisted of motion as such: long and endless, if possible. The position "commander in chief" made Markel think of the two-wheeled bicycle he had recently mastered: it stayed up only when it was moving.

A broad highway had been hacked through the Forest long ago and villages thrived on each side. The troops could move without stopping on terrain like that. Possessing all the means necessary for charging ahead to the South along the highway, Markel's troops denied themselves the joy of direct motion. They moved east and began a maneuver to bypass the Forest.

In order that the troops not think their movement seemed aimless, the commander in chief ordered them to pillage all the villages lying along their route. This yielded little plunder but it raised the soldiers' fighting spirit. The fact that the villages still belonged to the North had no effect whatsoever on the attackers' decisiveness: the spirit of lawlessness intoxicated them and they began to like this strange way of moving.

When the troops entered the southern part of the Island, every village they encountered turned out to be empty. The troops were deprived not only of foodstuffs but of victories too, and their spirits began to fall. The government army's route eventually reminded the soldiers of the Forest highway, since their path was now similar to that of a drunkard walking into a thunderstorm. The troops began grumbling.

And then, at Markel's order, the army suddenly changed tactics and moved directly on the enemy. Military commander Markel took the word *directly* in a literal sense: it corresponded to a red line charted on a headquarters map, crossing numerous mountain ridges, ravines, lakes, waterfalls, small rivers, and, most important, the deep, tempestuous River. To the question of how they were to overcome all those natural obstacles, the military commander invariably answered they would do so in kind: naturally.

The line sketched on the map led to the most fortified places in the South. Now neither Markel's troops nor the enemy troops understood Markel's strategic scheme. Both sides suspected him of mental deterioration. That suspicion deepened after the government army overcame inconceivable barriers and entered into combat with the South.

To the amazement of the commander in chief himself, his soldiers won their first battle. They crossed the River and entered into battle with all the strength of their despair as well as the habit of killing they had developed on their march. The southern troops had no such experience – they lacked bitterness. But it made its appearance after the first battle.

188

General Polikarp, who had so recently been a part of the government's General Staff, led the southern army. Polikarp was born and raised in the South. After realizing war was in the making, he secretly departed for his native soil and worked there on building defenses. When that news reached the commander in chief, Polikarp was sentenced to the firing squad, in absentia.

Since shooting someone in absentia is not an efficacious measure, Polikarp went about his tasks with even greater decisiveness. The government troops' unusual maneuvers gave him sufficient time for that. Prior to the first battle, neither he nor his troops were prepared for a bloody skirmish: the opponent's army still remained his own army. A civil war usually begins in complexity but once it has begun, it progresses with particular bitterness.

General Polikarp carried the day in the second battle, yet he behaved humanely. He could have destroyed significant enemy forces, who retreated beyond the River. Those stationed on rafts and crossing the River by water were good targets, for their motion was slow and predictable. One needed only reload a rifle or change an ammunition belt and then shoot.

Polikarp did not do that. He ordered a ceasefire when bullets rippled the surface of the River's black water. During that battle, he saw his enemies' faces – he knew many of them by name. The general soberly evaluated the situation and expected no changes in the commander in chief's plans after allowing Markel's army to retreat. General Polikarp did not want to cause an escalatory spiral of evil and counted on God and time to offer an opportunity for a peaceful resolution.

And so Markel managed to win two months that received the moniker *The Great River Stand*. When the mental ferment in his troops reached a dangerous level, he gave the command to attack and his soldiers began lowering their rafts and boats into the water.

There was round-the-clock monitoring from the River's other shore and the appearance of floating watercraft provoked heavy fire from that side. The River grew red in those days.

The commander in chief established daily classes in the evenings to lift the spirits, inviting Guards of the Future from the capital to tell, fittingly, about the future. They brought a *magic lantern* with them and introduced the soldiers to the frescos in the Church of the Bright Future as well as historic sites where Chairman Kasyan, who had departed before his time, spent his childhood.

They also introduced the war cry *Revenge for Kasyan!*, which was to be shouted upon entering the water and, with luck, when coming out on shore. The point of this cry was not completely understood since it was doubtful those guilty of Kasyan's demise were to be found on the other shore, and who were those guilty parties anyway? The serpent? The manufacturers of the Rolls-Royce? The guards who told Kasyan of his fate? Or maybe (and this question was heard ever more frequently) Markel himself? But the soldiers, as was proper, asked no questions. The war cry rolled off the tongue well and was easy to pronounce. That was enough for shouting it.

As the days passed, the troops' attention to the depiction of Kasyan on frescos as well as to details about his childhood weakened noticeably. And it was harder and harder to shout words of revenge on an empty stomach. At the spirit-lifting classes, the soldiers asked more often to hear about the food that could purportedly be found on the other shore.

In the end, they stopped speaking about anything but food and the magic lantern began showing sample dishes from the Palace kitchen. It was with that goal in mind that photographs of selected dishes were ordered for urgent delivery (the photographs, not the dishes) to the army's disposition in active duty. The photographs were accompanied by a brief, nasty note: *Here's what they eat in the*

South. These were the images the magic lantern beamed before the most momentous battles.

After the Palace kitchen's offerings had run out, the Guards of the Future recalled the Island's second opponent, with whom they were engaged in a long-term and grueling, albeit still unnoticed, war. They ordered photographs of dishes from Parisian restaurants. The French captions that landed in the shots were explained away as the South's collusion with the enemy. After victory over the South, the soldiers were promised they'd seize Paris along with all its culinary delicacies.

The personnel began howling when they surveyed the new portion of dishes. Suspecting they would not make it to Paris, the viewers were agreeable to simply eating on the other shore. The only problem was that the other shore was as inaccessible as Paris. From somewhere at the pit of Markel's stomach, which was filled even in that hungry time, a gut feeling made its way to his head and he realized that a rebellion was under way. And here he fell back on a remedy that was even more unexpected than those he had previously used.

PARFENY

Artemy Nikitin, the owner of the villa, comes over in the evening. We eat supper with him and Jean-Marie. Artemy is about fifty. He's wearing a light linen jacket, without a necktie. This is what French professors look like.

He thanks us, in French, for staying with him. Hopes we don't need anything. Ksenia says it is difficult to need for anything here; Artemy answers with a half-bow. I like that *half*; I have no love for extremes.

Jean-Marie speaks of tomorrow's filming. He's used to being the center of attention, which makes life easier for everyone else. He's sharing his small discoveries that will be shown tomorrow: an unusual camera angle and the corresponding lighting. Only the weather worries him (he signals to the waiter that he likes the risotto) but there's nothing even Artemy can do about that. Our host's face expresses moderate grief.

Jean-Marie's gaze focuses on a new portion of risotto. It appeared out of nowhere. Top-notch: thumbs up in the waiter's honor. There's who he can't find for his films: a good waiter. No, he's not joking. Perhaps the most difficult role is *Dinner is served*. There's very little space for expression there. Black olives appeared on the director's plate after he'd pointed at it with his knife. Meanwhile, those three words – *Dinner is served* – should hold everything, including *Figaro here, Figaro there* and *The sound of a breaking string* and maybe even *To be or not to be*.

Artemy clinks glasses with Ksenia and me.

"You left the chronicle in the living room. Based on the miniature, it must be opened to the War of the North and South…"

Ksenia nods:

"A strange war, wasn't it?"

"May I ask a question?" Artemy shifts his gaze to me. "Why did you save Chairman Markel back then? If you hadn't accommodated him, that matter might have ended with his fall and the end of the dictatorship. Pardon me if I've committed a faux pas."

Questions about history are always faux pas. Otherwise there would be no point to them. Ksenia asked me this same question back then. I pretend I'm thinking about the question though I'm actually not thinking. I'd already decided everything for myself then.

"I saved people from slaughter. But the dictatorship would have remained anyway, with or without Markel."

Leclerc takes several swallows of wine and examines the bottle.

"Port, vintage 1964.... Bravo."

"I think our guests have drunk even older," says Artemy, turning to us again. "For me, that's a question about Russian history. If Stalin had disappeared in the thirties, would the dictatorship have gone away? What was linked to its beginning and end?"

A good question.

"The rhythm of history."

I don't have a better answer.

KSENIA

Markel came to us one night and said:

"I want to ask you for help."

He had never asked for help. Essentially, he had never asked for anything. He took whatever he needed but apparently this time he'd realized that would no longer work, that you couldn't grab life by the collar forever.

By that time, we'd been resettled in a communal apartment by the city gate. That's where Markel came to see us. He sat with us in the communal kitchen since only a bed fit in our room. The neighbors nearly fainted. A neighbor's teakettle sitting on the Primus was boiling down, uncomplaining, but nobody dared come in. Parfeny turned down the flame under the teakettle. He listened silently to the commander in chief, who spoke incessantly. We could see he feared Parfeny's *no*.

I went into our room for a third cup. None of the neighbors were even in the hallway. Two sentries stood at the front door. After I returned to the kitchen, I lit our Primus and put the kettle on. Markel didn't look at Parfeny as he made his request. His gaze hovered on a cockroach that was walking broodily along a tightly wound wire.

I saw Lukyan, the owner of the teakettle, glance out of his room. The low-intensity war between us had been going on for a long time: Lukyan accused us of stealing kerosene, using his toilet seat, and switching on his kitchen light bulb. From where he was standing, he couldn't see that his Primus was shut off so he was seething over the burning kerosene. What was left of it, of course, that we hadn't already had a chance to steal. I was overcome with malicious pleasure.

Markel unexpectedly stopped speaking and pointed at the cockroach:

"You need to be rid of neighbors like that."

Lukyan disappeared behind his door as if a draft had pulled him in. A moment later, something dully thudded in there.

Markel was asking for mediation. It turned out he was against bloodshed. An innate pull toward peace brought him to Parfeny because His Highness (a surprised look from Parfeny) was the only person both sides trusted. When the chairman reminded those present that *blessed are the peacemakers*, Parfeny's lips broke into a smile. For the first time in many years, he was hearing a catchphrase that had not belonged to Kasyan.

But the commander in chief was not just seeking peace: he was also concerned about bread. Understanding that peace would not save him without bread, he convinced Parfeny and me to approach the world community and request food aid. He was certain they would not refuse us.

Markel did not attempt to buy us off. He knew enough about people. Human lives were to be our reward and the Island's chairman spoke of them in Parfeny's terms. It seemed to me that I even heard Parfeny's voice in some of what Markel said. I thought about how the new regime had succeeded best at imitating.

The commander in chief did not slow down as he also promised to immediately cease the war with France, something that, in his opinion, should turn into generous help from grateful Paris.

Yes, sly Markel had not attempted to buy us off. He simply mentioned a small gift for Parfeny and me, in passing: our own apartment. As if he'd mentioned it by chance, as if he were staring at a cockroach.

Like everything else in the world, the chairman's speech finally concluded. I poured tea into the cups and Markel took a few sips. We had nothing to go with the tea. Markel did not have it in him to stand the silence that had set in so he started drumming a strange march on the table with his fingers. Parfeny kept silent.

The commander in chief returned to the capital for one night, where he met with Parfeny and Ksenia. It is unknown what sort of conversation they had, but the next day Parfeny arrived at the government troops' position. His appearance evoked universal joy. It reminded everyone of the good old days, the precursors to the bright future. Old times. And good ones.

Parfeny spoke in front of the troops and said that any war ends in peace and he had come to speak not of war but of peace. Eyewitnesses maintained that if Parfeny had declared himself commander in chief at that moment, there was no doubt the position would have been his.

But Parfeny did not do that. He sat in a boat with two oars and rowed off to the River's other shore. People there already knew who was in the boat and they greeted Parfeny with three *hoorays*. General Polikarp saluted His Royal Highness and reported that the South's troops were prepared to hear him out.

Parfeny was brief:

I speak to you not by right of power, for I do not have that, but by right of love and by right of Agafon's prophecy. The North and South have lived together and gone through numerous ordeals for centuries. And now we must seek a route to peace together. This is why I have come.

Agafon the Forward-Looking's name was not mentioned by chance. It reminded the South's residents that Parfeny and Ksenia's pious marriage served as security for the Island's unity and, possibly, the Island's very existence. Southerners also understood that seceding from the wealthy North would occasion many difficulties for them. Beyond that, both sides were unbearably tired and throughout history deathly tiredness has been a weighty reason for negotiations. And so negotiations began.

Parfeny crossed the River several times during the course of the day, then representatives of the opposing forces crossed it too. Parfeny, meanwhile, contacted countries on the Mainland and requested their help. Nobody would have considered speaking with Markel, but they answered the prince with agreement. Several weeks later, the first ships with foodstuffs had reached the Island. The days had come when people who had voluntarily taken up arms began returning home.

Chairman Markel saw that life was gradually improving but that brought him no relief. His anxious mind had already discerned a new threat that he associated with General Polikarp's strengthening. Polikarp's position in the South was now unshakable and Markel considered it highly dangerous to leave the general there. He transferred Polikarp back to the capital in order to watch over him night and day. After the general's arrival, it became clear to the chairman that he was even more dangerous in the capital.

The royal couple caused Markel no less anxiety. Parfeny and Ksenia, whose life had taken its course in the communal apartment, were still called Their Royal Highnesses, whereas hardly anybody now called Markel himself (who resided in the Palace) His Brightest Futurity. The chairman felt he was only serving as the country's chairman as long as the royals allowed him to, and this deprived him of sleep.

The war between the North and South had ended. Another unfinished war remained and though it bore no disasters, it was still called a war and thus gave rise to waves of anxiety. Against the chairman's promises, no armistice with France was ever concluded. Markel had not maintained that it was impossible but rather explained that the time for an armistice with France simply had not yet arrived.

In the twenty-fifth year of the Revolution, an event occurred that stirred the entire Island. General Polikarp was fatally struck by a car while crossing the street in front of his home. The government's obituary wrote of fateful happenstance that cut short this steadfast person's life.

A short while later, eyewitnesses turned up who saw the car hit Polikarp twice. When Polikarp was able to rise to his feet after the car hit him the first time, the driver put the car in reverse, accelerated, and hit Polikarp again. Given that, many people wondered if it was possible to speak here of fateful happenstance.

It is said that Parfeny requested an audience with the chairman and asked him that question in the sharpest terms. A new obituary was released the day after the meeting, now without mention of fateful happenstance, though it confirmed that fate had obviously *haunted* the general.

The automobile that struck Polikarp was not found, something that, from the perspective of knowledgeable people, opened the way to new fateful happenstances. Everyone should remember this, particularly Prince Parfeny. Those same people also said, in lowered voices, that Markel's tenacious memory forgot nothing.

The chairman also did not forget that his, Markel's, freshly painted head had fallen off the fresco *Saint George and the Dragon* during the earthquake. He went to the Church of the Bright Future one day to see if the lost head had been restored to the fresco but the head was missing, as before. The perplexed chairman appealed to the Guards of the Future for an explanation. The guards answered that the head had been restored several times but had repeatedly fallen off.

When asked what this was supposed to mean, they ventured a guess that the plaster manufactured in the bright future was not firm and that it had been far stronger in the dark past. Suspecting a coverup of the truth, Markel paled and asked directly:

Might a fact of this sort point to my being forced to part with my head?

Well, answered the guards, that sort of interpretation is not out
of the question – it's even likely to a high degree, which is why we
consider it expedient to hold on to your head with your hands.

After that, people began to notice that Markel kept touching his
own head, as if checking for its presence, as if he seemed to think the
connection between his head and his body had weakened. Now he
tried not to rotate his head unnecessarily, turning his whole body instead. In order to ease his turning, he ordered that a swiveling chair
replace an ordinary model in the chairman's office.

After revealing his apprehensions to Vlas, the head guard,
whom he trusted as much as himself, Markel obligated Vlas to be
present around him at all times in case his, Markel's, head began
to detach itself. He taught Vlas that under those circumstances, he
needed to affix his head to his shoulders and turn it counterclock-
wise until it clicked.

Other persons began to surmise that the chairman was not right
in the head. And there was nothing surprising in their surmises since
whenever the chairman of the Island entered a place, he immediately
requested a mirror so he could assure himself that his head was in the
right place.

In the twenty-seventh year of the Great Island Revolution, when
Markel entered his office accompanied by Vlas, he found no mirror
there. It later emerged that the mirror had been removed for restoration. In the absence of a mirror, the chairman thought his head
had begun detaching from his body and Vlas was willing to swear
that truly was happening. Remembering the prescribed measures,
the head of security quickly began taking steps. With strenuous effort, Vlas managed to significantly turn the specified head counter-
clockwise. He noticed the chairman was dead just when he heard
the click.

During the medical examination it was revealed that a head should be turned clockwise, but Vlas had fulfilled the chairman's order precisely. When asked if the deceased had said anything prior to his death, the head of security answered that he had spoken. The deceased's voice broke with emotion. It was a blessing for him, Vlas, to take the post of Island chairman. The momentous words were uttered at the last instant. Before the click itself.

VLAS

After the death of Chairman Markel, Chairman Vlas began ruling the Island. He was the son of a beekeeper and had attended two years of church school. After becoming Markel's bodyguard, he rose but did not become proud. He was generally not a malicious person despite the threatening nature of his service. And he was not dishonorable. After discerning those characteristics in Vlas, Chairman Markel had drawn him closer, trusting only him. And it was not Vlas's fault that he turned the chairman's head in the wrong direction at the critical time.

Knowing Vlas as the head of security, Island residents expected that many would share Markel's fate when Vlas took up his post. Taught by bitter experience, however, Vlas was now cautious and only turned heads in cases of extreme need. He also slightly improved the living conditions of those relocated to the Camp and even increased their allowance.

In the twenty-eighth year of the Great Island Revolution, Vlas's wife Glafira gave birth to their daughter. Recollecting the chairman's childhood spent at the apiary, they named the girl Melissa. The child turned out to be unusually lively: she ate a lot, cried a lot, and tossed toys from the cradle. Glafira and Vlas's hearts melted at the sight of the babe in arms whose first tooth was celebrated by a state salute with one salvo. Subsequent teeth were celebrated, accordingly, with two, three, and more salvoes.

The quantity of salvoes naturally grew, signifying increased difficulties for the wet nurses whose breasts the child bit. The number of teeth – and the number of salvoes along with them – increased with startling speed. The Island's citizens could not hide their surprise when the number of salvoes reached thirty-six. But Melissa's white-toothed smile was so enchanting that the child's insignificant excess of teeth did not trouble anyone.

In the thirty-fifth year of the Revolution, unlike his predecessors, the chairman of the Island addressed cultural questions. In a meeting with writers, he questioned them about how the topic of bees was reflected in contemporary literary works. Vlas was distressed to hear that bees had thus far eluded writerly attention and briefly told attendees of bees' industriousness and their relationship to women and mothers, as well as the use of smoke to calm bees.

The hall full of writers was excited beyond belief when Vlas finished the story. His concluding statement – *The bee is a teacher for us all* – made a particular impression on everyone. Those seemingly simple eight words comprehensively defined the role of the bee in forming any writing person. Inspired by the chairman's speech, attendees assured him that the prerevolutionary regard for the bee would now change fundamentally.

In the thirty-seventh year of the Great Island Revolution, a bee-keeping department was opened at the University. That same year, the first volume of a family chronicle, *The Hive*, was released. The publication was intended to be multivolumed since the original concept stated that literary portraits of all the hive's bees should appear. The volumes were to be dedicated to individuals and they would be assigned among the Island's writers. After clarifying that an average of sixty to eighty thousand striped worker bees inhabit a hive, it was decided to focus on those with the most interesting destinies.

PARFENY

Filming was supposed to start the day before yesterday but it's been pouring down rain for three days now. We're

sitting inside the villa, no walks. Sometimes we go out on
the covered veranda and listen to the rain drumming on the
awning. Every now and then, one of the villa's workers comes
and uses a T-shaped device to raise the awning where it sags
under the weight of the water. A light waterfall flows into the
stone gutter.

There's nothing special about that, but it would be too
bad to lose even that picture forever. How much more time
will we be given to listen to rain? To observe whirlpools
in the gutter? We've seen everything so many times in our
oversized life that it would somehow even be embarrassing
to mourn parting with those. A person is built strangely: the
more one receives, the more one wants.

We saw Artemy again yesterday at supper. We took
advantage of Leclerc's absence and talked for a long time.
Artemy asked me what, in my view, the main difference is
between people in the Middle Ages and people today.

My view. People are becoming ever blurrier, and there is
nothing anyone can do about that.

"Perhaps the difference is in sensing time," I answer.
"It was like slow motion then, like in an underwater filming.
It flickered: now it's time, now it's eternity."

"And how do you sense time now? As it was before or as
it is currently?"

"Now? As it was before. But all the eternity has been
drained out of it."

The rain intensifies outside and the glass becomes
matte.

"That means you feel like you don't belong?"

"No, no …" I answer. "I don't think so."

I would have felt like I didn't belong if, let's say, I'd jumped out of that time into this one. If someone had taken away a hundred and fifty years, as happened to the chronicle. But, if you will, I lived all those years – right down to this one – without any break.

I understand why the chroniclers were so afraid that a part of time would be lost, why they so valued continuity. They counted each reign in order that there not be a single precipice, even a crack, along the trodden path. Otherwise, there's no unity to history and one piece of it's here, another's there. Of course it's there, by and large.

"Pardon me, I've already worn you out …" Artemy places his hand on Ksenia's. "What does longevity teach?"

Ksenia places her hand on his. Three levels of mutual fondness.

"It teaches that everything repeats in some way or other." She thinks for a minute. "It teaches you to wait for troubles, there are so many … You don't understand that in your youth. But at some point living becomes scary."

"And the longer you go," I note, "the scarier. Senility, might that be a defensive measure? Is it a kindness?"

Leclerc appears at the table. He wonders what we're talking about.

"About life? A narrow topic."

He laughs. They serve his salad.

About life. So many other lives have fit into our – defiantly long – life that somehow it's embarrassing to even discuss. We've observed them as they passed through. Each of them.

He. Just yesterday he was young, thin, and quick. Roared with laughter. Jumped and picked an apple from a

tree as he walked. Told of a new love. Mimicked a saleslady
with a fish. But today, here you go: fat and gray-haired, but
still solid. And still tells stories. A day later, you'll find out he
is no more. He's silent.

She. Combing her hair in the foyer before a show starts.
Smiled at someone in the mirror as she put the comb in her
purse. Walked through to her spot in a row of seats that were
already filled and everyone stood in turn; a wave of perfume
preceded her. After sitting, she pushed aside some hair,
spoke quickly and excitedly. Now she's silent too. And many
hundreds we'd seen are silent. They lived in different ways but
keep identically silent.

How many meetings and partings did we have, how
many gifts and losses? When meeting a beloved person,
you don't know if they're a gift, a companion in your life,
but when you part, it's obviously a great loss. It works out to
more losses.

We remember all the faces we had the chance to come
to love, all the words, voices, and gestures. We parted with
so many that parting became our primary occupation as
they all departed and departed, leaving us each time in our
solitude. Duosolitude, I would call it.

V las read the new volumes about bees with unflagging
attention. After praising the writerly effort, the chairman
expressed some quibbles as well. The beekeeper's sharp
eye noticed that the writer had confused two bees in volume three,
attributing to one what had fallen to the lot of another.

One character's appearance was described differently at the
beginning and end of volume six. In the first case, it was said that the

bee was attractive until she turned gray and that she possessed pliant wings and shapely little legs. In the second case, it was stated that the aforesaid individual had walked with a limp since childhood, was untidy, and always had remnants of pollen hanging from her antennae too. As time passed, she became more and more partial to nectar, grew flabby, and led a fast life with the drones. She let herself go, no longer flew, and just crawled lazily along the ceiling of the hive.

In volume seven, a reference to the "wasplike waists" of certain female hive residents aroused Vlas's displeasure. That expression spoke of the writer's weak differentiation between bees and wasps. Despite those isolated blunders, though, the chairman was satisfied with the Island writers' efforts.

Reading those books opened up the magical world of Island literature for Vlas. Something unexpected happened: he suddenly transformed from a reader into a writer. Having forgotten grammar during the years of political strife, the chairman avoided writing on his own. There was always a scribe with him. More precisely, he was accompanied by a person who jotted down what the chairman said. When noticing a melancholic expression on the ruler's face, the scribe would quickly take the inkwell hanging from his belt, as well as pen and paper, for he knew his work was about to begin. One could not say the leader's speech flowed like a deep river: it was a mountain brook, sparse and intermittent. In it one heard the clatter of stones and the booming of rapids:

My father said:
The bee is our ancestor. And was honored by the Egyptians.
He said:
When people died, a bee flew out of their mouth. Meaning the soul flew out. The soul, do you understand?

And the pharaoh was called the Lord of the Bees. I would also like to be called that, it sounds beautiful, does it not?

But stings hurt. I was walking around in just a shirt, barefoot too. And one time they almost stung me to death, but my father came just in time.

I shout to him:

They could have stung me to death!

And he says:

They would have been right. You, he says, do not understand bees.

In the forty-fifth year of the Great Island Revolution, Vlas took a new title: Lord of the Bees. That title thrilled Island residents since everyone on the Island, large and small, knew what the image of a bee meant. But the meaning of the new title was not just figurative. By that time, a significant part of the Island population was already engaged in beekeeping.

Honey, wax, and propolis, as well as flower pollen, royal jelly, bee venom, drone brood, ambrosia, dead bees, and comb cappings, were exported to the Mainland in huge quantities and transformed into an important line of government income. That line, however, was spent solely on procuring a variety of items since almost nothing else was manufactured on the Island.

That same year, Melissa, daughter of the Lord of the Bees, ran away from home, leaving a note asking that nobody search for her. Against his daughter's will, Vlas ordered that the young maiden be located. Island troops combed the Forest for two months because Lord Vlas thought the runaway might have hidden there.

Everyone escapes to the woods, Vlas said at the time, recalling how bee families acted when leaving the apiary.

And though Vlas's wife, Glafira, knew her daughter and said there was no sense searching for her in the Forest because it lacked amusements, nobody dared object to the Lord of the Bees. They searched for Melissa in the Forest.

Vlas's daughter was discovered, however, in the City – it turned out she never left. Melissa and the famous magician Valdemar had hit it off and she was hiding at his home. When hosting guests, Valdemar hid Melissa in a box for sawing his assistant. It also turned out that the smitten couple had married one night at the Church of the Bright Future. Misleading the church's guards, Melissa announced to them that the marriage was her father's will. The bridal couple walked around the lectern three times, kissed the portrait of Chairman Kasyan, and went home.

The Lord of the Bees was beside himself when he found out what happened, but there was no longer anything he could do. Nonetheless, he was happy his prodigal daughter had returned. In the end, Vlas was simply afraid of his daughter and made peace with her requests that he not buzz.

As the years passed, the family chronicle *The Hive* was expanded with many new volumes. The Lord of the Bees was forced to decline many state obligations in order to read the chronicle. Vlas, who had experienced an attraction to foreign books in the past (*Love of Worker Bees*), had become convinced over time that there was nothing better than domestic literature.

World literature somehow seemed superficial to him, as if it did not touch on anything topical. Vlas's final disappointment was the book *The Wax Persona*, where he learned nothing new about wax. It was around that same time that he also stopped paging through binders of *The Northern Bee* and focused solely on *The Hive*.

In the forty-eighth year of the Revolution, the Church of the Bright Future was renamed the Church of the Revolutionary Swarm and slated for restoration. The Lord of the Bees had not forgotten his daughter's secret wedding and the restoration did not lack for bitterness.

At the same time, Vlas acted to accent the succession of his predecessors: he did not remove their portraits, ordering only that they be depicted in the form of bees. On the solid wall that remained empty, they installed a panorama of a fight between bees and bears. The exploits of the spy bees were illustrated in particular detail, fearlessly taking root in the enemy's lair and warning the swarm of danger.

KSENIA

We had to wait four days for good weather. Today I woke up at dawn and was the first to realize that the day would be sunny. An orange ball rose out of the water in the course of a couple of minutes, as if it were making up for lost time. I glanced at it every now and then as I read on the balcony. The ball was still rising but no longer as quickly. At ten o'clock, we were on the set.

And there I saw my eight-year-old self: a blonde little girl with a narrow face that was unchildlike. A song rang out. *Your hair is like unharvested wheat* ... No: *Wheat the scythe has not touched* ... I forget. And then there's *Your eyes are like the morning sky*. The song didn't describe anyone in particular, there was one song for everyone. And everyone tried to correspond to it.

A roomy woolen tunic; a thin burlap shirt underneath. A stand-up silk collar fastened by several buttons. Decorative gold embroidery, pearl applique, red taffeta along the upper edge, that was the collar. Inside was a strip of birch bark for shape. That birch bark made me suffer – how it irked me, pressing at my throat. The collar seemed like a living creature that would one day strangle me.

I walk up to the girl Ksenia. I don't know her real name but I don't want to know because I'm walking up to myself. I unbutton the top two buttons of her collar:

"Is that better?"

"It's better, madame."

The costume mistress sighs and asks (whom?) that the collar be buttoned: that was Auntie Klavdia's favorite thing to do. She explains to those present that buttons should have been buttoned in the Middle Ages. She doesn't look at anyone in particular. I inform her that I did not button my buttons in the Middle Ages. The costume mistress nods politely; she has done all she can.

And so Ksenia walks, looking straight ahead. To the left, paralleling her motion, a camera slides along rails. To the right, with the sea as a backdrop, are a milkmaid, a miller, a blacksmith, and a fisherman. All in a row: an impressive, unnatural frame. Gap-toothed, beaky-nosed. Gnarled fingers scratch stubbly cheeks, all of them but the milkmaid. The girl's motion is endless. Those standing turn their heads, gazes following Ksenia. She's organizing a public showing of the Middle Ages. Her hair is unharvested wheat . . .

Auntie Klavdia pops up, as if out of the sea; this is her manner.

"Did you come from the mysterious depths?" asks the girl.

Klavdia doesn't hear her through the sound of the surf. Waddling like a goose, she keeps stopping to catch her breath. The camera trails after her, capturing the hills on the horizon: blueness and motionlessness. The two hills of the aunt's rear end, however, are in powerful, unhurried motion. Gathering up her skirts, Klavdia plods into water up to her ankles. Ksenia turns sharply and shouts:

"Knife!"

Her voice and mine merge into one shout. There is bewilderment on Klavdia's face. Everyone turns in the direction from which the shout has flown. There is only blue sky there – like your eyes. My eyes.

There's pressure in my chest. Two doctors lead me to an ambulance and put me on a stretcher. Parfeny ... Where is Parfeny? I feel his touch. He's sitting at my feet. The ambulance slowly drives off. Surprising historians of language, my question to Klavdia about her legs is already sounding without us.

The attack gradually fades. We're not driving to the hospital but to the villa: Artemy has a good doctor.

At supper, Jean-Marie asks if I'm feeling better. Artemy's meditatively drawing something on a napkin. Yes, I'm feeling better.

But I had been feeling very, very good then. I was living in childhood for several moments. But now my hair is like snow and my eyes ... What do my eyes look like?

"A very beautiful little girl," I say. "I wasn't like that. I was chubby, rosy-cheeked."

I feel Artemy's gaze on me. As he draws, he looks first at me, then at the napkin:

"There were different perceptions of beauty then. Jean-Marie is filming in accordance with the current ones."

211

"So it's clear to the audience why Prince Parfeny loves you so much," laughs Leclerc. "And the main thing: for so long."

Artemy reaches across the table to give me the napkin with my portrait. I examine myself. It's a surprisingly good drawing. My hair is as white as snow. My eyes are like ash.

In the forty-ninth year of the Revolution, Brother Galaktion passed to his final rest. Not long before his demise, he blessed me, God's servant Innokenty, to continue the chronicle. This became my work of penance because times and events must be depicted until the Lord ceases them.

That same year, Vlas's daughter Melissa rose higher in the world. A position – Commissar for Bee Matters – was created for her. In realms far from us, that position might not be paramount, but it meant a great deal here, something everyone on the Island understood.

This was not the first year that hearsay circulated, saying that the Lord of the Bees had not lorded it over anyone for a long time and was keeping to himself more and more, remaining aloof from state matters. Melissa's appointment became obvious confirmation of that. People also told of Vlas ordering a bespoke drone bee suit to wear while walking around the Palace, dragging his wings. It is told that at night he crawled into a honeycomb that was built in the bedroom and that he made Glafira do the same thing, saying that a hive is not a hive without a queen bee. When the Lord of the Bees still needed to be present at state receptions, he occasionally lapsed into buzzing. And it was obvious to all that it was becoming ever more difficult for him to run the government with that sort of mentality.

212

Many now called Melissa the Island's sole ruler. In actuality, power was divided between her and her enigmatic husband, Valdemar, who was appointed Minister of Development and Magic Tricks. He kept in the shadows in the true sense of the expression, not revealing his presence at all. When that necessity did arise, he popped (more than once or twice) out of a top hat, to the flapping of doves' wings. Valdemar had not sawed his assistants in a long time: he had transferred that sort of activity to carving up the Island's treasury.

The peculiarity of his tricks consisted of the fact that once monetary assets had disappeared, they never reappeared. And if key rings, watches, and banknotes had invariably been returned to their owners in the past, that was all different now. Valdemar astounded the distinguished public with the art of disappearances. He proposed they watch his hand, but so great was his gift that watching proved useless. In a short time, army salaries, money for road repair, and even the funds for beekeeping (the Island's main budgetary expense) vanished without a trace.

In the fiftieth year of the Great Island Revolution, large festivities were organized to celebrate the anniversary of the arrival of the bright future. Melissa ordered that commemorative coins be issued for the commemorative event. Chairman Kasyan's profile was embossed on one side of the coin and Lord Vlas was on the other, releasing a bee. Each citizen of the Island received one of those coins.

On the day of the anniversary, the Main Square and the adjoining streets were filled with people. When the cannon shot at noon, Lord Vlas appeared on the Palace balcony wearing brand-new drone bee vestments. Melissa, Commissar for Bee Matters, stood on one side of the Lord of the Bees, and Valdemar, Minister of Development and Magic Tricks, stood on the other.

Valdemar spoke first, saying that the country was greeting the fiftieth anniversary of the Great Revolution with new achievements and victories. And although development had slowed slightly (do not forget we are waging war on France), the government had achieved unprecedented heights in the area of tricks. To confirm that, the minister proposed that the attendees take out their commemorative coins and place them on the palms of their hands.

Watch the hands, said Valdemar.

He snapped his fingers and pulled a dove out of his hat. At that very same moment, the coins disappeared from the palms of those in attendance.

There was no applause.

I will reveal a little secret to you, smiled the minister. You watched my hands but should have watched your own.

Despite the partial explanation of the trick, the coins were not returned to their owners.

Melissa spoke after Valdemar. After noting that the country had traveled a glorious path ever since the day the bright future set in, the commissar called on her fellow citizens to find meaning in that path so that new heights could follow. At those words, the Lord of the Bees flapped his wings and began buzzing. Melissa nodded as if supporting her father's upward aspirations.

Over the fifty years that have passed, the bright future has successfully become the past, Melissa continued. That is the nature of time. Some might say that this past, as well as the present, are not as bright as we might want them to be. I consider it my duty to remind everyone that the Great Revolution promised a bright future and has kept that promise.

Melissa scanned the crowd for a long time:

The future remains bright, as before.

The square resounded in ovations that strengthened when the Lord of the Bees approached the balcony railing. Rustling his wings slightly, Vlas heeded the crowd's roar and smiled. Never before had he seen such a multitudinous swarm. The sun came out from behind a cloud at that moment, and the Lord of the Bees raised his hands to it.

By its nature, a bee strives for the sun, he proclaimed, unusually distinctly.

Island residents who had long not heard articulate speech from Lord Vlas responded with new ovations.

Vlas swung a leg over the railing with unexpected agility and then shouted:

Let's fly!

His words soared over the square and then began glimmering on the sun. Before they dissolved into the heavens, Vlas took a step into the aerial expanse. Melissa and Valdemar rushed to him but were too late.

Vlas's flight was brief. A dull thud cut short his happy buzzing. Leaning over the railing, the commissar and the minister saw the dead body of the Lord of the Bees on the marble Palace steps.

215

Chapter the Nineteenth

MELISSA

After the death of Vlas, Lord of the Bees, his daughter Melissa ruled the Island. People had become so accustomed to Melissa's rule during the final years of the deceased's life that it seemed inevitable that she would be endowed with higher power. She returned to an ordinary title for a head of state and was now known as Chairwoman of the Island. It is worth noting that, despite her name, Melissa devoted far less attention to bees than did her father.

In the fifty-first year of the Great Revolution, there was a horrible earthquake on the Island. It lasted for a short time but the aftereffects were great. The main jolts were in the South, near the Mountain. And for the first time, insofar as Island residents' memory could attest, smoke was observed at the Mountain's summit and everyone knew that ruin would threaten the Island if the Mountain awakened.

It was not only the homes of simple people that suffered. Even part of the Palace was damaged: the wing where the Lord of the Bees had lived with his wife Glafira collapsed. Those natural jolts caught the elderly woman in the latrine. The ceilings, however, collapsed favorably for Glafira: The oak beams landed so there was a small space between them. Glafira was fortunate to have been in that space. The widow was shivering hard when she was freed. She could understand nothing and incessantly repeated that she was not guilty of anything, that she had only wanted to flush the water.

The Church of the Bright Future also suffered losses. Guards told of how the church, which was built long before the time of the bright future, ended up being unusually sturdy. It withstood the main earthquake without losses. Several hours later, during additional jolts, the so-called *aftershocks*, all the frescos painted on the church's walls after the victorious Revolution crumbled. Once the dust had settled, The Church of the Transfiguration had taken on its initial appearance, right before the eyes of the dumbfounded guards.

This miraculous event was reported immediately to Her Brightest Futurity Melissa. After arriving on the scene, the chairwoman ordered that the guards allow her to be alone in the church, where she spent three hours and thirty minutes. The guards, whose position had also become a bit shaky as a result of the earthquake, observed her through a crack in the door and later said that Melissa had not simply stood but had moved around the church, speaking with the icons.

The chairwoman came out enlightened and announced for all to hear that from now on the church would be dedicated not to the Bright Future but to the Transfiguration of Christ. That news spread at once over the entire Island, occasioning fervent joy among residents. It turned out that many had prayed for this their entire lives, transforming rooms of their residences into home churches.

And the Monastery filled with monks who had previously carried out secret duties in the secular world. Father Georgy of one hundred nineteen years – who remembered the Monastery's former glory and the monks' dormitory life – was installed as prior. And so, upon thanking Our Lord Jesus Christ, Father Georgy said:

The Island's authorities needed to be shaken up pretty well in order for them to reopen this cloister.

I, a sinning man who was here by dint of my position as a custodian of the past, continued to draw breath and was now ranked as a monk.

KSENIA

I think Father Georgy was correct: if the earthquake had not happened, everything would likely have remained the way it was. But tectonic processes – please forgive my play on words – shook Melissa and she did what she had not intended to do the day before: she returned the church to the clergy.

There were no changes to the government structure. At least that's how things seemed. Looking back on events years later, though, we can confirm that this became the beginning of change. In a surprising sense, Melissa reminded me of her mother Glafira, who had wished to flush something unclean. By returning the church to the world, the chairwoman caused her own sort of earthquake, which finally swallowed the bright future, along with its arrests, murders, and labor camps.

As far as Parfeny and I go, we never did see the apartment Markel promised us so we continued living in the communal apartment. Yes, our life became slightly easier after Markel's visit. Lukyan, who had exasperated us more than all the other neighbors combined, grew meek. He was no longer interested in what toilet seat we used, didn't ask which bulb we switched on in the kitchen, and even stopped checking the amount of kerosene in his Primus.

The Primuses themselves went away over the years. Four gas cooktops were installed in our communal kitchen, for use by the eight households living in the apartment. Bunny, the cat, who didn't fit her inoffensive name at all, made her home in the space under the cooktops.

Bunny was a staunch misanthrope. She hissed maliciously when greeting anyone who neared the cooktops, though she dug her claws into people's legs even more frequently. Nobody knew which cooktop Bunny was resting under at any given time – she knew how to keep everyone in suspense. Everyone but Parfeny, whom she had singled out for some reason; sometimes she would even rub up against his leg.

People tolerated Bunny because of her phenomenal ability to catch rats. If not for her, I think the rats would have ended up driving us out of the apartment. Before Bunny, they darted around on the tables, gnawed bags of flour, and ate everything that could be eaten. They jumped off the tables with a dull plop that sometimes woke us up at night. We recalled those trying times on days when Bunny rested, especially at night. The cat's absence under the cooktops meant it was impossible to go to the bathroom at night. The rats weren't afraid of us but they feared Bunny.

Cockroaches and bedbugs were another adversity in the apartment. Even Bunny was powerless there. With our combined efforts, we somehow got rid of the bedbugs over time but the cockroaches were part of our life in the communal apartment right up until the last day. We poured boiling water on the bed's joints and sprinkled various kinds of poison along the baseboards but the cockroaches quickly adapted to them and even began to eat them.

Lukyan once asked how we fought cockroaches in the palace. When we said there weren't any in the palace, he looked at us in disbelief. He had never in his life seen a place where there weren't cockroaches.

PARFENY

At dinner, Jean-Marie says he doesn't know how it could
be possible to get used to a communal apartment after the
palace. I answer that we got used to it fairly quickly. Though
of course we thought back to palace life the way people
think back to movies. As something that was not immediate
for us.

"So could you have lived in a communal apartment?"
Jean-Marie asks Artemy. "After these princely conditions of
yours?"

Artemy shrugs:

"I did live in one. When I was a kid."

Leclerc asks for a few scenes from communal life. I say
that it's boring, that it's been written about a hundred times
and our life was no different from what's described.

"Was no different?" Jean-Marie raises his glass and
we clink. "You want to say there were former princes in all
communal apartments?"

"To some extent, yes," says Ksenia. "If you'd had a look at
our neighbors."

Jean-Marie looks at Artemy.

"And what did you experience? Disgust, hatred for
those around you, a feeling of desperation?"

Artemy puts his napkin to his lips.

"Disgust dulls. Hatred? When you're standing in a common line for the bathroom, it's hard to experience hatred,
it's more like weariness." Artemy smiles at Ksenia and me.
"Right?"

Right. Of course desperation came over us at times,
but there were also moments of joy. Closing the door to our

room, we would sit in the evenings on an old sofa and listen to readings of classics on the radio, in trained, old-fashioned voices. With background noises of rain and the wet sounds of tires outside. Or we'd just sit and keep silent.

Even so, there was a border dividing us from the outside world. That border can even exist in a mass prison cell, not to mention a communal apartment where we did, after all, have our own room.

"But rats, cockroaches, bedbugs?" Jean-Marie wasn't letting up.

Sometimes they were less annoying than the people, imagine that. Unpleasant company, of course, but they weren't the slightest bit underhanded. After all, cockroaches don't fly into the soup pot by themselves.

Yes, when you got right down to things, the neighbors weren't so bad. In the days when the bright future was in its heyday, we celebrated Easter with them. We baked kuliches. Someone brought vodka, another brought sausage and everybody sat – who would have thought it – at the same table!

"We don't consider those years a time of unhappiness," says Ksenia. "If that hadn't been in our life, we wouldn't have learned anything about our own people."

Leclerc's gaze stops on something outside the window:

"I want to find some episode that makes it clear to the viewer that you remained Their Royal Highnesses even in the communal apartment.

Ksenia joins her palms together.

"A lovely idea. However I, for example, quarreled with one of the women there, and His Royal Highness separated us. You cannot even imagine what an unlovely episode that was."

"Which is why it would be incorrect to summarize a life in an episode," says Artemy.

Ksenia buries her face in her hands and her voice sounds dull: "Life minces people like a food processor."

I pat her on the shoulder. "You talk as if you quarreled there for the entire half-century. It was just a day when you were a complete nervous wreck."

As a result, we often recalled our neighbors even after very august European families gave us an apartment in the city and a house on the Embankment. We continue to recall our neighbors now.

I probably stretched the truth by saying we miss them, but now that they're no longer of this earth we consider their absence an irreplaceable loss. And a loss is a loss even though we're not searching for others to replace them. Yet another part of our life that's irretrievably gone. And now we mourn those people, when our life seems to consist only of these sorts of gulfs.

Who do they quarrel with now?

Meanwhile, new ordeals awaited Chairwoman Melissa. Once the Island's residents had recovered from the demise of the Lord of the Bees and the earthquake that followed, memory returned them to the anniversary celebrations and they realized they had been deprived of their commemorative coins on the day of the celebration.

Someone said the Minister of Development and Magic Tricks had secretly transferred them into pillows that lay in his bedroom. That news spread like wildfire and soon a huge crowd stood by the Palace, itching for the return of the coins. To avoid bloodshed,

Chairwoman Melissa ordered that five representatives of the agitated people be allowed into the bedroom she and Valdemar shared.

The representatives were permitted to tear open all sixteen down pillows on the premises and check them for the presence of financial instruments. After an hour of meticulous searches, the representatives went outside to those who had gathered. Their faces were covered in down, which hid expressions of obvious embarrassment, for it turned out there was no money in the pillows.

Even so, the disappearance of the coins was an obvious matter and – under pressure from the infuriated public – Melissa was forced to institute an investigation of the losses. Army salaries were subject to inquiry too, as was the money for road repair and the funds for beekeeping. No papers were found to confirm the transfer of commemorative coins into Palace pillows. The only papers found concerned a transfer to a Swiss bank. All the other resources being sought resided there too.

Valdemar sat tight in a giant top hat all those days, until the morning Melissa could not find him there either. A little more than a month later, the Minister of Development and Magic Tricks was located in the southern part of the Island. Valdemar had reportedly been meeting with a slew of people who were speaking openly about dividing North and South.

One of those people was a certain woman named Varvara, who headed up the Southern Liberation Society. That made a thoroughly unfavorable impression on the chairwoman. Brief announcements about *intensive consultations* between Valdemar and Varvara definitively embittered Melissa. She could have turned a blind eye to her husband's state treason but spousal treason was not subject to forgiveness.

Melissa conquered her pride and wrote Varvara a detailed and admonishing letter in which she described Valdemar's negative qualities and insistently advised having nothing to do with him. The letter concluded with a warning that, true to his habit, Valdemar would, in the end, saw her, Varvara, to pieces.

The answer was brief and disheartening. And it was signed not by the head of the Southern Liberation Society but by her deputy, Vassa. The letter dryly announced that no feeble attempts at sawing had been observed thus far in Valdemar, who had offered tricks of another sort to Varvara.

The letter left Melissa speechless. She pondered her answer for several days and, given the circumstances, realized she could only respond with action. The chairwoman declared that Valdemar and Varvara had committed high treason and signed an order that they be taken into custody. After handing the order to a senior official in the Guards of the Future, her eye caught a certain tentativeness. In answering Her Brightest Futurity about the reason for wavering, the official responded that fulfilling the signed order would be challenging given that the guards in the southern regions had stopped obeying him.

And I thought, said Melissa, that this sedition was gone for good. But it turns out . . .

The chairwoman went silent, staring into the official's eyes.

Your Brightest Futurity left but then returned, said the official, with a click of the heels.

Valdemar had managed to charm the local population during the short time he had spent in the South. These were not the evil spells that black magic textbooks describe: the former state minister was too flimsy of spirit for those and he lacked the necessary focus. It was enough for the South's residents that he simply performed tricks and talked a lot.

Valdemar's speeches flowed like an endless silk scarf pulled out of a top hat. He told of transferring money from bank to bank via mental gymnastics and pledged to forward all the monetary holdings of Swiss banks to southern residents. He promised to create natural conditions that would enable the North's oil to redirect its flow to the South via secret underground routes.

He planned to drain swamps in the southern part of the Forest, though that was no simple matter. The River would need to be sent into reverse to fulfill the task. Valdemar promised nothing on that count. He fell silent when speaking of it, dropping a hint that even he had his limits. But even what he did promise was more than enough to win over southern residents' hearts.

Valdemar accompanied his stories with astounding tricks. He moved watches from one audience member's pocket to another's, motioned with his hand to restore banknotes that had been torn to shreds, and, in everyone's plain sight, sawed up women without harming them in the least. Coupled with the stories, those tricks acted on people like magic. His primary trick was that nobody doubted the validity of his stories, which were as florid as the ribbons he cut. Valdemar conquered the residents of the South in just a few weeks and they were prepared to follow him anywhere. He led them to the North.

KSENIA

We returned home from Tuscany two weeks ago. The first episode of the film was shot while we were in Italy.

Phillip, our editor, came to see us after learning of our return. He wants to publish our notes right in the text, denoting them with a different typeface. Parfeny is against a different typeface. My Parfeny does not like superfluous gaudiness. He considers it poor taste.

225

"But then how," asked Phillip, "can we differentiate your text from the chroniclers' text?"

Parfeny thought a bit and said:

"You can simply make larger margins on the page. Or not differentiate it: for the most part, it's the same text."

Phillip did not believe him.

Jean-Marie flew in unexpectedly two days ago. He'd finished a sample edit of an episode and wanted to show it to us. It's odd: during the filming, it seemed it was about us. But we watched... The film's good, like all Leclerc's work. But it's unclear who it's about. About someone who was born and lived inside Jean-Marie.

After we watched, he asked for our impressions.

"It's beautiful," said Parfeny. "Maybe even more beautiful than life."

Jean-Marie wondered what was bewildering us. He said he was willing to adjust details. I answered that everything was actually fine with the details. He looked noticeably sad.

"Then what's wrong?"

"Life," Parfeny smiled. "Life on the whole."

Then we went out for a walk, to the sea. A woman walking toward us reminded me of my aunt.

"Klavdia," Jean-Marie said, unsurprised.

Her advice has stuck with us. She shows up again and again, as she did the first time, always in a new guise, but in her we flawlessly divine Klavdia. What would we do without her?

The nice lady takes Parfeny by the arm and excitedly explains something to him. She points at rocks sticking out of the water. Parfeny nods politely. He kisses her hand when they part.

"What did that woman say?" Jean-Marie asks Parfeny.

"She pleaded with us not to go into the water by those rocks. She said she foolishly went in right there, then had trouble getting out. She nearly broke her legs."

Jean-Marie pensively watches Klavdia as she walks way:

"She might not have broken them, but she really bent them."

In the fifty-second year of the Revolution, southern troops began moving north on the twentieth of May. Seething with their love of freedom, the southern troops launched a two-day forced march, arriving at the Southern Highway that served as the approximate border between the Island's two parts. This was the first time a civil war had begun from the southern side.

The troops were volunteers, poorly armed and untrained. Their commander in chief fit them perfectly – Valdemar had been chosen unanimously. At the border, his detachments' rapid motion changed to motionlessness and the Island's regular army, radiating battleworthiness, was on the other side, awaiting the attackers.

The troops under Field Marshal Serapion's command conveyed their full devotion to Melissa, whom they considered their Fair Lady. Serapion was tall, gray-haired, wise, and terse. He was surprised when he used binoculars to scrutinize the strange assemblage that had already been making noise by the border for several days. The southern military's daily pursuits involved alternating fiery speeches for independence with lavish drinking bouts.

To raise the soldiers' fighting spirit, Valdemar performed tricks of a liberating character. He performed the usual cutting of a scarf with a happy ending (the scarf was returned to the owner completely whole) and then loudly demanded an Island flag too. After that, there appeared implausibly large scissors that required two hands to operate. Two soldiers unfurled the Island banner and the commander in chief cut it in half to the troops' approving shouts.

Are you waiting for the halves to unite? There's no use. Nobody can unite them. Not even me.

That trick was so successful that Valdemar had to perform it many times a day. He no longer needed to say anything. Everyone knew the words and the troops uttered them all together. In the course of a week, the commander in chief managed to cut so many banners that they had to be delivered from the most distant corners of the South.

Meanwhile, the commander was in no hurry to continue the attack. The reports coming in convinced him more and more that there was no reason to hope that magic tricks would work successfully in a battle with the regular army.

During those same days, Valdemar declared himself released from his marriage to Island Chairwoman Melissa. In a radio address to southern residents, he told of his many years of love for her, saying he might have continued to love her if not for her imperial essence. The thought of Melissa pressuring the freedom-loving South had gradually fettered his mind, heart, and absolutely everything that could be fettered, so in the end he could no longer share the chairwoman's bed. Valdemar's love for the South ended up being stronger than his love for Melissa. He had made his choice and here he was.

Her Brightest Futurity had devoured each piece of news about her fugitive spouse and so she listened to this announcement from beginning to end. Melissa's opinion on that score remained unknown because she was befallen by a stroke at Valdemar's final words. The chairwoman gasped and plaintive bleating came out of her mouth instead of human speech.

Her Brightest Futurity was somehow put back on her feet thanks to her doctors' efforts; however, the gift of speech never returned. Melissa's interest in government matters abandoned her along with speech. Nongovernment matters did not concern the chairwoman either and nothing caught her attention but the radio. She sat night and day by the radio set, which was turned up, at full volume. Its sound was so powerful that it resounded not only in all the rooms of the Palace but in the nearest streets.

It was at that same volume that Valdemar announced a week later, over the airwaves, his marriage to Varvara, who headed the Southern Liberation Society. The commander in chief informed radio listeners that he was henceforth united with the South's freedom movement, in the person of Varvara. Valdemar also told of how his love for the liberation movement had gradually shifted within him to a love for Varvara, though Melissa was no longer listening. She was found at the end of the broadcast, as the song "Libertà!" played. The chairwoman's head rested on the table, her hand squeezed the radio set's antennae, and her soul bobbed among the AM radio waves.

After learning of the chairwoman's death, Commander-in-Chief Valdemar announced that the attack would begin the next day. Those thirsting for immediate victory demanded the attack begin that same day instead, while the government was still confused. Valdemar answered that today was early but the day after tomorrow was too late. That explanation satisfied everyone because it was mysterious.

Valdemar was, in fact, waiting for the regular army to scatter after learning of the chairwoman's death. But the army was not scattering. In memory of the chairwoman, who had departed in such an untimely manner, the army instead decided to restore order within the government and thus prepared for battle with morose focus.

Some even saw Melissa herself floating among the radio waves and calling for vengeance.

The southern military leader grew downhearted after hearing of the regular army's mindset. People said he experienced a certain trepidation after realizing his former spouse was opposing him even after her death – that posthumous opposition genuinely frightened Valdemar. He was overwhelmed by the thought that punishment would come from Melissa's hand, which had once caressed him and which he had once kissed.

The commander in chief appealed to the troops, saying that the attack was postponed because of newly revealed circumstances, but now nobody was listening to him. The freedom-loving volunteers were preparing to attack. They saw only one place for Valdemar: heading up the troops, as is proper for a military leader.

The commander in chief shivered all night. A hand holding a pistol stretched toward his temple every now and then but something held it back each time. The next morning, the adversaries crossed the last several hundred meters that divided them. Now they stood opposite one another, on either side of the Southern Highway.

Field Marshal Serapion proposed that Valdemar surrender. His voice was filled with confidence and calm. Downhearted, Valdemar answered with something inarticulate and even proposed performing a card trick. The southern troops considered their commander in chief's behavior unseemly and a dull muted rumble passed through the ranks.

Serapion looked at his watch and announced that the southern army had an hour to prepare to surrender.

It is now eleven o'clock, said Serapion. I will open fire at twelve.

According to those soldiers prepared for battle, time had never been so palpable and rattling. Only Valdemar's muttering broke the silence as he tried to convince his troops to make a temporary retreat. Fifteen minutes before the appointed deadline, there was motion in Serapion's army and the audible clicking of breechblocks.

Just then, a dust cloud appeared on the Southern Highway. It seemed to be standing still, as if it were a faltering tornado, but several minutes later it was obvious the cloud was nearing. The troops on both sides turned their heads toward it, as if rescue could arrive from that direction.

It arrived.

His Royal Highness, Prince Parfeny, was sitting in the open automobile. Field Marshal Serapion was the first to approach the automobile. He saluted and helped the elderly prince out of the car. Valdemar also approached the automobile. He was keeping his own counsel, though witnesses described the expression on his face as happy.

An armchair was brought from the field marshal's tent. Parfeny sat in it, then several of the tallest soldiers raised the chair in their outstretched arms. They brought a bullhorn to the prince.

Peace to you, said Parfeny. I answer for all of you. That is my work of penance since, alas, you cannot find an answer yourselves. Filled with sorrow, I say to you: Go to your homes and embrace your wives and children, for if they lose you, what is the point of everything else?

A shared sigh of relief resounded. It was strong enough that the trees began swaying on both sides of the highway. Valdemar, whom that wafting did not touch, walked out to the middle of the highway. Taking care about the impression he made, this flexible person decided to display his unbendingness. They brought him the Island's banner and large scissors. After cutting the banner, he waited for his troops to utter the usual words. But the troops kept silent and he uttered them himself.

In the quiet that had set in, Valdemar raised the two halves of the banner over his head and repeated that nobody would unite them. Then he passed them to Parfeny, who took the two pieces of fabric and folded them together. When he unfolded them, everyone saw an undamaged Island banner in his hands.

And the soldiers of both armies understood that something unusual had happened and so they removed their hats and stood in silence. Then, without uttering a word, they went, as they had been told to do, to their homes and embraced their wives and children.

The next morning, Field Marshal Serapion announced that, in light of the death of Melissa, the Island's chairwoman, he was taking the full range of the country's power upon himself.

There is nothing worse than a power vacuum, said Serapion, for it reveals the darkest abysses within people and transforms life into hell.

The field marshal also announced that he was taking power for only a year, until the election of a leader who fit Island residents' expectations. Serapion himself gave his word as an officer that he would relinquish his powers in exactly a year, to the day, and retire.

Chapter the Twentieth

SERAPION

In the fifty-second year of the Great Revolution, Leader Serapion's first ukase was the announcement of a pardon for all who took part in the turmoil at the Southern Highway. With his second ukase, the Island returned to its previous chronology. The fifty-second revolutionary year thus became the first year of Serapion's rule. The first and only, according to the leader's promise.

Not all Island residents could make sense of the changes in the numbering of the chronology so voices even began saying that Serapion had taken away fifty-one lived years with the sole goal of depriving the country of its bright future and returning it to the dark past. Serapion answered those people by saying the future cannot be taken away since it exists only in the imagination. Due to his vocation, he, Serapion, was completely deprived of imagination and worked with the present. It was mandatory to remember the past, too, in order that its mistakes not be repeated and history not form a vicious circle.

Valdemar had fled overseas, believing in neither the announced pardon nor Serapion's promise to relinquish power. From outside the country, he contradicted Serapion and proposed adding fifty unlived years to the Island in order to stride into the future without expending unnecessary effort. In confirmation, the fugitive cited and lavished all sorts of praise on overseas experience in establishing lifestyles. Serapion, however, alerted Valdemar to the fact that unlived years contain no experience, making them a pointless addition.

One may declare a child to be an adult, said Serapion, but will that make its intellect wiser and strengthen the soul?

Sputtering from the Mainland, Valdemar said: He is likening the people to a child. That is in denial of folk wisdom and therefore shows a lack of faith in government by the people.

The field marshal did not reject government by the people but he did not believe in its unlimited possibilities. Serapion thought that a democratic way of life demanded feelings of responsibility from every human soul. He had not observed that on the Island.

When the spine does not hold up the body, said the field marshal, a corset is put on the person. That corset is harsh rule.

He is denying his people's high awareness, Valdemar responded from beyond the sea.

If a government by the people arrives only as a shamanistic incantation, said Serapion, then great difficulties await us. New words should arise through internal changes.

He is proposing to wait, but I demand action, objected Valdemar.

Let them live according to their own hearts' inclinations, said Serapion. My task is to set elections.

In order to learn how to swim, one must enter the water, announced Valdemar.

And we entered the water.

Various forces began preparing for the Island's election of a leader, and a variety of views immediately manifested themselves. In the struggle for power, the supporters of the bright future put forth their protégés, as did the adherents to the past. A Bee Party also formed to continue the work of Lord Vlas, and that party nominated its own person. The Progress Party became a new social force on the Island, headed by none other than Valdemar, who remained, in body, overseas.

He fulfilled his promise of transferring money in an unexpected way, albeit in limited quantity, although he sent it not to the South but the North, to the capital, where the newly formed party had launched its activity. The South's liberation movement no longer attracted Valdemar and he soon announced for all to hear that there had been a transformational change in his worldview. The former military leader no longer wished for the South to secede – he dreamt instead of strengthening the Island's unity.

The first victim of Valdemar's transformational change was Varvara, since all the politician's personal connections were inseparable from the public ones. Love's invisible threads now connected Valdemar to Mainland Oil Company, which was the source of his funds.

Captured by a new passion, he sought the reinforcement of existing relationships but understood that marrying an oil company (or even its owner, Mr. Brand) would be challenging. And so Valdemar took the only possible route: he married Cecilia, Mr. Brand's daughter.

Unlike Melissa, that news did not kill Varvara. Having grown accustomed to cataclysms along her liberating path, it only steeled her. Varvara sent the newlyweds a congratulatory telegram with the promise to personally present them with a gift. Valdemar, who had thoroughly studied his former comrade-in-arms, felt disquieted, but the die was cast. His Rubicon became the sea separating the Island from the Mainland. After receiving Serapion's written assurances of safety, Valdemar and Cecilia arrived on the Island.

Valdemar immediately dedicated himself to campaign activity, without even giving himself a day to rest. To general surprise, his first meeting with voters did not take place in the capital. Sparing neither time nor effort, the candidate headed for an oil-producing region on the northwest part of the Island. With oil derricks as a backdrop, Valdemar told of the prosperity that awaited the country under his governance, and the rhythm of his speech coincided with the rhythm of derricks that looked like gigantic well sweeps.

After finishing his speech, he performed a trick. He raised a transparent vessel filled with oil, which he only called "black gold," over his head. Valdemar approached the first row of the audience and allowed all who wished to sniff the liquid in the vessel. He even smeared their noses with it so it was obvious to everyone that he was holding this same black gold in his hands. The magician called over an old drill technician and asked him to take off his jacket and show it – including the inside – to those present. The jacket was dirty on both sides, which meant nobody would think it had been readied for the performance. The technician was above suspicion too, since in all his years working at the well he had never displayed the slightest inclination for magic tricks. At Valdemar's request, the technician covered the vessel of oil with his jacket. When he lifted the jacket off the vessel, the vessel turned out to be empty. The technician and the other oilmen were stunned since they had never imagined that oil could disappear without a trace.

KSENIA

Phillip came and discussed details of the upcoming publication. He certainly wants to open it with an epigraph. He decided against an ordinary typeface and hired a well-known graphic designer. He handled the job in two days. He brought it to Phillip this morning. Would we like to have a glance at it? Yes, of course, how could we not? And what sort of epigraph is it?

Phillip takes out a sturdy, rough sheet with stylized ancient letters.

"Here... This is Prokopy's addition on the last page of *The True History*..."

Bent over the sheet, we read: "By Agafon's coffin will

not find a prophecy are so vessel is the source of information about the future of the Island."

Ah, so that's it . . .

"A well-known phrase," says Parfeny. "Primarily because its meaning is not very clear."

"What could be better for an epigraph?" laughs Phillip.

He takes a photograph of the manuscript page out of the folder, along with a copy of the calligrapher's work. He places them at the edge of the table. He's leaving that for us, just in case.

Parfeny asks: "So how do you understand that note anyway?"

The editor understands it approximately like this: even by Agafon's grave, no one is in a condition to utter a prophecy that is a source of knowledge about the future of the Island. Prodded by our silence, Phillip explains that in the absence of a prophecy, all that remains for us is history, which we must study scrupulously. And publish.

He smiles. "Of course everything would have been simpler with a prophecy."

Well, yes. A reliable prophecy is more authentic than history.

After the editor left, I picked up the photo he left with us. I knew the inscription in its published form but had never held the manuscript in my own hands. "ByAgafonscoffin . . ." To my taste, Prokopy's handwriting was far more pleasant than the calligrapher's exercises. According to the custom of that time, there are no periods or commas, the words aren't even separated. Then again, there's a whole slew of diacritical marks that are beautiful and mean nothing. I called Parfeny over.

"Look at this, where the edges of the sheet are damaged, there could have been a few more letters. Do you see the pale strokes? They look like parts of letters."

"Maybe starting with an n?"

"Maybe ... Adding a few letters, it could work out to something else: 'By Agafon's coffin ... will not find a prophecy. A reso*nant* vessel is the source of information about the future of the Island.'"

"If we add a few more letters, we have, 'By Agafon's coffin *one* will not find a prophecy. A resonant vessel is the source of information about the future of the Island.' It's talking about a resonator, an acoustic niche in the church wall."

"It works out that Prokopy hid the prophecy in a resonator and that the resonator is located alongside Agafon's grave."

We called Phillip and told him our hunch. For some time, there was just a snuffling sound in the phone. I shook the phone and it answered:

"I'll try to contact the Ministry of Culture tomorrow morning. Any work in the Church of the Transfiguration is only possible with their permission."

It works out that Prokopy was certain that nobody would make their way to the prophecy. And he simultaneously gave a clue about how to find it. That is so like him.

Never before had the Island been so caught up in social strife. The Island dove in headfirst, just as the pharaoh's troops in ancient times drowned in the depths of the Red Sea and, much later, Prince Konstantin's troops were pulled into a forest swamp. The Island needed to elect a new ruler who would, henceforth, be called "President." A president was being chosen for the first time and the elections were the first, too, and not one soul in the country knew how it would end.

Discussion of political protégés took place everywhere: in newspapers, on the radio, and even inside the television boxes that had gradually entered Island residents' daily life. People argued on streets and public squares, in trams and taxicabs, and even on the high-speed train connecting North and South.

One day, the chairman of the Bright Future Party made a televised speech. He announced to television viewers that certain truthtellers had brought him a paper labeled *Declaration of Intentions*. The document evidenced Valdemar's intentions, which coincided with the intentions of the Mainland Oil Company. In the event that Valdemar won the election, he would be obligated to take the Island's oil production out from under government subordination and transfer it to the company.

The power of the televised speech lay not only in the fact that Island residents heard it. They also saw it. *Declaration* was shown in a close-up shot and remained on the screen so long that everyone had time to familiarize themselves with it, including those who did not read quickly. The paper was countersigned with handwritten signatures from both sides.

Valdemar made a televised speech the next day. Contrary to everyone's expectations, he used television's possibilities to far greater advantage than had the whistleblower. The whistleblower had the paper and dry details of the agreement on his side; Valdemar had fervent feelings on his side.

Nervous and even stunned, Valdemar asked television viewers how they could believe some sort of paper instead of him, Valdemar, who had never deceived his compatriots. Tears ran down his cheeks and his voice cracked. He explained the appearance of the paper as the whistleblower's sleight of hand, saying that trick was well-known to any magician.

To prove what he said, Valdemar took a copy of *Declaration of Intentions* and crumpled it, but the sheet was blank when he smoothed it. The candidate's actions were so convincing that his compatriots, who knew the contents of the paper as well as Valdemar's dubious past deeds, believed him unconditionally.

Valdemar was unstoppable now that he'd convinced himself that he could prove and refute anything at all. He showed his trick at every appearance and explained away all attempts to reveal his true nature as machinations from the enemies of progress.

Portraits of Valdemar were delivered from the Mainland on cargo ships and pasted up all over the Island. Valdemar appeared differently in each of the portraits. At times there was a jacket tossed over his shoulder, signifying his industriousness. At times he had no jacket but his face was wise and tired, reflecting the strain of all his powers.

This toiler, however, also knew the value of merriment. A portrait of Valdemar laughing and showing implausibly white teeth spoke to that. It was obvious that this person, like simple Island residents, also knew how to relax: a photograph of Valdemar on a carousel confirmed that. With each new docking ship, voters learned ever more details about the candidate: Valdemar at the library, Valdemar at the theater, Valdemar at the gymnasium.

It was worthy of amazement that those portraits invented a new Valdemar: book lover, connoisseur of the liberal arts, and gymnast. Someone whose heart bled for the Island's land, someone who had never signed a declaration of intentions and had no intentions anyway. Who had not appropriated monetary assets but had ridden the carousel, carefree. Who had served as guardian of the insulted

240

and humiliated, people who began vying amongst themselves to tell Island residents about their experiences. Never before had so many interviews with the poor, orphaned, and widowed been published. Few people did not want to vote for that sort of man.

So many Island residents came to cast their ballots on Election Day that the closing time for polling places was moved back four hours. The ballots were counted for three days and three nights. Valdemar was elected as the country's president.

Chapter the Twenty-First

VALDEMAR

In the first year of President Valdemar's term in office, Mainland Oil Company gas stations began appearing on the Island. They popped up like the endless scarves coming out of Valdemar's top hat and Island residents took to them enthusiastically. Bright and colorful, the gas stations differed favorably from other Island structures, which were remarkable only for looking faded.

Even Island residents who did not own automobiles gladly patronized the gas stations because they sold not only gasoline but numerous other small, lovely things, namely: lighters, potato chips, hard candies in tins, aftershave lotion, glossy magazines, and chewing gum. Unlike previous filling stations, the new ones smelled not of gasoline but of mysterious cleansers and eau de toilette.

After those visits, Island residents returned home with spirits raised, smelling sweet, and crunching chips. Given the high prices of name-brand goods, some attempted to cut thin potatoes and fry them in a pan, but that did not make chips. That resulted in burned potato slices that were difficult to scrape out of the skillet and just as difficult to eat after all the scraping.

Toward the end of Valdemar's first year, it emerged that Mainland Oil Company had purchased all the Island's oil wells. It was announced that the company could extract greater utility from the wells than the Island government. The oil derricks nodded at the acquisition of a new master, confirming what had been said, keeping quiet only about the fact that the utility of the wells was evidenced not on the Island but on the Mainland.

Accordingly, some recalled the *Declaration of Intentions* and asked the president about it at the first convenient opportunity. Valdemar answered that there had been no such intentions and oil production had been inadvertently switched over to Mainland Oil.

PARFENY

After lengthy discussions and agreements, permission was received for exploratory work in the Church of the Transfiguration. First and foremost, Agafon the Forward-Looking's burial place needed to be found since a new floor had been laid over the gravestones during restoration.

As Phillip told us, they came across Agafon's gravestone fairly quickly while dismantling the floor. After that, they carefully checked the resonators in the vault of the church where the grave was discovered. They all turned out to be empty. Then they examined the resonators located a distance from Agafon's resting place and found nothing there either. They decided not to cover Agafon's gravestone with boards, leaving it open for those who prayed.

Ksenia is crushed. Quite honestly, so am I. Our discovery had seemed so beautiful to us that we had no doubt of its truthfulness since beauty and truth accompany one another. We had nothing left to do but offer apologies to Phillip and everyone we had disturbed.

"I feel that manuscript, do you know what I mean?" Ksenia asked me. "I know for sure that it isn't lost."

Tomorrow we're supposed to fly to Paris where Jean-Marie is expecting us for filming yet more episodes.

In the third year of Valdemar's presidency, a multitude of buildings for branches of Mainland companies began to rise on the Island. Valdemar never tired of repeating that the Island was greeting the world with open arms for the first time in its history. That wide-openness had made itself known primarily through increased exports of extractable resources and timber. Island residents received an abundance of unfamiliar items in return. Beyond what was already for sale at the gas stations, there were additions of novels by King, records by Sting, rhinestones, stringy thongs, and a great number of other items impossible to list.

The companies' buildings were called "offices." Once the offices were built, the companies filled them with people from the Continent. They looked exhausted and there was a sense they were better than Island residents and knew how to do everything. The newcomers jokingly called Islanders "natives," though they did not joke much and preferred making serious lectures about how people should work, relax, receive medical treatment, make love, and, basically, arrange their lives.

By watching people from the Continent, Island residents gradually began to resemble them. Many actually did become like those from the Mainland. They would saunter around, leisurely, with a hand in a trouser pocket and say: *That's your problem.* They'd say: *I hear you.* They'd ask: *What's it going to cost me?* Those who were not made for that sort of thing felt sick at heart because they had not kept pace with the president, who was so light on his feet, leading his people into the bright realm of progress.

Those from the Continent, however, felt a bit ashamed of themselves when they saw their own clumsy reflections, though there was nothing they could correct. They recognized their gait, appearance, and speech, and though their own reflections resembled something in a funhouse mirror, they understood that the distortion was not accidental and served to underline their own specific traits.

Island residents who were used to leisurely eating had difficulty mastering *fast food*, but willpower helped them succeed there too. The overall pace of life picked up and the expression *time is money* was firmly imprinted on the Island consciousness. Time had not yet transformed into money for Island residents, but everything accelerated noticeably as they awaited that transformation.

Children on the Island played at being entrepreneurs, bank workers, and notaries, taking toy credit cards and traveler's checks out of toy wallets. By assimilating into that new life, they became more successful than the adults who, for their part, also felt like children because the adults on the Island were from the Continent.

Even Valdemar's tricks had now begun to carry an exclusively monetary character and only took place without an audience. Valdemar himself had shriveled, shrunk in size, and (in the view of the Island's citizens) begun to look unpresidential. This was not a question of great size: it was greatness that citizens missed. Valdemar lacked the presence that had distinguished previous Island rulers. He rode from one continental country's embassy to another, participating in *roundtables* and *presentations*, after which he ate *sushi* and *canapés* off plastic plates.

Valdemar initially attempted to invite the royal pair to accompany him, as if their presence would gain him some missing dignity, but Their Royal Highnesses declined his invitations time after time, preferring dinner in the communal kitchen to embassy receptions. They also declined the invitations of continental ambassadors. Perhaps because those invitations possessed a pointedly imperious character, as the ambassadors themselves were only guests on the Island.

Meanwhile, people from the Continent played a growing role in ruling the country. They advised Valdemar, and since the advice came with money, the president gratefully took it: it was no secret to him that those two forces of nature were inextricably linked. When the advice touched on transferring government property into private continental hands, Valdemar transferred it. When requests came to fit some article or other into Island newspapers, he fit it in.

Overall, people were satisfied with Valdemar, noting that his individual administrative shortcomings – the disappearance of government monetary resources, falling economic indicators, and the like – were excusable, given his insatiable hunger for progress.

KSENIA

We're back in Paris and we're going to the studio today. According to Jean-Marie, they reconstructed our city there – several episodes have already been filmed. Now they're filming yet another. Jean-Marie spoke about that rather oddly, as if it were almost something intimate. I'm feeling slight anxiety because my premonitions often come true. Parfeny and I are very different from Leclerc: we speak different languages, not only in the literal sense. It's doubtful he'll start speaking ours.

Parfeny is reserved, as always:

"We'll see."

"Well, yes," I say, "if there has never been anything intimate in our lives, at least we'll see it."

He laughs.

"It's a bit late to start, don't you think?"

The director's assistant greets us at the studio. He drives us to the set in an electric car. Everything is well under way there. Bedroom scenery. A bed of unbelievable size. Two young creatures in identical studio robes are sitting at its edge.

"We want to film it chastely but juicily," Jean-Marie tells us.

"What '*it*'?" I ask.

Leclerc's finger cuts through the air like a wave.

"Well, it's . . . You weren't monks, after all."

"We were," Parfeny says. "That's why we don't have children."

I keep silent. Jean-Marie runs a hand over his face. The corners of his lips separate and at first it seems as if he's crying.

No, he's laughing. He apologizes, it's from nerves. He simply doesn't know what to say. He takes a cigarette from his assistant. I'd never seen him smoke. Sure, he doesn't smoke it – he takes the cigarette with his lips but doesn't light it. Now he's attempting to explain everything. He clicks the lighter and smokes anyway.

He wants to film a scene about Tristan and Isolde, about a wonderful young couple (he shows us the wonderful couple) living in challenging medieval conditions . . . In the viewer's eyes, any medieval couple is Tristan and Isolde. How can you describe that . . .

Parfeny shrugs:

"But, really, there's nothing to describe."

"I don't understand what's troubling you." Notes of annoyance. "Lovemaking? But I only have a hint of that in the script. None of *that*."

Parfeny's calm.

"Well, there wasn't any of that. We lived according to perfect love. Like brother and sister."

Jean-Marie burns a hole in the bedspread and asks for another. Parfeny and I understand the pressure is on us.

"The thing is, that in the script…" He leaves the sentence unfinished and silently sits.

He has a script but we have a life, so there's room for comparison. Particularly since he doesn't have a script in the usual sense of the word.

"I could say," Leclerc is looking at the floor's even, ornamental pattern, "that it's impossible to film perfect love – chances are it's uncinematic."

He raises a hand, anticipating our objections but we don't object. Chances are it's uncinematic.

"But I'll put it another way. It's fine, let's say, that you lived an angelic life. But wouldn't you like to see how it could have looked different?"

Parfeny's surprised gaze.

"Undress!" Jean-Marie shouts to the young people without turning toward them. He's in hysterics, looking only at us. "This wonderful couple are you! Try to live out *another* life thanks to their efforts. You had every experience but this one, so why deny yourselves? Out of stubbornness?"

Parfeny smiles.

"Yes, of course. Any choice demands stubbornness."

I shout.

"It was," I'm shouting, "my choice! And he made it his and that's why there's no person dearer to me. And now I don't know if I should have decided for both of us. I think about that all the time, but what do your Tristan and Isolde have to do with it? After all, he wanted a child but I deprived him of one. And your foolish film doesn't correct anything here!"

I'm sobbing like I've never sobbed. Jean-Marie's scared. We leave for the hotel.

Jean-Marie comes to see us about two hours later and suggests we have a walk around Paris. None of us bring up what happened at the studio.

"I read that there was a *yellow vest* demonstration today in the city center," says Parfeny.

Leclerc nods. "Indeed there was, but it's already over. We'll go for a walk *after* the yellow vests' demonstration."

"And we'll have coffee," I say.

After what happened at the studio, I feel like saying something reassuring. Jean-Marie doesn't react at all to my suggestion.

We go in three cars. Jean-Marie and Dominique are in the first, Parfeny and I are in the second, and the third is a jeep with security. The cars stop near the Grands Boulevards. The policeman who approaches explains that it's not a throughway. We continue on foot.

Today turns out to have been a day of catastrophes. Tow trucks are hauling away burned-out cars. All the cars here are burned. There's a collection of charred motor scooters at the edge of the sidewalk. The majority of plate glass windows are smashed, many have plywood nailed over them. The bank's bulletproof glass is covered in web-like cracks but not smashed. There are several compact stereo systems in boxes by an electronics store. Someone wanted to listen to music. The store's workers are carrying them back through a window that no longer has glass.

"The fight for justice," says Jean-Marie, "usually ends in robbery."

"What do they want?" Parfeny asks.

Jean-Marie points at the empty boulevard: "That."

We turn onto the street where our cars are already waiting. Leclerc looks at me.

"Coffee's complicated here right now. We'll go to another part of town."

We drink coffee in the Latin Quarter. We sit on an open veranda. They serve espresso and water to everyone, adding liqueur for Dominique. Jean-Marie takes the baseball cap off Dominique's head and puts it on his own, backward. He looks at me:

"Foolish film, foolish director – trendy and pointless."

I look away.

"Forgive me, I didn't want to offend you."

"The saddest part is that it's true." Leclerc tears open a sugar packet and sprinkles half of it in his espresso. "You think I don't understand that Tristan and Isolde have nothing to do with it, but that there's a completely different love here? That doesn't change anything, though, because the viewer isn't planning to understand anything about your love. Either they're watching a movie about Tristan and Isolde or they're not watching anything at all."

"The viewer is stupid," says Dominique.

Jean-Marie returns the baseball cap.

"It's simply that one time refuses to understand another. And modernity won't look in history's mirror if it doesn't see its reflection." Mischievous Leclerc sprinkles the rest of the sugar in Dominique's liqueur. "Will modernity watch, Dominique?"

"Filming the story of a spiritual marriage is suicide."
Dominique tastes the liqueur and pushes it away with a sigh.
"There's all sorts of marriage now, all but that."

A group of students sits down at the next table. After
quietly conferring, they approach Leclerc for autographs.
They've read about us too; can we also give them an auto-
graph? Well, of course we can.

As he signs, Jean-Marie asks if young people will watch
a movie about a spiritual marriage. The students smile. They
know the director loves to joke. Everybody knows that.
They'll watch anything Monsieur Leclerc makes.

Jean-Marie asks them to confirm it in writing. One of
the students takes out a notebook and writes a statement
that they all sign. After reading it carefully, Leclerc folds the
paper into quarters and sticks it in the back pocket of his
jeans. He sternly says: "Good. I'll think about it."

I n the seventh year of Valdemar's presidency, five casinos and
two houses of ill repute opened in the City. The best prac-
tices from the capital spread around the whole Island with
incredible speed.

Many said:

There has never been anything like this in our land.

President Valdemar answered those people:

Perhaps you will say people have not sold their bodies? That,
perhaps, they have not gambled?

His face broke out in crimson spots from his excessive directness.

He answered:

I can't handle sanctimoniousness. Or hypocrisy either. We have
simply regulated what exists.

People took exception to that:

The fact that they're regulating – it's as if they're making it into an example for society. But sanctimoniousness has nothing to do with it.

Progress's gait was becoming more and more certain. News spread fairly quickly that people had seen Valdemar himself in dens of vice. He initially denied his presence there but so many people had seen him that it became pointless to deny the obvious. He announced that he had visited those sorrowful places for inspection purposes, but when the extraordinary detail of that inspection was clarified, there was nothing to deny.

Valdemar was summoned to the Mainland, where he had an awkward discussion with his father-in-law. Gossips said that after the conversation, all the president's urge for communication with women (not to mention gambling) had vanished and only his passion for money remained.

Unlike her father, Cecilia, Valdemar's wife, did not react so grievously to what happened. She had already tired of her husband's tricks by that time and found solace in horseback riding lessons. Dealing with horses and, to an even greater extent, with Sozont, the riding instructor, had a salutary effect on her. Everyone noticed Cecilia's newly rosy cheeks as well as her general physical vivacity.

It was soon revealed that the president's wife was in the family way. Valdemar, who had not returned to the marital bed after the meeting with his father-in-law, suspected infidelity. Finally, overwhelmed with doubt, he timidly asked Cecilia if her pregnancy was connected with her horseback riding lessons and, if so, who sired the child.

Cecilia's answer was brief and crude:

The horse, dearest. Does that explanation suit you?

The explanation did not suit Valdemar but he did not let that show. Cecilia's answer had been uttered in a loud voice, meaning that Valdemar as well as many others in the Palace heard it. The entire country was discussing it the next day. Little by little, the Island community began to believe that the president's wife was carrying a centaur. That, however, was not subsequently confirmed.

Once the requisite time had passed, Cecilia gave birth to a sturdy male-gendered baby with puffy cheeks. He did not look a bit like Valdemar and there was nothing equine about him either. Meanwhile, the child's resemblance to Sozont was striking. Rarely can one say that babies look like someone but that was all one could say about this baby. Per Cecilia's wish, he was named Hippolyte, meaning *freer of horses*. By that time, Cecilia herself was unbridled to a certain extent, too, and found it unnecessary to hide her affair with Sozont.

The most important personages from the North and the South attended a formal reception held in honor of the birth of the president's first child. To everyone's amazement, Varvara turned up at the reception too, arriving at the celebration accompanied by her deputy Vassa. The happy parents noticed them when Vassa pushed her way through the crowd, breaking a trail for her boss to reach the couple.

Valdemar recalled that Varvara had promised a gift. He assumed there were two possible offerings: a sharpened knife or a nine-gram bullet. Knowing Varvara, he was leaning more toward the bullet because his former comrade-in-arms was a sure shot. Gripped by those thoughts, Valdemar was surprised to find himself behind Cecilia's back.

Varvara drew closer and now Vassa no longer needed to push aside those standing in her path: the attendees gave them wide berth on their own, freeing the way to Varvara's former intended. The bellicose women took their final steps in full silence. After stopping, Varvara said this to Valdemar:

Do you remember that I promised you a gift? I set it aside until the day your first-born would make an appearance, in order to kill the three of you. I wavered between a knife and a bullet, though my heart leaned toward the bullet. But now I have come empty-handed. You're pathetic and your life's pathetic. And your best punishment is to leave you with your life, so don't expect me to rid you of it.

Who are you, wonderful unknown woman? Cecilia asked Varvara. Everyone knows my husband is pathetic, but you chose particularly poignant words.

I am his death, answered Varvara, who loathes even approaching him, which is why I'm letting him live.

Dear, I think it would be appropriate to perform a trick here, Cecilia said to Valdemar, but her husband just threw up his hands. Now it turns out you're not even capable of a trick.

Cecilia smiled at Varvara:

It really is too bad, isn't it?

Too bad but not that bad, said Varvara.

She turned around, crossed the hall at a march and then vanished out the door, along with Vassa. A sigh of disappointment carried through the hall since the attendees had counted on more.

In the tenth year of Valdemar's rule of the Island, laborers were brought in. Nobody knew their ancestry or their language or their names or their customs. All that was known was that they were undemanding and worked for very little money. Foreign companies insisted that they come because they were finding that Island residents lacked both the quality of being undemanding and the desire to work for next to nothing.

The laborers lived in barracks and ate whatever their masters brought them. This labor force provoked surprise rather than bad feelings among Island residents. These people did not interfere with Island life and they communicated only amongst themselves, in their own language. They wore identical robes that were issued to them, and to the Island residents their faces looked identical. When invited for visits, the arrivals smiled politely and pointed at their barracks, making it unclear if their hand motions meant they were forbidden to leave the barracks or that they were proposing to invite the whole barracks on the visit. People soon forgot about them.

PARFENY

Ksenia and I are feeling more and more favorably disposed toward Leclerc. We initially thought he seemed talented but superficial. That's not a reproach. It's not everyone who has a talent for depicting superficiality. He could tell of something else, but he's horribly dependent on moviegoers, sponsors, and advertising. He's connected to so many people and organizations that it's unclear what's under discussion, creativity or production. That's what I thought until the tempestuousness that spread over the set.

I don't doubt that it all started as a staging. Both the oversized bed and the young people in the robes were elements of that. Ksenia and I were the audience. Afraid of hearing a refusal, Leclerc decided to show his ideas to us rather than describing them: You'll live the life you haven't lived. Look at how it could have been. Did he really think that would attract us?

There's another possibility, though: Leclerc wasn't trying to convince us. He wanted us to change his mind.

He apparently felt the film he'd come up with didn't mesh with us.

The next day, when we were walking around at the Louvre, Jean-Marie suddenly said:

"After all, I have reached a position where I can film however I want. And nobody dares disagree with me."

He said that near the *Mona Lisa*. The director in him is undying. We, contemplating the painting, and he, standing with his back to it. He points over his shoulder.

"La Gioconda can be brought closer to our time, drawn laughing so there'd be more drive. But she's smiling. Or rather almost not smiling and that's what makes her interesting."

Leclerc returned to that conversation when we were in the car. He said he'd decided to change gears, to shift from his to ours. And for that, he needed to understand what ours was.

He said he was risking but that the risk wasn't too big: the film would just flop.

KSENIA

Jean-Marie comes to the hotel to see us after the day on the set.

He's barely inside when he announces that the film won't be anything like how he initially envisioned it. It won't just be about Parfeny and me, it will be about something much larger.

Leclerc considers the narrative about the Island a metaphor for the history of the state in general. Maybe even for world history. That thought was already hovering in his previous conversations with us, but now he's convinced of it. Even the Bible is history, in one of its dimensions, with its light and dark times.

We're sitting at a low glass table. There's a bowl of fruit on it. A pitcher of apple juice with a tight circle of stemmed glasses. Jean-Marie asks us to answer one question that's important to him.

"There's life on the Island and things I can comprehend. Political power, for example." Jean-Marie takes one of the glasses and places it in the center of the table. "Power realizes itself in history."

Another glass appears next to the first. Leclerc reaches for a third and fourth.

"The Island's history is stretched between prophet and historian. And all this," here Jean-Marie's hand hangs over all the glasses, "functions as a single system. What place do you hold in that system? I know that place is great, but where is it?"

The question isn't clear to either me or Parfeny, despite the shift of the glasses.

"You're not prophets, not historians, and haven't been in power for a long time, so who are you?" Jean-Marie returns the glasses to their original places. "The answer to that question is the key to the film. Who do you feel you are on the Island? The embodiment of history? The spirit of your people? Conservators?"

"Those who live a bit longer than usual," smiles Parfeny.

Leclerc leans back in his chair, exhausted.

"But *why* are you living so long?" he asks. "Or, maybe this: *What is the reason* you are living so long? You can't help but ask yourselves that question! You have, haven't you?"

Sad, Parfeny looks at Leclerc.

"We have."

"And what is your answer?"

"That the question needs to be addressed at a much higher level."

In the twelfth year of Valdemar's rule, reforms began on the Island. Hearing "form" in that word, the president decided to begin with uniforms. The old dark blue military uniform became green, the square toes of the coated fabric boots became rounded, buttons for military personnel began indicating the type of troops, stars on epaulets were enlarged, and headgear could remain off while saluting.

In educational institutions of a nonmilitary character, however, uniforms were changed from green to blue, the boys' belt buckles now showed the government seal, and the cut of the female students' pinafores changed significantly.

Publications allied to the government celebrated the depth and irreversibility of the reforms.

But the transformations were not limited to uniforms. It was resolved that right-lane traffic would become left-lane traffic, an issue that provoked unfeigned anxiety in Field Marshal Serapion. He warned that the reform would lead to many victims because it had been poorly planned. As a person from another way of life, he recalled a folksy saying:

It is not difficult to remove a head, it is difficult to attach it.

Unfortunately, nobody heard the saying. The country's traffic patterns were changed the day before they were announced. There hadn't been time to change road signs either, thanks to reasoning that reform should not be delayed for that sort of trifle. As Serapion had warned, there were victims.

The concluding reform introduced the post of vice president in the country. Valdemar's father-in-law had suggested the innovation, proposing his daughter, who was Valdemar's wife, be appointed to the post.

PARFENY

This evening Phillip called us in Paris. He found a good illustration for the book: Saint Jerome the Blessed. The cave. The scroll. The lion. That fresco is right over Agafon's grave.

We're talking on speakerphone.

"Over Agafon's grave?" Ksenia's surprised. "I remember that fresco; it's on the opposite wall."

Patience enters Phillip's voice. He's describing the fresco's location in detail. The left-side chapel, the church's load-bearing wall. But. Ksenia seems to think that Agafon was buried in the right-side chapel. She's convinced of that. And I think she's correct.

"Good, I'll clarify it," Phillip meekly says.

Or maybe he won't, that's how his voice sounds.

He calls back two hours later. He's excited.

"How about that, Agafon really was buried on the opposite side! They moved the burial site during the restoration of the church, under Vlas. Vlas wanted to install a sculpture of a bee in its place. Do you understand what this means?"

"I do. We were looking in the wrong resonators."

"Exactly! It's simply that at the Ministry of Culture they didn't remember about the reburial."

Of course they didn't remember. They have a lot of other things to do.

Valdemar quickly tired of reforms, and government matters generally concerned him less and less anyway. In the evenings he watched *Columbo* on TV, drinking beer in quantities that are bad for the health. In one *Columbo* show, Valdemar saw a trick with a guillotine that warranted surprise.

A magician placed his head under the blade and the blade fell without harming him. The whole trick was in the restraining assembly, which was set up, unnoticed, to prevent the blade from falling. Only the empty frame came down, while the audience thought the blade was falling. This trick was used to murder a magician. After familiarizing himself with the mechanism's action, a certain villain switched the catch and the guillotine worked according to its intended purpose.

Valdemar ordered that this same sort of guillotine be prepared for him and then rehearsed relentlessly so he could perform the trick at the Island Day celebration.

Valdemar, however, was not the only one who watched *Columbo*. As was later determined, the guillotine's catch mechanism was taken off the "safety" position just before Valdemar's performance, so the president lost his head before the eyes of his celebrating countrymen. The head rolled along the scaffold and Cecilia stopped it with a refined soccer move.

The next day the Constitutional Court met and announced that in the event that the president is unable to fulfill his duties, those duties, by law, were entrusted to the vice president. It was up to the Constitutional Court to establish that inability.

Photographs of the previous day's event appeared on a large screen, across which the chief justice drew a pointer. Recalling Serapion's gloomy saying, the judge noted that it was actually impossible to affix the president's head to his body. At the same time, it was equally out of the question that presidential duties could be fulfilled headless. Those considerations led the judge to the conclusion that Valdemar needed to leave his position and transfer his authority to the vice president. The judge wrapped up by allowing himself to joke, saying that power, like Valdemar's head, had fallen at Cecilia's feet.

Cecilia joked, too, after sensing that a relaxed, almost friendly atmosphere had arisen. She announced that her deceased husband had actually lost his head long ago, though that had not prevented him from ruling the country.

However, said Cecilia, if you insist, I am prepared to accept power.

The judge insisted. He reminded those present that new presidential elections should be held in the country within the next year. To avoid a power vacuum, Cecilia should immediately take office and work on preparations for elections. Agreeing that there is nothing worse than a vacuum, Cecilia accepted presidential power.

PARFENY

Phillip calls at around three in the morning. They found the prophecy. Just where it was supposed to be, in one of the resonators over Agafon's initial burial spot. Phillip exhales and apologizes for waking us up. Why apologize?

I shout:

"What does it say?"

Phillip starts reading but stumbles. I ask him to photograph the text and send it to my phone. Five minutes later we have the prophecy.

The text turns out to be very short. The paper is profoundly deteriorated but with effort, what's written can be made out. The handwriting is definitely Prokopy's. There's no doubt at all that this is Agafon's prophecy. I don't know how many times Ksenia and I read it. Fifty? A hundred? We discuss each word. We understand all the words. The same cannot be said for the prophecy as a whole. Here it is, in full:

Agafon the Forward-Looking's prophecy for times to come

I, unworthy Agafon, address my words to our descendants. I am speaking about the coming and, perhaps, final times of our Island in the hope that these words of mine will make their appearance opportunely.

You will open up to the world and that will be for the good. But it has been said that there is a time to embrace, and a time to refrain from embracing. Days will arrive when ailments will seize you and good will turn to harm, for you will not rid yourself of your own ailments but rather acquire unknown ones.

And strangers will inundate the Island. You shall reside among them, as a crow upon ruins. Your woe, however, will not be in the strangers but in you yourself.

For depravity will multiply and you will become embittered and begin to crowd one another. And a great hostility will flare up between you, so brother will strike brother and son will strike father.

The earth, which is sensitive to the bitterness of people, will itself become embittered.

262

A trying hour will come, when a stone will appear that can be softened only with the blood of the goat.

And the ground will shake and black water will ignite in the North and a fiery water will begin to flow in the South.

And ash will float from the heavens and your hearts will turn to ash.

And you will be unable to pray to the Lord for salvation for He will turn His face from you.

And if three righteous people are not found among you, to climb the Mountain and speak with Him, your life will remain in smoke and darkness.

Chapter the Twenty-Second

CECILIA

In the year of Cecilia's reign, the Island prepared for elections. This was the country's second election, so Island residents had already gained some experience. Experience hinted to them that elections undoubtedly influenced the flow of life but then the influence had its limits. More specifically, elections determine the name of the president rather than the president's decisions. The shrewdest citizens even expressed their conjecture that the victor in a presidential election does just as any other candidate would do upon winning. Someone recalled unforgettable Bishop Geronty's story about the crow and the cheese, but that recollection was deemed inappropriate and even dangerous.

Fulfilling presidential duties changed little in Cecilia's life. She still went horseback riding and spent her free time with Sozont, considering all her time to be free time. People her father sent to the Island worked on election preparations. They acquired Cecilia's signature on various papers when necessary, not burdening her with too many details or explanations. Only once did she ask who would be president. Upon hearing that it would most likely be Sozont, Cecilia clapped her hands and asked no further.

It upset her a little that Sozont now frequently went to events with voters, diverting him from their horseback riding together. Cecilia was told, though, that the trips were only temporary and the previous calm would return to their life after Sozont became president.

It should be noted that the trips did not gladden Sozont himself in the beginning since he was nervous about public speaking.

He was a man of few words and in his previous life he conversed primarily with horses. His vocabulary was not large, for a horse's vocabulary is small: they know only basic commands. Commands are important for fulfilling presidential duties, so staff sent from the Mainland considered Sozont redeemable. Matters gradually took a turn for the better and he became talkative.

Sozont turned out to have a good memory, so he easily memorized election speeches as well as answers to frequent questions. His aides who attended the events were always able to help him out; this happened when questions touched on details. In those situations, he held out a hand, as if calming a horse, and said that his aides knew those matters better. It was obvious to everyone that this was a person able to think big. In the eyes of the electorate, his stately lack of knowledge about trifling matters elevated him above humdrum life.

PARFENY

We went to the set today. They were filming an episode about how Prince Averky, Ksenia's uncle, attempted to give me a different wife. Scenery for the church, glimmer of candles, air teeming with tension. I liked the uncle very much: an inspired schemer. Unalloyed evil. He wants to put his own daughter on the throne instead of Ksenia. And he calls himself an uncle . . .

The actor playing me is good too: nervous (sweat on his forehead), prepared for decisive actions. His finger motions, beckoning to the head guard. Barely a motion. He's not even beckoning: the head guard is next to him after just the flash of an idea. The uncle is to be seized at the exit. The daughter could be taken too; that's a safer approach.

The camera glides along the church walls. The miracle of Saint George and the dragon. George. Dragon. A close up of Averky, the dragon.

Everything was resolved without the guards' interference; it could not help but be resolved. Through the strength of the love between Ksenia and me.

It was in those days that Sozont and Cecilia's wedding ceremony took place. The wedding was notable for its opulence and large invitation list. The same people working on the groom's election campaign planned the wedding. The carriage for the young people was drawn by twelve white horses that the planners thought symbolized chastity and the marrying couple's devotion to family values.

Horses were provided to the guests too, producing a certain confusion in their ranks since not everyone knew how to ride. Sozont and Cecilia wanted to offer the attendees the joy of horseback riding, but that joy turned to woe for many. With many people present, the lumbering and unwieldy guests unsuccessfully attempted to clamber up on their mounts. Observers quickly surrounded them. Those standing to the left of a horse lifted riders and placed their feet in the stirrups as those standing to the right took them by the arms and pulled them into the saddle. To general laughter, those who clambered up were called *those saddled* by wedding rituals. Now that they were on the horses, the riders participated in the wedding procession with tense faces. Those faces remained the same as they kept sliding to the ground.

The wedding ceremony exceeded all its precursors in terms of equine participants and was immediately dubbed The Horse Wedding.

KSENIA

Parfeny and I couldn't close our eyes again the night they found the prophecy. What had been considered lost for several centuries had now been shown to the world. We read it again and again but just could not stop.

Agafon hoped the prophecy would become known at an opportune time. He was a person whose hope was firmer than hard knowledge. From that it follows that the information is addressed to us as we are now and everything stated in the prophecy should come true in the foreseeable future.

We are frightened.

Paris's morning newspapers come out with a statement about the prophecy. They give one line but promise that details will follow. People in Paris have a vague notion of the Island, but everybody knows about the prophecy. A lot has been written about it: everybody here loves historical mysteries.

Almost every newspaper mentions that Parfeny and I are in Paris and that we will doubtless clarify the situation. The hotel director calls us and announces that a crowd of journalists has already gathered in the lobby. What are our wishes?

Our wishes are to not see anyone. We are not yet in a position to comment. The director promises to station security by our room.

Jean-Marie arrives an hour later. We ask that he be allowed to visit us. Jean-Marie is worked up. Never before has a future film had such advertising.

"I already read the prophecy in French," he says, "but I didn't understand everything. Maybe there's something peculiar in the translation?"

"Those are the peculiarities of the original," says Parfeny.

In fact, the prophecy is clear to Parfeny and me, at least almost clear. We call what we don't want to believe unclear. We think that if we interpret it line by line everything will come true. We explain this honestly to Jean-Marie. He nods. He will attempt to understand everything on his own. He stands and says goodbye.

"A conversation with Him, that's an attempt to justify the Island, isn't it?" Leclerc stands. "If you don't mind, I'll make that conversation the final scene."

Parfeny looks attentively at the director.

"Yes, that scene really could become the final scene."

Leclerc turns around when he's in the doorway:

"I'd say you are the justification of the Island."

He disappears.

Just as in the previous election, ships with portraits – of Sozont – reached the Island. The portraits underscored the candidate's industriousness, his boundless honesty, and his boundless love for children and horses.

This time there were no photos taken at the theater and library, although horses were a presence in multiple guises: they leaped over obstacles with the candidate on their backs, he led horses by the bridle, and they even stood on their hind legs, aspiring in vain to fling the powerful rider. Photographs of the rider on a rearing horse as he stands in the stirrups with a hand stretched forward seemed to depict not a riding teacher but the statue of an emperor, for all emperors galloped just like that and the horses under them preferred to get around on two legs. The forward-stretched hand promised the pacification of not just the horse but also everyone whose abuses stood in the way of progress.

With all the differences in the candidates and their highly diverse abilities, nobody could compare with Sozont's ability to sit on a horse. Sozont's proud bearing, hewn profile, and innate terseness quickly gained him love among the people.

Sozont's aides from the Continent initially made him memorize long speeches, but once they realized his strength was in his terseness, they began writing his addresses in short, punchy phrases similar to commands at the riding arena.

Having grown up in a peasant family, Sozont attracted primarily the peasantry, a significant majority of the Island population. When that became obvious, they began pasting up photographs of Sozont wearing peasant shirts and blacked boots. He patted horses on the withers, harnessed them to carts laden with hay, and sometimes simply conversed with them, kindly and soulfully.

His envious rivals said that a horse could be elected president with the same success, but even that didn't scare off the voters. They recalled how the Lord of the Bees led the country in days of old and now found that Vlas's time in power had not been the very worst. By election day it was already obvious that Sozont would be the Island's next president.

And Sozont became president.

KSENIA

Jean-Marie asked: "What was it like living with your aunt in the house on the coast?"

I answer: "It was a spacious stone house: there were stone quarries in those parts of the Island. That's why houses still stand on the coast, while many parts of the city, which is primarily wooden, have not remained intact."

In the winter I loved going to the scullery and watching the cook, bright red from the fire, prepare lunch for us. I remember her pudgy arms, bared to the elbows. The cook herself was immense and her body filled the entire small scullery. The floorboards where she always stood sagged, she could reach anything from there. Only her arms animated her motionlessness.

I would sit on a small bench with my back leaning against the stove. Sometimes I fell asleep there but woke up in my own room – those arms of hers had carried me there.

Auntie Klavdia loved the cook. She was no longer fragile then, my aunt, and it's possible she liked that she and the cook were of similar proportions. People value a reflection of themselves in others more than anything else.

Of course there were thin servants moving about the house in great numbers. The motions of the thin are bustling, unconvincing, and often goalless. Auntie Klavdia knew that if the cook was headed somewhere there must be weighty reasons for it. Other menials scurried around the house, moving things from place to place. I do not exclude the possibility that the moving about of those in motion was not always meaningful, despite always being benevolent.

When walking past, those people would tousle my hair or crouch and talk with me about something. Sometimes they treated me to sweets. They called me Your Royal Brightest Highness. If I seemed to think that *Brightest* corresponded to my appearance, then *Highness* made my cheeks turn red. Addressing me that way felt like an advance: I wanted very much to be high in terms of height.

I saw Parfeny as being the same height as me in the future. In my childhood fantasies, we stood like two thin trees reaching out to one another. Foreheads touching, hands interwoven. Between us was Auntie Klavdia, small and fat. Located in that arched composition, she would turn to either me or Parfeny, reminding us of a pot on a potter's wheel. We would look each other in the eye, as if we had forgotten about Klavdia.

Parfeny was brought to Auntie's house in the summer. What is now a beach was then a deserted sandy space. Through present-day lounge chairs and beach canopies I see the shore of that time, along with us, going for a walk. We build our sandcastles where the waves no longer roll in; all our castles were somewhat reminiscent of the royal palace. The wave's border is agile and the elements finally destroy the castles. They stand for a time as smoothed sandy ruins but then those disappear too.

There are many sandcastles now. And many builders: they're bent (a fragile line of vertebrae) over their structures, crouched in front of them and then, still crouched, they circle them like ducks. After six in the evening, though, it's deserted again here. The beach is a temporary phenomenon in all senses.

In the evenings we sit in a gazebo overgrown with grape vines. We drink warm milk with honey, listening to the nannies' leisurely storytelling. Their stories are endless and continue one another. And thus we sit, holding hands and, destined for one another, experiencing happiness. We already knew then that this was happiness. For some reason we suspected that we would never again experience it with such completeness.

SOZONT

The first year of Sozont's rule fell in the Year of the Horse according to the Chinese zodiac. Nobody on the Island had previously known about the Chinese Zodiac. Knowing Sozont, however, everyone understood that this year could not have been any other animal's year.

The president decided to mark this calendar occurrence on an unprecedented scale, establishing International Equine Games that called for gathering every living horseback rider on the planet. Or at least a significant portion of them. All the Island's financial resources and human energies were thrown into preparations for the event. Numerous horse arenas were constructed on the Island and a huge hippodrome was erected in the capital in short order.

Despite round-the-clock work, it was obvious from the very start that it would not be possible to hold the games during the Year of the Horse. A presidential ukase later announced that the next decade would be known as the Decade of the Horse. From then on, all that held the builders back was the president's impatience, which was mighty.

Sozont began his mornings by touring building sites and the production facilities associated with them. He did the same for the entire rest of the day. Anything related to horses brought him immense joy. He saw the presence of horses in everything and his inquisitive mind even divined them in unobvious things.

And so, during a visit to a concrete products factory that supplied building materials, Sozont's gaze fell upon Firs, an aged accountant. Firs was bowlegged and not very tall. The president interrupted the factory director's speech and then approached the accountant to ask:

You a cavalry man?

Firs, who was a bit blind, straightened his worn oversleeves and answered:

Yes, sir.

And he clicked his heels.

Muffled laughter could be heard from the back rows. Everyone knew that this person had tried many occupations at various times, even serving as an expeditor of eau de vie. In his spare time he was keen on card games and forged bond certificates. The cavalry was probably Firs's only untrodden path.

The president was extraordinarily satisfied after his brief interaction with Firs and mentioned that *The cavalry should play a leading role in the manufacture of concrete products.* According to old Island tradition, that remark from the president was posted over the factory gates that same day.

A week later, the accountant was invited to the Presidential Palace, where he was awarded the Order of Island Valor and allocated a personal pension. After getting tipsy at the ceremonial banquet, the honoree suddenly began speaking about the peculiarities of transporting eau de vie by rail. Small openings, he said, were drilled in oak barrels and the eau de vie was siphoned out through a straw. The openings were later plugged with woodchips and smeared with clay. The barrels were generously doused in water at stations, making them swell and weigh more. That procedure allowed them to deliver the product at its initial weight.

The story came as such a surprise to the ceremony's guests that their faces gradually began dropping. Fortunately for the awardee, Sozont was absorbed in conversation when the tale was told. Once that conversation had finished, the president asked Firs if he had any personal requests. The honoree, who had managed to sober up a bit by that time, asked to institute horse escorts for shipments of liquor and spirits. The request was rapidly approved.

In the fourth year of Sozont's rule of the Island, the International Equine Games took place. Fifty thousand riders from all corners of the world gathered and displayed their art to audiences for ten days. An announcement was made at the closing ceremony stating that any of the fifty thousand participants who wished could rightfully stay on the Island. They would receive a worthy allowance in monetary form as well as feed.

The Games' participants came primarily from places lacking both money and feed so all fifty thousand agreed to stay; oddly, when entering the names, the number grew to seventy thousand. A detachment of *rapid-deployment cavalrymen* was formed from some of those individuals.

Soon after, however, the detachment ran into difficulties with the local population. This was due to the fact that the cavalrymen had not been told precisely what, exactly, they were supposed to react to. Their reactions to residents, particularly the women, caused dissatisfaction on the Island. Many residents demanded harsh measures for the cavalrymen.

I, a sinning man, fear that this will lead to nothing good. The suppression of someone who lives in the same place as you is destructive most of all for those who do the suppressing because it destroys them too. According to an Island saying, when fighting with a dragon, you yourself become a dragon. Others can ask: How does one avoid this?

I have no answer to that question. Perhaps one cannot.

What causes peoples to move? What was the reason for the migration period of the fourth through seventh centuries? A search for living space? An unaccountable urge for motion? Curiosity?

Alexander the Great and his troops reached India *wishing to see the edge of the earth,* but that explanation has always felt unconvincing to me. These days, becoming like Ecclesiastes, I shall propose that there is a time to remain on one's own soil and there is a time to go to another's. To ours, for example.

PARFENY

Jean-Marie wants to learn more about the nature of Ksenia's and my relationship.

"What," I ask, "can relations be like between parts of the same whole?"

It's hard for Leclerc to imagine how much two people can become intertwined over three hundred years. That can even happen in less time. We think alike, react alike. If need be, we answer letters for one another because there aren't any situations we haven't gone through together. And there generally aren't any situations we haven't gone through.

Married couples only have differing childhoods, but that's not the case for us. Destined by events to unite our unfortunate land, we even spent our childhood in close communication. And those rare moments when we were apart have long been known to us from the stories we tell each other.

We don't just think alike, we feel alike. I think that if, contrary to our dream, one of us departs sooner, the one who remains will serve as eyes and ears for the other, so the departed can still see a warm summer day and the pensive swaying of grass from a residence beyond the clouds.

In the fifth year of Sozont's presidency, seismologists from the Mainland came to our country. After studying the Mountain in the Island's South, they declared that the volcano could awaken. The seismologists appealed to residents of the villages surrounding the Mountain, calling upon them to find other places to live, to the extent practicable. Of course that was not practicable for the residents.

The seismologists made their statement at dawn, when they left the Mountain, meaning the neighboring residents did not respond in the necessary way to the news about the awakening volcano – they themselves had only just awakened. In essence, there was nothing new in what the seismologists said, since warnings of the sort had been conveyed before on the Island. And so the seismologists left, heading in an easterly direction for further research.

A certain vagueness sprang up with regard to the seismologists. Some said they'd seen them in the eastern part of the Island, an area of deserted plains that's far from seismological threats. Others maintained the visitors weren't seismologists at all but rather geologists and that their visit to the Mountain was only a cover for some other sorts of goals. Since nobody could name those goals, the accusation was considered unproven and the seismologists were forgotten.

In the sixth year of Sozont's rule, Brand, the chairman of the Mainland Oil Company, bought from the Island government those same lands where the seismologists had allegedly been spotted. The lands were purchased for a song and when the buyer was asked why he wanted that desert, he answered that he was seeking seclusion. And although Brand had not previously revealed any inclination toward seclusion, the answer provoked respect.

Brand began receiving numerous letters of support. Pious people turned up and expressed their readiness to found their own isolated hermitages within the bounds of Brother Brand's daily perambulations from his hermitage. On one hand, that would have supported the anchorite, but on the other, it would not have broken the seclusion he sought, given the remoteness of the new hermitages. There were also people who proposed helping the hermit build a church, since even a recluse needs confession and communion.

It turned out, however, that the reclusive new arrival needed nothing of the sort. His isolated hermitage ended up being a complex of contemporary structures intended for mining and cutting diamonds. And it was not Brand who toiled there but numerous diamond mine workers.

The land purchase – and more important, its underlying rationale – became a serious mistake for Brand and Sozont if, of course, one considers that Sozont was part of the decision-making. For some reason it particularly stung Island residents that Brand turned out not to aspire to seclusion. Perhaps that is because any island is seclusion and in those sorts of places, people receive Brand's sort of explanation with particular sympathy.

Brand was genuinely concerned, because another presidential election was supposed to take place on the Island in another year. He attempted to declare that his remark about the life of a hermit was a joke, but that only aggravated the situation, since people on the Island did not joke about such matters. Sozont explained nothing and his terseness reached unprecedented levels.

The presidential campaign began on schedule. Varvara unexpectedly became Sozont's primary rival. The external enemy she saw in the foreign companies seemed far more dangerous than those she called *northern neighbors*. The change that had taken place in Varvara surprised both the North and the South. Varvara's charisma was so great, however, that she was quickly able to win everyone over.

When ships loaded with portraits of the main candidate reached the Island yet again, they were not allowed to dock. And although the vessels eventually docked after long negotiations, Sozont won nothing from the situation: all his portraits ended up in the hands of Varvara's supporters. The portraits appeared in very visible spots, as planned, but the sight of them gave Sozont no joy, since they had been reworked into a variety of collages.

And so, the candidate himself was cut out of all the horsy images and his head had been attached to where the horse's head should be. Sozont's head actually took on a slightly equine appearance when attached to a horse's withers. The thick mane, powerful jaws, and, most important, large teeth bared in a smile, left no doubts regarding the candidate's true ancestry.

A portrait depicting Sozont as a horse with Brand sitting on him as a rider attracted the most attention. The effect of the visual propaganda intensified because Varvara called her rival none other than *that stud*.

Varvara's speeches were notable thanks to her rich imagery, vivid similes, and a fullness of feeling that Sozont lacked. People looked forward to her appearances, and each one became an event that was later discussed for a long time.

Varvara's primary passion was now extractable resources rather than independence for the South. She urged ridding the Island of the domination of foreign companies and their leaders and workers. When promising to return the depths of the earth to those they belonged to – the people – she did not forget about Brand and his inclination for solitude, something Varvara said lay ahead for him, in a prison cell.

Sozont and Cecilia did not wait around for results after voting on election day. Seeing nothing good for themselves, they used the final day of Sozont's presidency to leave the Island unimpeded, for they did not aspire to the solitude Varvara promised.

When the presidential plane began gaining altitude, Sozont spoke to his fellow citizens in a live broadcast. Since he had not seen the text of the address until it was given to him on the airplane, Sozont had no chance to memorize it and so he read it from a paper.

Things went awry for him from the very first sentence. After assessing the battle for the presidential post as having very *high stakes*, Sozont announced that he had not lost. Unfamiliar with the text, he then read the words incorrectly – and absolutely clearly – as *hot steaks*. The burst of laughter on earth was so deafening that its echo reached the airplane and forced Sozont to correct himself. When he explained that his departure from the Island was a necessary measure, the echo of a second burst reached him. This time they laughed over the correction.

When referring to the *bitter bread of banishment*, a cart with lunch rolled into the picture. It was rolled right back out and braked but Sozont's fellow citizens' hungry eyes had seen all. A dish of black caviar adorned the foreground, and clusters of grapes hung picturesquely on a beheaded pineapple. The rest was hidden away in silver salad dishes and covered platters. Perhaps one of them contained the steak he mentioned.

The remainder of the text explained the cart's appearance to some extent: Sozont promised to take care of himself until such time as his return was required. That, however, could not fully correct the vexing blunder, leaving an unpleasant taste in everyone's mouth.

In conclusion, there was a mysterious and audible call to *Walk away from the tail side*. That statement was a stage direction to Sozont that (according to the director's notions) Sozont should stand and walk off, leaving his seat empty. The statement became popular and was used eagerly on the Island for highly varied occasions, since the text itself allowed that.

Sozont was already far away by the time all the votes had been counted. He was in Brazil, in the state of Minas Gerais, where the couple had already bought a horse farm. Sozont was calm and joyful with the horses, and he realized he had found his purpose in life. And he was surprised that his path to that goal had been so winding.

Based on the election results, Varvara was declared president of the Island.

VARVARA

I n the first year of Varvara's rule, during the first day of her rule, she received a call from Brand, and that was her first call too. Brand congratulated the president on taking office and said he hoped to continue his collaborative work with the Island. As Varvara later told newspapers, her response to Brand was this:

Our collaboration can only consist of one thing: you return extractable resources to the Island's people.

Brand proposed that Varvara think a bit and find a resolution under which there would be enough room on the Island for both of them. When Varvara responded that unfortunately there was only one Island, and there was no place for him on that Island, Brand said:

That means we will have two Islands.

Not a week passed before it became known that Varvara's long-time assistant Vassa had accused her, Varvara, of neglecting the South's interests.

The blow was doubly painful. Varvara had been betrayed by a person she had trusted as much as herself. It was also significant that the majority of residents in the South supported Vassa, although Varvara had been certain the South was fully on her side.

The new president's first decree declared that all the Island's extractable resources were government property. It also directed that the Mainland Oil Company hand over the reins to the country's government as soon as possible and leave the Island.

The company truly did leave the Island, but only the northern part. The company had no plans to leave the southern part and continued mining its diamond deposits. Diamonds had not been the company's primary mining objective, but since the seismologists who turned out to be geologists had stumbled on the diamonds, the company did not consider neglecting them either. After Vassa's decree, it became clear that it would not be very easy to dislodge Brand from the Island's South.

PARFENY

A branch sways under a strange bird. A squirrel goes still in its flight from tree to tree. Children in burdock hats step on soft moss. There's duskiness among the dense trees, but it's sunny in a clearing. Warmth replaces coolness. The trail-blazers' tread is cautious, senses are keen. A little girl picks a dandelion and blows at its gray cap. White sap flows from its stem. Invisible threads tickle the face. The forest thins.

Plantains line the road. The nearing clop of hoofs blends with dust. The horse is dappled. In the boy's hand is an apple. He bites, crunching. He holds out the apple to the little girl:

"Want some?"

She bites too.

The apple is large and they eat it for a long time. Maybe for a hundred years. White has turned brown where they first bit.

The children pick up their pace. Fast-moving wanderers, they walk along a narrow strip between two ruts. Fervid pilgrims, they hurry to an invisible goal, not knowing that the land is like an apple, that if you walk a long time on the road, a very long time, you'll return to your previous location. Which will not be the same because you'll no longer find anyone there.

Jean-Marie is quickly noting down what he heard, even drawing something: deep ruts in the road, trees on both sides. A few strokes and Ksenia and I appear . . . It turns out he draws fairly well.

"An excellent sequence," says Jean-Marie. "I need small scenes for all seasons; I still don't know what will go in during editing. Do you have any other recollections left?"

Recollections remained. Recollections are all that remain for old people.

In the second year of Varvara's rule, she sent an ultimatum to Vassa. Varvara demanded that Vassa recognize the supremacy of the Island's governmental powers and fulfill its orders. She reminded her that the primary demand at present was to turn the diamond mines over to the government. Varvara promised to take appropriate measures if the orders from the capital were not fulfilled. The missive was brief and stern, as an ultimatum should be.

Vassa's answer was even briefer but more mocking than stern. It contained no greeting or signature. It said that the South's government would decide on its own how to handle the diamond mines. In response to Varvara's threats, Vassa only contemptuously wondered: *Or what will happen?*

Only after receiving Vassa's response did Varvara realize the full complexity of the position she had found herself in. It had become clear to her that she had lifted her hand but lacked the opportunity to strike. That she had no actual possibility whatsoever of forcing Vassa to submit. The Island's army was in a sorry state and it was common knowledge that Vassa was mustering militiamen in the South. The militia, which initially seemed to be a figment of Vassa's imagination, had grown with extraordinary speed because rigid ideas have the property of capturing minds. Varvara had obviously underestimated Vassa's charisma.

The ultimatum did not just reveal Varvara's weakness. It became the first of many regrettable events. Even if one supposes that those events would certainly have happened one way or another, one must admit that the ultimatum hastened them.

And so, as if by command, newspapers on the Continent began expressing doubt about how democratic Island life was. People had begun accusing Varvara of preferring to speak the language of ultimatums. The expropriation of private property for the benefit of the government was acknowledged as undemocratic too. *Predatory expropriation*, wrote the newspapers, as if they were publishing carbon copies.

After that, a series of articles and television programs appeared on the Mainland, glorifying specific qualities of southerners: peaceableness, industriousness, thirst for knowledge, and a lack of desire to come to terms with the northerners' centuries-old yoke. By dint of a natural anomaly, the northerners ended up bellicose, lazy, lacking the desire to learn, and feeling an irrepressible passion for enslaving those similar to them. Having learned of the existence of such varying peoples on one island, the Continent did not tire of its amazement at that natural phenomenon.

A speech by a certain Philon, a ufologist from the Island's southern shore, was a real bombshell. Since his early childhood, Philon had been devoted to observing aliens who traveled from the Southern Fish constellation and frequently landed near his native village. After noticing the inquisitive lad, the extraterrestrials quickly found common ground with Philon, befriended him, and occasionally took him for rides on unidentified flying objects.

They told Philon that in the Southern Fish constellation there had long been an interest in the southern part of the Island and that some Southern Fish residents had even dreamt of establishing ties between their two regions. The South attracted the guests with an ancient civilization unlike any other, luxuriant cuisine, and folk arts. In the latter category it was riddles reflecting the paradoxicality of southerners' thinking that made the largest impression.

Philon immediately responded to the extraterrestrials with a riddle: *What bites by day and swims by night?* Try though they might, the extraterrestrials could not solve the riddle. When Philon told them the answer, they were struck by its simplicity: *dentures*. In answer to their question about where that amazing device had been invented, the young ufologist answered that of course that happened in the Island's South. How else, he asked, could everyone in these parts have dentures?

Philon also acquainted his two-headed visitors with Chairman Kasyan's catchphrases, which he'd known by heart since he was a child, though he passed them off as his own. The extraterrestrials applauded him with all six hands, though they admitted two heads were not enough to understand those phrases.

In a moment of candor, they admitted to Philon that they had directed two beams at the Island back in the day: one was positive, aimed at the South, the other, accordingly, was negative, aimed at the North. This was the moment when the origin of sublime civilization in the South and its utter absence in the North became clear to Philon. He explained away his many years of silence about these important things by mentioning his extended stay in the Southern Fish constellation.

Information about the irradiation spread through the world news agencies within a day, and it became clear to all that northerners themselves were not to blame for being so unattractive. A day later, however, the cosmic theme had disappeared from news roundups just as suddenly as it had appeared.

Roughly a month later, a brief item came through news agency feeds saying that it turned out that Philon had never been to the Southern Fish constellation and had spent all those past years institutionalized.

Meanwhile, publications shifted to discussing what could be done about the situation that had arisen. People of goodwill answered: help the South. Shuddering from the unexpected suggestion, the press asked in dismay: But how? And then, the cold word *weapons* was heard for the first time. People of goodwill uttered it not without regret.

KSENIA

It's dark: darkness falls early in autumn. It's still warm and we eat supper in the yard at Auntie Klavdia's house. There are oil lamps on the long oak table. With no wind, the flame is strong and even. Anticipating Caravaggio, it draws eyes, cheekbones, and hands out of the darkness. A quiet conversation flows between the adults, making us feel calm and even a bit sleepy.

We don't want to go inside and the servants bring us cloaks. We're sitting next to each other, listening to words that float, unhurried, from lips, without combining.

"The sea is choppy."

"They say it is much colder now on the mainland."

"You should drink ground onyx when you have a stomachache. And of course you really must pray."

On their own, the words are familiar, but the meaning of the speech slips from us, melting in the darkness like the smoke from the wick.

We feel someone's strong arms carrying us off into the house.

Morning. Jean-Marie asks us to tell about an autumn morning. Preferably on that same road we walked during the summer.

The air is sharp and spicy. We are walking behind a cart. The leaves are yellow. Some of them are no longer even leaves but only joined threads. The wheels in front of us turn, pressing the leaves into the damp ruts. Some leaves that are stuck to the rim rise to the wheels' full height before again falling to the ground. Ferris wheels. They squeak and move unevenly, following the slow striding of the horses, as if they really were inseparable. They move, seemingly apart from one another, but they are in fact inseparable.

We sit in the cart and merge into that general rhythm. Our legs bob to the right and to the left. There is soft hay beneath us. Ahead of us is a route that keeps going and going. Our trip is farewell and sorrow because when moving forward, one must turn around and say farewells and feel sorrow.

After sustaining a loss in the international arena, Varvara set her sights on local Island life. She craved a quick victory that could divert the spotlight away from failures on the domestic front. Varvara announced that she would restore order with an *iron hand*. She wanted to use that exact expression and so she did.

Varvara's iron hand came down on the heads of foreigners. She declared that their unrestricted presence was a time bomb that would explode years later and transform the Island. The ruler pointed out that a foreign workforce is, first and foremost, a *force* that should not be underestimated. That force did not wish to *integrate* and so another people was developing alongside the Island's people.

These people are already restless now, said Varvara, and that restlessness will only grow in the future.

The head of state forbade inviting workers from overseas, a measure that provoked a sympathetic reaction from Island residents. Varvara did not stop there, however, and issued an order to begin deporting foreigners from the Island. Since those people had no-where to go, they became embittered and then moved on to muted opposition. The police captured them on the streets, but the police's powers turned out to be insufficient and so the army was brought into play.

Quite a number of Island residents also pitched in as volunteers to catch the visitors. The foreigners who remained at large began taking Island residents hostage, demanding that those captured be released. Varvara called on her fellow citizens to be patient, saying that it was better to nip evil in the bud than to experience an all-out war as a consequence.

What was happening looked more and more like war with every passing day. A true battle took place when army units attempted to disarm the seventy thousandth detachment of the *rapid-deployment cavalry* that Sozont founded. It could not be disarmed and the detachment had not reacted to any government orders. The detach-ment rushed through the entire country, from North to South, at a Spanish trot before dividing into small groups and dispersing around the Island like spilled mercury. Some cavalrymen earned their living by helping in peasant enterprises, although others found monetary satisfaction and feed through less onerous methods.

Their Royal Highnesses Parfeny and Ksenia were visiting Paris in those days. They appealed to Varvara in an open letter, warning that the path she had chosen was increasing hatred and leading to catastrophe. In the letter they said that actions like those liberate the worst that is inside people. Recognizing that the unlimited entry of workers had been an obvious mistake, they cautioned the president against new mistakes. Changes, wrote Their Highnesses, should touch on general rules, not on the fates of people.

There was also discussion in the royals' letter of prohibiting foreign manufacturing. In Ksenia and Parfeny's opinion, the first order of business was to sort through what manufacturing served the Island's interests and what did not – only then could a decision be made. The letter asserted that the truth never lies at extremes and correcting harsh decisions with other harsh decisions would not lead to harmony.

Varvara flew into a rage after reading the letter. She accused the royal couple of being from the fifth column and of deserting the Island too. The president regarded Parfeny and Ksenia's visit to Paris as fleeing to a country with which the Island was at war.

Varvara's statements were quickly circulated by the Island's newspapers and television, and since the media outlets feared the cavalrymen would *react*, they went to war with the elderly couple. Acting as a discordant choir, they sent maledictions to Parfeny and Ksenia, publishing more new revelations of their traitorous activity each day.

And so, after rummaging around in binders of old newspapers, reporters showed the world both the ancient accusation that the royal couple had embezzled from the State Treasury and the accusation that Parfeny had defiled the underage Lukeria. The Island police responded to that news readily because they had doubts about the age-old conclusion regarding Lukeria's intact virginity.

By that time, Parfeny's supposed victim had long been resting in the city cemetery. Despite the protests of her son Sysoy, Lukeria's body was extracted from the ground. Nothing in her disrupted dust pointed to the presence or absence of virginity and Lukeria was again laid to rest.

Even so, the matter was sent to court, where it became one of the most notorious cases in recent years. Sysoy declared in court that the question troubling the investigation regarding his mother's virginity could have been resolved without experts' examinations. The answer was Sysoy himself, in the flesh. Sysoy called himself the fruit of a happy marriage entered into by Lukeria and a person of like mindset, five years after the events had been investigated. During his court appearance, Sysoy also cited his mother's statement regarding the essence of her relationship with Parfeny: *I have never seen him.*

In announcing the acquittal, the press emphasized the cunning of the prince, who had done all he could to cover his tracks and destroy the accusation that had been leveled against him. An embezzlement investigation had also been brought against Parfeny and Ksenia by the Island police but, sensibly, it was not brought to trial after the defilement case.

The detailed discussion of royal matters stirred up the Island's citizens. The Internet was filled with profanities whose point consisted of the majority of the population having felt for a long time that something wasn't right: Parfeny and Ksenia seemed too righteous. The most common of the printable expressions turned out to be *demons hide in quiet places* and *wolves in sheep's clothing*, as well as several other examples of folk wisdom. Parfeny and Ksenia's life was described by Internet users as an unending series of defilements and embezzlements.

Stones flew regularly through the windows of the royal house on the Embankment but one time a Molotov cocktail was tossed.

The fire was extinguished and the house did not completely burn, though the library was ruined.

Observing history's current-day developments, I wonder why the Internet is so harsh. Because nobody knows who is writing? Because those who write were not born for making public statements? In the past, of course, only a few could speak up nationally: they weighed their words and they were deliberate in their responsibility. I also do not understand why Their Royal Highnesses, from whom the Island residents have seen nothing but love and goodness, became their victims. I will express a thought that scares even me: perhaps this is how the people's love for them manifests itself?

The persecution of Parfeny and Ksenia did not remain un-noticed on the Mainland either, where voices began to be heard in their defense. The most noticed was undoubtedly Brand's speech, announcing that he would like to see the royal couple as allies. The dauntless elders' answer soon followed, though, making it clear that sort of alliance was impossible for them. The explanation was brief but crushing: they saw Brand as something of a rogue.

Their Royal Highnesses had to pay a price for that statement too. The day after their refusal was marked by a full U-turn from the press on the Continent. Parfeny and Ksenia, who had been *a pillar of humanism* on the Island the day before, had been instantly transformed into *enemies of progress*, *native princelings*, and *bellicose obscurantists*. Did they live so long to hear *that?*

Who had they been and who do they continue to be for all of us? Guardian angels? I doubt that, since that is not a position for a human. I think about the prophecy and wonder if perhaps everything is explained by the fact that Parfeny and Ksenia were supposed to live until its fulfillment while supporting us, who are powerless.

Do many people, one might ask, live three and a half centuries?

I will answer: No, not many do.

292

PARFENY

Children walk along a snowy road, dressed in short fox-fur coats. Reddish-brown on white. Fingers balled into fists inside mittens, so as not to freeze. Snow falls and falls from huge spruce branches. Snow crunches on the road. It preserves their tracks.

They approach Island Monastery of the Savior. They walk among the graves in the monastery cemetery. Tearing themselves away from their business in the afterlife, the deceased wave to them from their snowy slabs.

The boy clears the snow off the closest slab, carefully, so as not to disturb the departed. Prince Feodor, who Christianized the Island. Seeing that Feodor has a cross, the children kiss the cross.

"Why are you silent?" asks the little girl.

"Properly speaking, everything has already been said," answers Feodor. "What else can I add?"

The children clear the snow off the inscriptions of two neighboring graves: Konstantin and Frol. During their lifetimes they led the War of the Genealogies.

"We are now neighbors," laughs Konstantin. "Almost friends. Many things are re-examined after death."

Frol breaks a bent bough from a tree and brushes the snow from his gravestone. He looks somehow dissatisfied.

"And what could we divide? Our legendary great-grandmothers? Yours, by the way, as well." Frol points at the gravestones at the beginning of the row. "Can someone tell me what is in those graves?"

Filming from above with an infrared camera. A black-and-white image consisting primarily of contours. Skeletons lying in all the graves. The graves of Melania and Ilaria are empty.

Konstantin looks sorrowfully at Frol:

"You are becoming a grumbler, my friend."

"And where is Augustus' grave?" asks the little girl.

"In Rome, one must think," says Frol. "He ended up not being very kindred, our grandfather Augustus . . ." Frol turns around. "And this is for you."

Princes Mikhail and Andronik slowly approach along the cemetery path. Their tread is light so their striding is more like gliding.

"You have aged, son," Mikhail says to the little boy.

The boy shrugs.

"My children," says Andronik, "worry not, for only we see this. I am glad that you treat each other so reverently."

"A very touching pair," nods Konstantin. "I have no doubt that they will only enrich our community. Highly varied people lie here, but all are princes. Princes! Enjoying the fact that you are still alive, you may choose a suitable place for yourselves."

"I think that would look . . ." Frol tosses a spruce branch on the path. "Well, slightly tactless."

Mikhail dabs his eyes with a handkerchief.

"You know, I am not worried about them."

Meanwhile, the situation on the Island was becoming inflamed. Gangs of robbers had begun making their appearance in the City and its environs. They were composed of local people, but rapid-deployment cavalrymen later joined them. The bandits felled trees on the roads to stop cars and then mercilessly robbed the owners. In the evenings, the miscreants burst into theaters, restaurants, and gaming houses, and, not daring to interfere, the police drove away when they saw them robbing patrons.

In the third year of Varvara's reign, a meteorite fell on the Island. It fell on an oil tank, setting it afire, and that huge torch blazed until all the oil had burned up.

Certain people asked Bishop Kirill what that could mean.

The bishop replied to them that what happened held two meanings. The first was physical and meant that hydrocarbons are predisposed to burning. The second was metaphysical and was not absolutely clear to him either, but it most likely signified nothing good. This made people recall Agafon's prophecy. As is common knowledge, the prophecy was discovered recently.

In those same days, a diamond of inconceivable dimensions was found in southern mines. People said the earth's depths had not previously begotten diamonds like that and human eyes had not seen them. News of the astonishing diamond spread around the whole world and everyone looked at the images with wonderment. Others, unafraid of the tempers that had seized the Island, went to the mines where the stone was initially on display for viewing, under careful guard.

Once cut, a diamond is called an "adamant." The stone found on the Island, despite not having been processed, shone as if it had been cut and was thus called an adamant. It is known about the properties of diamonds that fire and iron are powerless before them so they can be hit by a hammer or cast into a crucible to melt and nothing will damage or soften them.

I shall liken that stone to the hearts of those who no longer feel a thing and no longer understand, who are not grateful for what is good, who are impervious to tenderness and reverence, are not mollified by supplication, and do not fear threats.

And if you attempt to split an adamant, it will only become harder. There is but one method on earth capable of removing an adamant's hardness: the blood of a goat. When soaked in it, the stone loses its properties and can be smashed by a hammer on an anvil, but even that is very difficult; the hammer and anvil will be damaged. The diamond that was found was soaked each night in fresh, warm goat's blood, but so hard was its nature that the stone-cutters doubted their own powers.

But the stone's faceting no longer concerned anyone. Everyone remembered the prophecy's words about the adamant and no one uttered them aloud because doing so was frightening. And it was frightening that nothing softened or damaged it. If the stone had softened even a bit or if even a small facet had broken off, that would, of course, have become slightly easier. And there was some-thing in the adamant's strength that was implacable, inhuman, and not born of the earth.

That same year, underground tremors resounded as if someone huge had been locked beneath the ground and was desperately straining to get out, all as pervasive smoke made its appearance over the top of the Mountain for the first time in many centuries. And those tremors in the country's midlands crumbled the prison and some of the incarcerated died. Others of them, freed of their fetters, scattered about the Island. Seeing what was happening, police officers began leaving their jobs, for there was no occupation more dangerous under the present circumstances.

Ambulances now came only for calls from the central part of the City, since it was still protected. It was not infrequent that doctors were called for one single reason: to rob them or take away their narcotic drugs. Several weeks later, ambulances no longer went anywhere.

An unprecedented number of prostitutes of both sexes had appeared on the streets. They were hungry and tugged at the sleeves of pedestrians, offering bodies ruined by vice. But there were not many pedestrians, since few people dared go outside after six in the evening. The City emptied out.

That same year, large numbers of continental ships began mooring in the southern part of the Island. They were carrying modern weaponry that the Island had lacked, along with trainers to teach weapon handling.

With the arrival of weaponry, the first battles began on the line of engagement between the two armies, and so brother lifted a hand against brother, and son lifted a hand against father. Those battles, however, slightly disappointed those who taught the art of warfare, for the weapons were not used to all their brilliant possibilities and the bitterness befitting armed clashes was absent.

This was all because, with the passage of time, moods had begun changing in the South. Southerners had run up against the same woes that gripped the North, albeit to a lesser degree, because a plague knows no borders, especially within the bounds of one island. Southern residents now had less forceful aspirations for a victory over the North. Vassa's bellicose war cries still hovered in the electrified air but they did not find their previous response.

Brand and his accomplices were filled with decisiveness to wage war down to the last Islander but realized the war they had dreamt of was now impossible. And then continental troops were sent to the Island, summoned to return a progressive way of life to the country.

Nature itself cued the continental troops' line of action. Seeing how long and brightly the oil terminal burned after a meteorite set it afire, they launched long-range artillery and began shelling the oil-bearing area. Three days later, it blazed like a giant candle that could be seen from the Mainland. The smoke from the flame was so thick and black that it enveloped the entire Island. North and the South were both plunged into darkness.

Island residents' desperation gradually began growing into rage. People came to the Main Square and expressed that rage openly. Everyone understood that the government had long been powerless to affect anything, but the rage was like water that had overfilled a dam: it sought a way out and was bound to vent itself on someone.

More and more people gathered near the Presidential Palace with each passing day and they were ever angrier. On the day the human ocean flooded not just the Main Square but also the adjacent streets, Island residents demanded that Varvara come out to them.

But Varvara did not come out.

She had escaped the previous night, dressed in men's clothing.

KSENIA

In May the children return to Auntie Klavdia's house. More than three hundred years later – time really does pass in the blink of an eye. They walk, holding hands because they don't know what awaits them in that house.

They walk along the open expanse and the house is already visible. The sea is behind the house, just as it was in the past. Alongside the road is fresh grass, still unsinged by the summer sun.

Sometimes the children leave the road and walk along the grass. Grasshoppers jump out from under their feet;

lizards slide along warm stones. The grass is in motion but the stones are motionless. If not for the stones, this picture would be crumpled and carried away by a gust of wind.

The house acquires details as they near. Fissures appear and there is moss on the walls, right by the earth itself; swallows are nesting under the roof. Swallows circle high up in the sky. The children look at them, heads craned. They and the swallows have a house in common.

The door is open, its rectangular blackness gapes. The children are already entering the house. They are still approaching but they are already entering.

And now they are on the threshold. To the left, something tin falls and rolls along the floor's stone slabs. After reaching the endpoint of its rolling, it turns into an echo and hits the wall. A child's shout flies after it: "Is anyone alive?"

A good question. The only possible question.

After the shout is silence, but after the sun is darkness. And uncertainty. Feet sense the seams of the slabs and lead in the proper direction. They have their own memory.

To the left is the scullery, which is slightly brighter, from the fire built under the kettle. Simmering; the matte gleam of bubbling.

They'd been awaited until the last minute – as long as they could. But that wasn't long enough. This is what happens in movies: people miss each other by a half-hour and everything takes a different direction.

The children's eyes grow accustomed to the semidarkness and they look all around. By the stove is a pile of logs, on a low table are several dishes.

The contours of the cook, on the bench by the wall, are now visible. She is lying on her back, one hand on her chest, the other hanging almost to the floor.

"Did she die?" asks the little girl.

The little boy walks over to the cook, lifts her powerful arm, and feels her pulse.

"She didn't die but she's sleeping."

The children leave the scullery on tiptoe and head off to wander the house. The servants are sleeping on trunks. The nanny's dozing, slumped behind a spinning wheel's spindle.

After going up to the second floor, the children enter Auntie Klavdia's room. She's reclining, drowning in feather pillows. Pillows have always been her weakness. People called her *A Dozen Pillows* behind her back – she knew that but there was nothing she could do about herself. She so loved pillows.

After counting them, the boy says: "Eleven."

The girl points out a servant woman with a pillow in her hands: "Twelve."

The servant woman rushes to Klavdia, sits on the floor, places the pillow under Klavdia's left side, and rests her own head on the bed.

The children go out on the terrace and look at the sea. They sit in oak chairs with armrests shaped like lions' heads. They wait for everyone to wake up.

Chapter the Twenty-Fifth

PARFENY & KSENIA

I the sinner Innokenty, who left my cell owing to a natural cataclysm, became eyewitness to much of what is described, although, of course, not to everything. This chapter consists of notes made by me, primarily during the events. Against my usual habit, they are not polished and are rather muddled. The publisher, Phillip, insisted they be published in this exact form. He seems to think they convey the true tragedy of events. I am not certain of that, but I am obeying.

May 25

A power vacuum has set in. For the first time in all the history of the Island, nobody wants to take power, for it is unclear what to do under these pitiful circumstances that have now come about through God's calamity.

May 26

News came from the South that the continental troops ceased their attack on the North and are beginning to urgently evacuate the Island.

May 27

The primary misfortune has arrived: the Mountain has begun to awaken. The weak puff of smoke emitted above it changed into a thick column of smoke breaking from its mouth. Its emergence is accompanied by vibrations from the earth, as if the unseen and huge one who was pounding there for all the last months joined forces with the Mountain and now welcomes its awakening. Fiery rivers have already begun to flow along one of the Mountain's slopes, burning everything in their path. Smoke is coming from the North, from the burning oil, and there is a cloud of ash from the South, from the Mountain. And the sky has dulled and the sun barely breaks through and the ash settles on the earth. It is not yet thick: it is still only dust on open surfaces since, by the grace of God, the wind is blowing in the direction of the sea and most of the ash is carried there. But if the wind changes and the ash falls on us like black snow there will be no rescue because it enters the lungs and stops the breathing. Yet another horrifying danger awaits us, however, something all Islanders know: the Mountain belongs to a type of volcano that has a habit of blowing up. The world is summoning the Island leadership to begin evacuating residents immediately, warning that little time remains until catastrophe. But the Island has no more leadership and there are no vessels for evacuation since most of them are already at the continental army's disposal, for saving its soldiers.

May 28

Ten o'clock in the morning. Everyone has gathered at the Main Square and nobody is leaving, knowing that it will be easier to find a path to salvation together. Beyond that, the square is an open place and when there are tremors it is less dangerous there than in buildings or on narrow streets. Everyone speaks of Agafon the Forward-Looking's prophecy; it is now obvious to all that it is beginning to come true. Old and young, rich and poor, believers and nonbelievers are all talking about it. Everyone knows the lines of the prophecy by heart and it is now sliding across the leaden sky like a crawling news ticker. We opened up to the world and that was for the good. But it has been said that there is a time to embrace, and a time to refrain from embracing. The days came when ailments seized us and good turned into harm, for we did not rid ourselves of our ailments but rather acquired others. And strangers inundated the Island; we reside among them, as a crow upon ruins. Our woe, however, is us ourselves, not strangers, for depravity multiplied and we became embittered and began to crowd one another. And a great hostility flared up between us so brother struck brother and son struck father. The earth, which is sensitive to the bitterness of people, itself became embittered. A trying hour came and an adamant appeared that can only be softened with the blood of the goat. And the ground shook and black water was ignited in the North and fiery water flowed in the South, and ash floated from the sky. And our hearts are ready to turn to ash. And we are unable to pray to the Lord for salvation, for He will turn His face from us. And if three righteous people are not found among us, to climb the Mountain and speak with Him, our life will cease, in smoke and darkness. And so we began to think of three righteous people capable of speaking with Him and no one comes to mind but Parfeny and Ksenia. We do not find a third righteous person but we keep in mind that the Lord who was ready to preserve Sodom for the sake of fifty righteous people, agreed to preserve it for the sake of ten who, alas, also were not found. And so, we dare to think, perhaps two instead of three will count for us? And we recall how we treated the Royal Highnesses and are ashamed of that. There remains only the hope that they will forgive us, the imprudent, and that everyone begs them for forgiveness as if with lips united, believing that this cry will reach their ears. People await the return of our royals in order that they accept power on the Island, if only for a short duration, climb the Mountain, and speak with the Lord.

303

The noon hour. News comes that the Island airport closed after accepting a final airplane: the thickening of the ash is so great that the air has become unfit for flights. And our final hope departs with that news.

Two o'clock in the afternoon. A news flash that Parfeny and Ksenia are on the Island. They arrived here unannounced on the last airplane and are currently on their way to the capital. Their Highnesses are fully accepting power and are ordering members of the government to report to the Presidential Palace at four this afternoon. Of course it is possible to allege that this is not an answer to our prayer but rather their free will, a decision made after Varvara's escape. We perceive it as an answer, which in actuality it is.

Three o'clock in the afternoon. Gray with ash, the first car of the presidential motorcade flies onto the square. An automobile with the Island's flag follows. This is Parfeny and Ksenia's automobile. The motorcade stops and the royals exit the car. They have arrived to confront chaos. The word *chaos*, which is making the rounds, wanders the square. There, they will confront chaos. Joyous news. Someone needs to confront chaos. They do not let the car go. People genuflect as they ask the royal couple to climb the Mountain and speak with Him. Those making the request understand now is not the best time to visit the Mountain, but what can you do when a prophecy is speaking? Someone must climb the Mountain. Apparently they must. It is frightening, but there is nobody other than them, for there are no righteous people and Parfeny and Ksenia are everyone's last hope. How will we accomplish such audacity, ask the royals. We will recognize ourselves as righteous people or something and dare to speak with Him? There is no need to recognize yourselves as righteous people, answers the crowd, since we have already recognized you as such. Simply go and speak. Pray for Him not to allow the Mountain to explode. Or have you no pity for us and our children?

Four o'clock in the afternoon. Means for saving residents are discussed at the meeting of Their Highnesses and the government.

Five o'clock in the afternoon. By supreme ukase, martial law is declared for the country. Field Marshal Severian orders troops to enter the City to secure order and help residents. Addressing the troops, the field marshal says that the battle will not be easy because, for the first time, our enemy is invisible. In light of the danger of new tremors, the soldiers hurriedly pitch their tents in open expanses and hand out gas masks and respirators on the streets. Women volunteers are sent to hospitals, textile factories, and stores to produce gauze masks. Men volunteers form detachments for handling rubble.

Eight o'clock in the evening. Parfeny makes a radio address to the people. He calls on Island residents to drive fear from their hearts and help one another, for the situation is complex but not hopeless. After a pause, he says, Nobody gave us the right to walk up the Mountain and speak with Him, thus we cannot go there. He says, Seeing your tears we cannot not go there and so, of course, we will go.

Ten o'clock in the evening. A column of military trucks forms in front of the Palace. At its head are two police SUVs because off-road travel is not unlikely. Bishop Kirill holds a prayer service for the salvation of the Island. His censer sparks as if it is a volcano of tiny size and the sparks preceding the column fly toward the Mountain. Field Marshal Severian announces five minutes until departure. Greeting the calamity fully armed, he is in full-dress uniform and carrying his field marshal's baton.

Eleven o'clock in the evening. The column heads off and sets a southerly course. Along the way it meets a multitude of people going north. They, people who have lived their whole lives near the Mountain, feel its restlessness. They say that although the eruption has settled down for now, the Mountain is ready to explode at any minute. Pitying those driving, they call on them to return.

May 29

Two o'clock in the morning. The vehicles draw closer to the Mountain from the side untouched by the eruption. Thousands of people who have gathered at its foot are awaiting the column. Who are they? asks Bishop Kirill. Are they those who have nowhere to go or those who believe in the power of royal prayer? Both one and the other, answers the senior priest of the local church, and methinks that those multitudes have united to a significant degree. The police cars at the front of the column turn on their sirens. The column moves slowly through the crowd. It stops at the serpentine road leading to the mountaintop. Spotlights protrude from the trucks; they are directed at the winding road. The first hundred meters of road are as bright as day. Their Royal Highnesses are standing next to the lead car. Someone brings them jackets, concerned it may be cold on the Mountain. The royals refuse the jackets, they have no need for them. It is important, they say, not to be too warm. They also refuse walkie-talkies, for they have other communication methods. In any case, walkie-talkies most likely would not work here. Bishop Kirill blesses them. As he lingers, he says: Prophecies need not always be understood literally. I have in mind that it is not necessary to go a long way along the road. Standing here, at its foot, it is as if you are already on the Mountain. That, as they say, counts. He makes an attempt to smile. Parfeny and Ksenia bow their heads. It counts, yes. For anyone at all, but not for Agafon.

Three o'clock in the morning. In the ensuing quiet, the royals take their first step toward the mountaintop. The bishop accompanies them. He stops at the beginning of the serpentine road: You will continue alone; may God protect you. What do those who are seeing them off think? That they are vulnerable? That their steps are not firm? Two soul-stirring old people. They walk, holding on to one another, just as they have walked their entire lives. Ksenia's dress flutters in the night wind. As they reach a bend in the path, they turn and look at all of us. They take a step into the unlighted expanse. Disappear. They will need to turn on their flashlights, nothing difficult there. They have strong bulbs and the charge will last several hours. If they do not use them simultaneously, the charge is, one might say, more than enough. In the absence of electric service, I light my cell with that sort of flashlight. Before, though, I lit candles. Speaking frankly, it is hard for me to imagine them with flashlights. Those walking toward the Light.

Four o'clock in the morning. A thundering sound. A horrifying cracking as if the earthly and heavenly firmaments have shattered. Everyone understands that He has begun speaking with Parfeny and Ksenia. A huge cloud, black and scarlet, rises over the Mountain. The voices of the elderly are weak – may He hear them. A new thundering crash. The crowd shouts, heartrendingly. The next jolt knocks down those who are standing. How long do we lie like that? I do not know. My mouth is full of sand and ash. The thundering echo rolls along the whole Island and hits in turn on the heavenly firmament and then the earthy firmament, yet becomes no quieter upon return, as an echo should. The buildings in the cities are covered in cracks, some fall. No ambulance sirens can be heard. Gray flakes glide in headlights. The headlights pierce this blizzard the distance of an extended arm, so cars move at the slowest pace.

They drive, undaunted, to the nearest rubble, from which volunteers carry wounded survivors. A people that was an embittered crowd only yesterday has tonight transformed into a convocation of fellow citizens, a throng of mercy. When those waiting at the bottom of the Mountain shake off the first wave of horror, people surround Field Marshal Severian. He intently watches the serpentine road, his face crimson with reflections from the flame. Wet from tears. People shout to him that Parfeny and Ksenia remain on the Mountain, as if he does not know that. They shout that they remain there, amidst this hell, that they should not have been sent up the Mountain. The army is idle. The army is powerless, the field marshal mouths, but was it not you who sent them there? Several soldiers approach him. He listens to them, not shifting his gaze from the Mountain. Nods. Two trucks start their engines and begin driving along the serpentine road. Parfeny and Ksenia could not have gone far. Everyone believes they will be found.

Five o'clock in the morning. The wind changes and clouds of ash begin moving north. The clouds seem slow, but of course they are swift. They are reminiscent of an aerostat's unprecedented size. Lightning flashes inside them, for the particles of ash are charged and coming into contact with one another. Drifting at an unseen height, the ash cools and sinks to the Island. There is lightning along the sky's entire width and tremors along the earth's entire expanse. Are these end days? It has, after all, been said that the sun will dim and the moon will not shine and stars will fall from the sky and the heavenly hosts will waver for a time. The main flow of lava is on the other side of the Mountain but several fiery tentacles are making their appearance on this side. The trucks return, rushing down the serpentine road. They are enveloped in flame. Soldiers jump out of the running

vehicles. Trucks roll to the side of the road and explode. Doctors
run to the soldiers. Parfeny and Ksenia were not located.

Seven o'clock in the morning. The eruption is losing strength but the
sun is wallowing in ash and there is no sunrise. It is not what is happening that frightens but the thought of an impending explosion:
the Mountain is still in its place.

Eight o'clock in the morning. The tremors subside. Streams of lava
turn to brooks and then harden completely.

Noon. It is now clear that the Mountain is calming. The sky brightens
slightly. The soldiers form a human chain and scour the Mountain in
accessible places. They are searching for Parfeny and Ksenia.

October 6
The searches went on for more than a week but Their Royal
Highnesses were not found. A three-day mourning period was
announced due to their death and bells tolled all over the Island.
It makes one's head spin to think of how many years they were
alongside us. Advanced in age and decrepit of body, what might one
think they could do? But it was Parfeny and Ksenia who defined
our life. With just their presence. The feeling has never left me
that we rushed with the mourning. It is hard to believe that people with such a lengthy attachment to life could lose it. They were
mostly likely taken by the One with whom they were conversing
that night. Maybe that is why they went to the Mountain. Others
say that a discussion of that sort could not have taken place since
there were only two righteous people. But it was said by the Savior:
Where two or three are gathered together in my name, there am I in

the midst of them. It works out that there were three of them because Christ was with them. My intent is not to argue with anyone, for it is not truth that is born in argument but wrath and anguish of the spirit. Whoever wishes may consider that the Mountain swallowed Parfeny and Ksenia. But the fact that on the night they disappeared the Mountain calmed and the earth quieted down convinces me that I am right. And also. It is known that history is but a path along which a person walks. Along that path, one may increase goodness or sow evil; that depends on each person's choice. A person may blend in with a crowd, becoming like the fiery stream creeping down the mountain. And then harden like it. But one can move toward the mountaintop, unafraid of tremors and rockfalls. Blessed is the land that gives birth to such rulers. For them, all are their children: The rulers grieve for them, feel joy for them, and climb a mountain to discuss their rescue. One can tell the mountain, Move from this place. And it will move. Or, the opposite, Remain in this place. And it will remain. The air is fresh now, as after a cleansing thunderstorm. There is no malice dissolved in it but rather mutual love and compassion. Yes, compassion, because it gives birth to love and defeats malice. In the days of the earthquake, for example, the steward priest did not give me paper to continue the chronicle. He said: It appears history is ending, so why, Brother Innokenty, are we going to use up paper for no reason? At first I took offense and wanted to direct some vexed words at him. To at least remind him that *it is not for us to know the times or the seasons*, it is for us only to take careful notes. But I kept silent, pitying him for his attachment to the earthly. Particularly because I still had paper left. Two days later he brought an abundance of paper, embraced me, and melted into tears: Forgive me, O brother, for my stinginess. Here is paper for you; write, as before, as long as history has not ended. Yes, I say, history is continuing, for now. But that, I say, is a final warning. And

310

peace and love set in between us, and all on the Island made peace with one another in the hope that their days would continue. Our country signed a long-awaited peace with France. I heard that those in that country were glad for the peace too, although far from everyone knew of the war there. With regard to France, I nearly forgot that news just came saying Jean-Marie Leclerc's motion picture *Justification of the Island* won some sort of important prize. They say Leclerc was apparently afraid his film would be incomprehensible. There was nothing to fear: What wasn't understandable? I am not familiar with the film but I was fortunate to know Their Royal Highnesses. There have not been more joyful people in our history. I think few people at their age would have had the courage for an ascent of that sort. That is comprehensible to anyone in the audience.

Eugene Vodolazkin was born in Kyiv, Ukraine, in 1964. His second novel, *Laurus,* won both of Russia's major literary awards, the National Big Book Award and the Yasnaya Polyana Book Award, and was shortlisted for the National Bestseller Prize and the Russian Booker Prize. His debut novel, *Solovyov and Larionov,* was shortlisted for the Andrei Bely Prize and the Big Book Award. Two other critically acclaimed novels, *The Aviator* and *Brisbane,* have also been translated into English. Vodolazkin was the 2019 winner of the Solzhenitsyn Prize. He has worked in the department of Old Russian Literature at Pushkin House since 1990. He is an expert in medieval history and folklore and has numerous academic books and articles to his name. He lives with his family in St. Petersburg.

Lisa C. Hayden's translations from the Russian include Eugene Vodolazkin's *Solovyov and Larionov, The Aviator,* and *Laurus,* which won the Read Russia Award in 2016 and was also shortlisted for the Oxford-Weidenfeld Prize along with her translation of Vadim Levental's *Masha Regina.* Her blog, *Lizok's Bookshelf,* examines contemporary Russian fiction. She lives in Maine.